'You are going to provide me with weekly flower deliveries to make the apartment look beautiful,' I responded.

Giles grinned. 'Oh, that's a fabulous idea. Ooh, yes, I'm going to start thinking about it now. Flowers that bring romance, flowers that boost your mood.'

'Yes, definitely those ones,' I said, rubbing my eyes. I hadn't been sleeping well, ever since Hugh's latest demand, and it was beginning to catch up with me. 'And de-stressing ones would be good. You know, for relaxation—'

'And mind-blowing sex,' Helen giggled. 'I know it's not on your list, but, trust me, you'll soon realize it's the only thing that matters.'

'Flowers that encourage mind-blowing sex,' Giles said seriously. 'Okay, I can't make any promises, but I'll see what I can do . . .'

Gemma Townley started writing when she was sixteen with a book review in *Harpers & Queen* magazine. She went on to become a journalist, writing for titles including *Company* magazine, the *Sunday Telegraph* and *Homes & Ideas*. She lives in London with her husband and two children.

By Gemma Townley

The Hopeless Romantic's Handbook
Learning Curves
Little White Lies
When in Rome . . .
The Importance of Being Married
A Wild Affair
An Ideal Wife

An Ideal Wife

Gemma Townley

First published in Great Britain in 2011
by Orion, an imprint of the Orion Publishing Group Ltd

An Hachette UK company

1 3 5 7 9 10 8 6 4 2

ISBN 978-1-4091-0290-8

Typeset at The Spartan Press Ltd,
Lymington, Hants

Printed and bound in Great Britain by
Clays Ltd, St Ives plc

The Orion Publishing Group's policy is to use papers that
are natural, renewable and recyclable products and made
from wood grown in sustainable forests. The logging and
manufacturing processes are expected to conform to the
environmental regulations of the country of origin.

The Orion Publishing Group Ltd
Orion House
5 Upper Saint Martin's Lane
London WC2H 9EA

www.orionbooks.co.uk

To Mark,

from his (nearly) perfect wife

Chapter 1

〜

'WELL, ISN'T THIS NICE?'

I looked at my mother with what I hoped would pass for a natural smile. She was right; of course it was nice. There she was, on the other side of the table with Chester, her fiancé and my biggest client, and here I was, on this side of the table with Max, my husband. It was so nice I could scream.

I closed my eyes briefly as my hand closed sweatily over my phone. The text message had come through moments before: *Thanks, honey, knew I could depend on you. I'll be in touch.* And as I'd read it, I'd felt sick suddenly, felt a layer of cold sweat leak from my pores.

The message was from Hugh Barter, and he was never going to leave me alone.

'Darling, are you all right? You look very strange.'

'Strange?' I forced another smile. 'Sorry. Just . . . thinking about something.'

'Well, it's very rude to think of anything other than the guests around your table,' Mum said pointedly. 'And your husband is sitting right beside you, too.'

Husband.

I still wasn't used to being married – it had been nearly a year, and I still got a slight thrill every time I introduced Max: 'This is my husband.' And he would always wink at me, like it was our own private joke, the first of many such

1

jokes that would bind us even more tightly together over the years. 'My wife and I would like to thank you for taking the time to stop by,' he'd say, his eyes twinkling, even if it was just my friend Helen, and even if she hadn't 'stopped by' but had barged in during supper, flopped on the sofa, and insisted that we listen to the latest installment in her dramatic love life.

'This *is* nice. In fact, "nice" doesn't really go far enough,' Max said, in that voice that no one could ever quite read or be sure whether he was teasing or not. I raised an eyebrow at him and his eyes widened innocently. 'What? It is nice. Especially the food.'

'You're only saying that because you cooked it,' I said, forcing myself back into the room, forcing myself to concentrate on the here and now instead of worrying about that sniveling little rat's request: £10,000. That's how much Hugh Barter had asked for this time. The time before it had been £5,000. Relocation costs, he'd told me. A loan, he'd told me. His trip around the world hadn't worked out as he'd hoped; he'd decided to come back to the UK. That was three months ago, and I thought the £5,000 would be enough, that he really did just need a bit of money to find somewhere to live, to tide him over while he looked for work. A favor, he'd said. Like the favor he was doing me by not telling Max the truth about us, by not telling Max that I'd been Hugh's for the taking when I was engaged to Max. God, how stupid I'd been.

'And I cooked it only because you threatened to order a takeaway if I didn't,' Max was saying.

'Yeah, well, cooking isn't my forte,' I replied, stretching my lips into another smile. The cooking thing was a long-standing joke; Max regularly called me the worst cook in the world. And he was absolutely right. I tried following recipes but invariably got distracted and ended up burning things or adding too much of the wrong ingredient, or putting it in the oven at the wrong temperature. I'd once, in a fit of enthusiasm and desire to please, made Max a fish pie – his favorite – only to discover that the fish was still raw when I went to serve it. He'd never let me forget that one; he'd laughed for about an hour in spite of my protestations and threats never to so much as boil the kettle again.

'And why should it be?' my mother said immediately. She couldn't cook, either. 'A woman's place is not in the kitchen, darling. Not anymore.'

'Of course it isn't,' I agreed. 'Is it, Max?'

Max looked at me wryly.

'No,' he said. 'Luckily for you.'

I thumped him on the arm and managed a little laugh. Inside, bile was rising up through my stomach; I felt dirty even having a text from Hugh on my phone. I wanted to delete it, wanted to scrub it clean. But not now. Things were bad enough; letting myself become preoccupied with Hugh now, when I was supposed to be enjoying myself with Max, would just make things worse. 'Anyway,' I said, 'it's not like you chop down trees or, you know, build camps.'

I took a gulp of wine and looked up to find Chester's gaze on me, a slightly bemused expression on his face. 'Chop down trees?' he asked.

'You know, like the traditional male role,' I explained. 'The woman's at home, cooking, and the man's out killing animals and building houses. The point is, you guys don't fulfill your side of that bargain, so there's no reason why women should be the ones to cook and clean, right?'

'I guess,' Chester said. 'Personally, I like to cook. It relaxes me.'

'Relaxes you?' My mother rolled her eyes. 'How can cooking be relaxing? So many instructions!'

'Exactly,' I said. 'Nightmare.'

'So,' Max said, turning to me playfully. 'You don't cook. And as I've said, I have no problem with that. I don't expect you to cook. I would be perturbed, upset even, if you so much as attempted cheese on toast. But where does that leave us?'

I frowned. 'What do you mean? You cook. We get take-away. I buy ready-prepared—'

'No, that's not what I mean,' Max cut in, smiling warmly. 'If I don't cut down trees or kill wild animals and you don't cook, what is it that we actually do? I mean, how do you define the perfect wife nowadays? Or the perfect husband, for that matter?'

I looked at him uncertainly. 'I still don't see what you mean.' I realized as I spoke that my voice sounded defensive, and I checked myself. The problem was, I *felt* defensive. Max was joking, I reminded myself firmly. Max always joked. He didn't know anything. This was not about Hugh.

'He means, what makes a marriage great?' Chester said, leaning forward. 'And that, my friends, is a question I can answer.'

'You can? I'm impressed.' Max grinned. 'So come on, then, what's the secret?'

'No secret,' Chester said firmly. 'An ideal husband looks after his wife. Makes sure she has everything she needs, everything she wants. Tells her he loves her. Makes sure he shows it, too.'

'And the ideal wife?' Max asked.

'Does the same,' Chester said. 'She looks after her husband, makes sure he's got ironed shirts in the morning and a good meal when he comes back from work. She listens to

4

him, gives him advice when he needs it, and is always there when he needs her.'

'A good meal and ironed shirts?' My mother turned to him in horror. 'But that's the most depressing thing I've ever heard. And, in case you've forgotten, I can't cook and I don't iron.'

Chester put his arm around her and grinned. 'And yet I still love you.'

Mum, realizing that he'd been teasing her, rolled her eyes crossly, but she didn't move out of his embrace.

'Although a man does appreciate a crisp shirt in the morning,' Chester continued wickedly. 'Am I right, Max?'

Max caught my eye. 'You're absolutely right,' he dead-panned, moving his hand over mine and giving it a squeeze. I had tried to iron one of his shirts once. Suffice it to say the shirt was no longer in his wardrobe. It was too singed even to use as a dishcloth. 'But we can pay other people to do those things and it makes no difference to the relationship. So we're still no further in our definition.'

Chester shrugged. 'I think I nailed it, other than the cooking and ironing. Being there for each other. That's the key, right?'

'But is that enough?' Max mused. 'Dependability, I mean?'

'The ideal husband, Max,' my mother said archly, 'should adore his wife and not be afraid to demonstrate it. And I'm not talking about gifts and flowers, lovely as they are; I'm talking about being with her, about making sacrifices in order to be with her, rather than being at work every day until nine P.M.'

Chester whistled. 'Here we go again,' he sighed. He turned to Mum, a serious expression on his face. 'Esther, honey, I am crazy about you. But I am also the chief executive of a big private bank. Sometimes I have to work late. Sometimes very late. It goes with the territory.'

'There's more to life than business,' Mum said.

'Yes, there is,' Chester agreed. 'But businesses don't run themselves. And it's not like I have control over my diary anyway. My personal assistant fills it up.'

'So get a new assistant,' Mum said crossly. 'One who knows how to say no. You say yourself that you regularly find yourself in meetings that you really don't need to be in.'

'I know,' Chester sighed again, 'but it's not that easy. I need to know what's going on.'

'You need to learn to delegate more,' Mum said tersely. 'Jess delegates all the time, don't you, Jess?'

Chester looked at me expectantly, and I forced a little smile. 'Yes, of course, but that's different. I mean, I'm not the chief exec of a bank . . .'

'No, you're not. And if you can delegate, then a chief executive certainly can,' Mum said.

'You've got to be realistic, Esther,' Chester said, looking ruffled. 'You've got to live in the real world, you know, hard as that is for you. The real world, which doesn't always revolve around you and your latest whim.'

'Chester, believe me, I know all about the real world,' Mum said, her voice tightening. 'And I do not have whims or expect the world to revolve around me. As you well know. Personally, I don't think an ideal husband would ever say such a thing. Certainly not in front of others.'

Max and I glanced at each other; this was obviously an argument that had been had a few times before.

Chester looked at her for a moment, then nodded. 'You're right,' he said apologetically. 'You're absolutely right.' He took her hand. 'I'm sorry. I got defensive. I know I need to slow down a bit. But it's not easy.'

Fed Up With Shaving, Plucking and Waxing?

Our New Aesthetic Clinic Now Open in Twickenham

Virtually Pain Free IPL Hair Removal

£39 per Area per Session or 6 for £195

Laser Hair Removal

From £39

Cryo Lipo Fat Reduction

Only £195

We Also Specialise in....

◆ Teeth Whitening ◆ Skin Tightening ◆ Stretch Mark Reduction

Cellulite Reduction ◆ Rosacea & Skin Redness Treatment ◆ Acne Treatment

◆ Skin Rejuvenation ◆ Advance Skin Care Products

All Treatments are Unisex & We offer Free Consultations & Friendly Advice

43 London Road, Twickenham TW1 3SZ Tel: 0203 727 7272

Email - twickenham@thelaserclinicgroup.com Web - www.thelaserclinicgroup.com

New Aesthetic Clinic Now Open in Twickenham ... Helping Look Better & Feel Great!

We offer a large range of non invasive aesthetic treatments to enhance your skin and keep you looking great. Our professionals and qualified practitioners will provide you with all the facts you need to make an informed decision about your treatment. We only use the most effective but yet the safest technology in the market today for Laser/IPL hair removal, fat loss, advanced skin care at affordable prices. Contact The Laser Clinic Group today for a free consultation.

Recommend Us To Your Friends and

Receive Free Treatments.

(Ask us for a Loyalty Card)

The Laser Clinic Group

0203 727 7272

twickenham@thelaserclinicgroup.com
www.thelaserclinicgroup.com

Franchising Opportunities Available

Scan Here For Our Web site.

'I know,' Mum said, looking slightly mollified. 'But you have to understand that it isn't easy for me being on my own all the time. I'm not like Jess. I get lonely.'

I frowned. 'Hey, I don't like being on my own,' I said. 'I mean, I don't mind it sometimes, but . . .'

'Yes, you do. You're one of these independent types,' Mum said, looking at me as though I'd somehow let the side down.

'Nothing wrong with being independent,' Chester said warmly. 'And don't suggest for a minute that you're not proud of your daughter, Esther. Rightly so, I might add. Max, you've got a great woman there. Someone I'm going to be very proud to call my stepdaughter.'

I looked up at him and felt two little tears prick at my eyes. I still remembered the first day I'd met Chester, the powerful American head of a major bank, sitting there listening to me present a pitch that had been poorly planned and researched by my former boss, who'd totally set me up. I'd somehow pulled something out of the bag and won the account, and since then Chester had been a firm fixture in my life – my number-one client and now my mother's fiancé. The very idea that he might be proud of me meant the world to me.

'Thanks, Chester,' I managed to say. 'That means a lot.'

'Quite sickening, really, isn't it? The perfect wife and the perfect stepdaughter,' Max said, grinning.

I shook my head. 'No. No, I'm really not,' I said nervously.

'Well, I'd disagree,' Max said. 'You couldn't be more perfect. But, come on, tell us your version of the perfect spouse.'

'Me? Oh, I don't know,' I said uncomfortably. What I did know was that kissing other men probably didn't come into it. Kissing business rivals and letting slip highly confidential information definitely didn't. As for letting your mother take the blame for your misdemeanors – well, I was pretty sure that negated any claim to being an ideal *anything*. 'I don't think perfection exists,' I said hesitantly. 'Does it? I mean, don't most of us have feet of clay?'

'Even me?' Max grinned.

'Well, obviously not you,' I said immediately, smiling involuntarily for the first time that evening. 'You are perfection itself.' And he was, I found myself thinking. To me, anyway. I loved him so much – I'd never been so happy in my whole life. And I couldn't bear to let anything threaten that happiness.

The truth was, I'd never really expected to get married. Never expected to fall in love, actually. I'd been brought up by a grandmother who taught me that love was a chimera, that men always left in the end, and that if I entertained any notion of falling in love, I'd 'end up like my mother.' As far as I'd known back then, Mum had died in a car accident, the result of fast living and wearing skirts that were too short. So I'd concentrated on my studies, gone to university, worked hard, and, to my delight, landed a job at Milton Advertising. Milton Advertising, where Max Wainwright had been deputy chief executive. And I still pinched myself that he'd been more than interested; he'd fallen in love with me, and I'd realized how much I loved him, too, just in time.

'I'm not sure that's a good enough answer,' Chester said, raising an eyebrow. 'Come on, Jess. You work up concepts for a living. It can't be that hard to sum up what makes a perfect spouse, surely?'

I forced another smile. 'You're not going to let me off the hook, are you?' I asked. Chester and Max shook their heads.

'Not a chance.' Max looked amused.

'Fine,' I relented, my flush deepening. 'I think love is all that matters, really. I mean, at the end of the day, if someone loves you deeply, then you might, maybe, possibly, you know, overlook her flaws.'

I glanced up hopefully; Max looked serious for a moment.

'You don't have any flaws, Jess. That's why I love you so much. You may not believe in perfection, but I do. I have it right here.'

'Well, that's nice,' Chester said warmly, evidently keen to keep the focus on me and not his busy schedule. 'He's right, too. Perfect wife, perfect account manager. Hell, I'm beginning to think you may be a little too perfect. There've got to be some flaws somewhere, right?'

I shot him a look; Chester knew all too well about my flaws.

'She does have one,' Max said suddenly, and I looked up at him in alarm.

'I do? What?'

'Your lack of flattery,' Max said seriously. 'I was rather hoping that you were going to mention perfect physiques and incredible intelligence in your précis of the perfect husband, with a strong indication that I have both of those things in spades.'

His eyes were shining and I grinned in relief. 'You didn't mention anything about me looking like Kate Moss,' I said, pushing all thoughts of Hugh Barter firmly out of my head.

'Absolutely not,' Max agreed. 'She's way too skinny.'

I raised an eyebrow and he laughed. 'So what you're saying is that John Lennon was right all along.'

'John Lennon?' Mum asked.

'All you need is love,' Max said. 'He's the genius who put that thought to music.'

'Oh, I see,' Mum said. 'Yes, I'm afraid I was never a great fan of the Beatles. I didn't really do the whole hippie thing.'

'But you agree, right?' Chester asked, suddenly looking less like the high-powered chief executive and more like the smitten teenager. 'Love's all that matters, isn't it?'

'Love is all that matters,' my mother agreed. 'Love and a roof over your head. Money in your pocket. And a husband who isn't home late every single evening.'

She looked at Chester archly, and he smiled easily.

'You know,' Chester said thoughtfully, 'it's funny that we're having this conversation.'

'It is?' Max asked.

Chester nodded. 'See, I've been thinking. Not about perfection in relationships, but about . . . you know, what makes a company a good one.'

'Work, work, work,' my mother groaned, annoyed.

'Ah, well, that's easy,' Max interrupted. 'Great management, good people, and lots of luck.'

Chester nodded. 'Yeah. About that luck thing . . .'

We all exchanged furtive glances. Chester was the chief executive of Jarvis Private Banking, and the truth of the matter was that the entire world hated banks at the moment, blamed them for economies that were spiraling out of control, for job losses, for summer holidays abroad being a distant memory.

'I would admit there's not a huge amount of it circulating at the moment,' Max said quietly. Business at our firm, Milton Advertising, wasn't exactly booming, either. Clients were going out of business and failing to pay, and even those who were still active had cut their advertising budgets back. Max tried to make out that he wasn't worried, but I'd noticed how tired he looked lately. So far we'd managed to avoid letting anyone go, but every time a new invoice arrived, I saw Max's expression tightening.

'Yes, times are not great right now. Let's face it, Jarvis is an investment bank. We're the bad guys,' Chester said gravely. 'We've just bought an Internet bank, and people don't trust them very much these days, either, do they?'

I bit my lip, not sure whether I should agree with him or attempt to reassure him.

'Not so much,' I conceded. 'I think people probably trust their mattresses more than banks these days, to be honest.' It was true; ever since banks around the world had gone to their governments for bailouts, people had started to see banks as the bad guys. At first they were hated for lending too much money and lots of bad debts, and then they were hated for not lending enough money and making housing markets collapse. Now they were hated for paying themselves huge bonuses when everyone else was feeling the pinch. To be honest, coming up with a positive spin on banking was proving pretty tough these days.

'Exactly!' Chester said, clapping his hands together. 'As usual, Jess, you have hit the nail on the head. People trust their mattresses more than they trust their banks. So what do we do about that?'

'Create a smear campaign against mattresses?' I suggested, smiling slightly. Chester was our client – our biggest client, in fact. Milton Advertising was responsible for Jarvis Private Banking's entire campaign schedule. Without it, the agency would be in dire straits.

Chester shook his head. 'No, Jess. We put our own house in order. We show the world just how trustworthy we are.'

'Good idea,' Max said, nodding thoughtfully, as he always did with Chester these days. He used to challenge much more. Then again, he also used to have a lot more clients.

'You want us to develop some adverts telling everyone? We could position you as the ethical choice, the safe choice, the—'

'No,' Chester said, his eyes gleaming. 'I have a better idea.'

'You do?' Max asked interestedly.

'An ethical audit,' Chester said triumphantly. 'An audit of every single employee at Jarvis Private Banking. And every single staff member of all our partner companies, too. Yourselves included. What do you think? Brilliant, huh? I can see the slogan now: "We make sure we can trust all our people – and that means you can trust us."' He caught Max's eye and grinned sheepishly. 'Or, you know, something a bit shorter. I guess there's a reason I don't work in advertising. Right?'

Max smiled, but it didn't quite reach his eyes. 'You really think this is a good idea? It'll be expensive. And how will your employees feel about being scrutinized like that?'

'They'll handle it,' Chester said lightly. 'These are tough times, and we need to use all the ammunition we've got. And so what if it costs money? You gotta spend money to make money, that's what I always say.'

Max cleared his throat. 'This is a really great idea. Like all your ideas, Chester. But perhaps we should pause before rushing into anything,' he said tentatively. 'Let's think this through, work it into an overarching strategy that encompasses your brand and your goals for the next few years and—'

'You know what?' Chester interrupted. 'I'm sick of overarching strategies. I'm sick of business-school speak. When I started out as an investment manager, I trusted my gut, and it was my gut that got me where I am today. And since I got here, all I've been doing is following strategies.'

'Safe strategies that meant you avoided all the chaos of the banking-system collapse,' Max pointed out.

'Sure.' Chester nodded. 'But we're not talking about anything major here. We're talking about an audit. We're good guys, and this is a chance to prove it to the world.' He sat back happily. 'You know, I have a really good feeling about this.'

'Well, if you have a good feeling about it, then we are very happy to be part of it,' Max said diplomatically.

'Wonderful. So we have a perfect wife, and now we're going to have a perfect company,' Mum said dryly. 'Now perhaps we can focus back on this evening and attempt to make this dinner party perfect. So no more talk about work, and, Max, perhaps you could serve pudding? I can smell something delicious coming from the kitchen.'

Max beamed. 'You're right. No more business. And as for pudding, my perfect wife is responsible for that lovely smell,' he said, taking a slug of wine. 'She may pretend she can't cook, but she made an apple pie this afternoon.'

I looked at him in horror. 'Oh shit,' I said, scraping back my chair quickly and jumping up toward the door. I hadn't *exactly* made the pie; I'd bought it from a deli around the corner. But it had been made by hand there, and perhaps by telling Max it was 'homemade' I might have given him the impression that it had been homemade by me instead of by someone who could actually cook. Now, however, I'd managed to ruin even that. 'I put it in ages ago,' I said desperately. 'It's going to be burned . . .' I shot a reproachful look at the table. 'I said I didn't cook. Why did you let me cook, Max? We both knew it was a terrible idea.'

'I turned the oven down half an hour ago,' Max said reassuringly. 'It'll be just done now. And I took out the ice cream, too, so it won't be hard.'

'You did?' My eyes widened – in surprise, in gratitude, in love. And then I ran back to the table and hurled my arms around him. 'I told you that you were perfect,' I said. 'You are the best.'

'Perfect because I turned down the oven?' Max asked sagely. 'Well, I'm very glad to hear that. Sounds like I've got a pretty easy ride ahead of me if that's all you're looking for.'

Chapter 2

∾

'MAX THINKS I'M PERFECT.'

It was the next morning, and all night I'd been obsessing about perfection, about the attainability of it. The more I'd thought about it, the more I realized how far from perfect I was. In fact, I was so not perfect it was laughable. Cryable, more like, even if that wasn't a proper word. When you looked at it properly, which is what I'd been doing, it was pretty clear that I was a crap wife. Awful. And once I'd realized that, I became preoccupied with the idea that Max wasn't really in love with me; he was in love with someone he thought I was. Someone perfect. And one day he'd find out that I wasn't that person and then he'd fall right out of love with me. And that was just too awful to even contemplate.

'Perfect?' Helen wrinkled her nose. We were drinking coffee in a café around the corner from where she lived – where we both used to live. 'Well, bully for you. Is that what you think the problem with John is? That I'm not good enough?'

Helen was my former flatmate and all-time best friend. We'd met at university, and despite our differences (she was a party girl; I preferred a night with my laptop, catching up with my studies), we'd been as thick as thieves for years. 'No,' I said quickly. 'God, no, I wasn't talking about you and John.'

'Oh,' Helen said, looking slightly affronted. She'd spent the past hour filling me in on every detail of her latest relationship and appeared less than enthusiastic about changing the subject.

'I'm sorry,' I said quickly. 'I thought we'd finished on John. So you called him last night?'

Helen raised an eyebrow. 'Exactly. And he said that he'd love to see me this weekend but that he had a lot of work on and didn't think it was fair to me when he wouldn't be able to give me any attention. So do you reckon he's married after all? Or is he just a nice guy who's being honest?'

I frowned. John was Helen's latest flame; she'd met him through work, and he had – so far, at least – been pretty perfect in that he'd called when he said he would, didn't appear to be hiding a wife anywhere, and was both handsome and self-sufficient. Naturally, being Helen, she smelled a rat.

'I don't know, Hel. I haven't met the guy. Does he seem nice?'

'Well, of course he does, dummy, otherwise I wouldn't be going out with him. But the wolf in "Little Red Riding Hood" seemed nice at first, didn't he?'

She had a point. 'So look a bit closer,' I suggested, slurping more coffee. 'Does he have big teeth?'

Helen rolled her eyes. 'You are not taking this seriously. What's up with you, anyway? You keep getting this funny look in your eye. Like you do when you're obsessing about something.'

I shook my head. 'I'm not obsessing,' I lied.

'But . . . ?' Helen prompted me.

'Nothing. It's just . . .'

'Just what?' Helen asked impatiently. 'Come on, Jess, spit it out.'

I sighed. 'It's just that Chester and Mum came over for dinner last night, and we were talking about what makes the ideal spouse.'

'Okay,' Helen said hesitantly. 'And?'

'And Max said he thought I was perfect.'

'That's terrible,' Helen deadpanned. 'Jeez. Husband thinks wife is perfect. Horror! I'm surprised the papers haven't picked up the story.'

I shot her a look. 'I gave Hugh Barter more money.'

'Oh,' Helen said, her face suddenly becoming more serious. 'You did, huh?'

'I didn't have a choice.' I sighed again. 'I mean, I did, but . . .'

'But you didn't,' Helen agreed. 'How much this time?'

'Ten grand. Another "loan," he said.'

Helen whistled. 'So what are you going to do?'

'I don't know,' I said wearily. 'Tell Max. But he's so stressed out about work right now. And then when he started on that whole I'm-perfect thing . . .'

'You don't want to burst his bubble?' Helen asked.

'I don't want him to realize how imperfect I am,' I said despondently. 'I don't want him realizing he's made a mistake.'

'Oh, don't be so melodramatic,' Helen said. 'No one's perfect. Max said that only because he's a nice guy.'

'Some people are perfect,' I insisted. 'Max is.'

'He is?' Helen asked dubiously.

'Yes, he is. He's kind, thoughtful, handsome, strong, hardworking, successful, and he even cooks.'

'He does cook,' Helen agreed. 'That beef bourguignon he cooked the other day was delicious.'

'I should be able to cook,' I said. 'I should be able to make him a delicious meal sometimes.'

'Jess?' Helen peered at me. 'Jess, what's going on?'

I shrugged. 'I don't think I measure up,' I said quietly. 'I wish I was a better person. A person who deserved Max.'

'You do totally deserve him. You may not be able to cook, but you're loaded, remember. So buy him takeaway,' Helen said immediately.

'That's not the same. It's about making an effort. I don't even iron his shirts.'

'No, and you also don't live in the 1950s,' Helen said, rolling her eyes. 'Ever heard of having a cleaner? Or using the laundry service? Ever heard of women's emancipation?'

'I know. And it's not that I want to be forced into doing those things. I'd just . . . you know, like to be able to. Sometimes.'

'So learn,' Helen said wearily. 'But you know this isn't really to do with home economics, don't you?'

'I know,' I said, biting my lip. 'So what do I do about Hugh? He's going to keep coming back. I know he is.'

Helen nodded uncertainly. 'Yeah. But don't rush into anything. Do you remember what happened when Max thought for a second that you'd cheated on him?'

I shivered. It had been horrible. A month or so before Max and I were due to get married, he started to be very evasive, and then I discovered that he'd been seeing a woman. A really attractive one. Anyway, I put two and two together, got five, and drowned my sorrows in a bar. And that's when Hugh Barter turned up.

Hugh used to work for Max and had moved to a rival firm; he was a terrible person, a scheming, self-serving schmoozeball. The night I met him in the bar, though, I was drunk and not thinking straight, and when he invited me to come back to his place, I agreed.

But the attractive lady hadn't been Max's bit on the side;

she was my presumed-dead mother, come back to find me. And before I knew it, Hugh had blackmailed me and brought Milton Advertising to its knees, stealing Chester's business and sending Max into a total meltdown.

There was an awful minute when I'd told Max the truth. I would never forget the look in his eye, the look of total devastation that left him only when Mum rushed in and told him that I'd been trying to protect her, that it was actually she who'd slept with Hugh, who'd kissed and told, drunkenly revealing company secrets. The look of relief on his face when she said that had haunted me every time I'd been tempted to come clean. I knew I'd never be able to forgive myself for what I'd done, and neither would Max, if he knew the truth – even though it turned out I'd only kissed Hugh, even though it turned out he was gay and had planned the whole thing to get at Max.

'So, what, I just spend my life on tenterhooks, waiting for Hugh to demand anything he wants?' I asked miserably. 'One way or another, Max is going to discover the truth: That I let him down. That I'm a terrible wife.'

'No, you're not. It was one indiscretion at a weak moment. And, anyway, technically speaking, you were a bad *fiancée*,' Helen pointed out. 'You haven't done anything bad since being his *wife*.'

I raised an eyebrow. 'I'm not sure it works like that, Hel.'

'Sure it does,' she said breezily. 'Anyway, perfection is overrated. Everyone's got skeletons in their cupboards.'

'Max doesn't,' I said miserably.

Helen looked at me sternly. 'I'm sure he does. And even if he doesn't, you can't let this Hugh thing take up more head space than it deserves. Max doesn't need to know. No good will come of telling him. So don't. And stop beating yourself up about it.'

'Easy for you to say,' I complained.

'Do you think telling him will make anything better?' Helen demanded. I shook my head. 'Then, can we move on? Can I continue telling you about John?'

'Yes,' I said firmly. 'Yes, please continue. So he said he was busy over the weekend?'

Helen nodded. 'All weekend. I mean, that's weird, right? No one works all weekend.'

She caught my eye and reddened slightly. 'Other than you and Max,' she said quickly. It had been over working weekends that I'd fallen in love with Max; we were both workaholics, both pretty uninterested in going out and painting the town red.

'Maybe it's weird,' I said tentatively. 'But maybe it isn't. I mean, maybe he's just swamped at work.'

'Yeah, it's possible,' Helen said, her forehead creasing into a frown. 'But what if it's a brush-off?'

I shrugged helplessly. 'Hel, you know I don't have much experience with men,' I said.

'You're married,' Helen pointed out.

'Yes, but—'

'You've been engaged twice.'

'Sure, but—'

'And you convinced a gorgeous, in-demand man to marry you in fifty days.' Helen raised an eyebrow and sat back, as if to say, 'Game, set, and match.'

It was true, but it wasn't the way it sounded. Helen was referring to a story that started with Grace, my grandma's neighbor at the old folks' home. I hadn't known that Grace was rich. I'd just thought of her as the sweet woman to whom I told stories, cheering her up in the process. The one she'd liked most was about me having a boyfriend, a story I'd made up about Anthony Milton, my boss. And before long, the 'boyfriend' had become a fiancé (egged on by Grace) and finally a full-fledged husband. I know, it seems a little far-fetched. But her eyes lit up when I told her about our (totally made-up) romance. And then when she died, I got the shock of my life – she'd left me all her money and an amazing house in the country. Except she didn't leave it to me; she left it to Mrs. Anthony Milton. So Helen and I hatched Project Marriage, an attempt to get Anthony to marry me for real. And it worked. Kind of. There was just one more twist in the tale. Turned out Anthony was actually Grace's estranged son; she'd known all along that I wasn't really married and had been angling to get the two of us hitched so that I could keep him on the straight and narrow.

Fortunately I'd realized, just moments before saying 'I do,' that I couldn't do it – not for Grace, not for all the money in the world. Because I loved Max and I couldn't imagine being married to anyone but him. Grace might have been disappointed if she were still alive, but I like to think that the romantic in her would be happy. After all, I got married eventually; I got my happily ever after.

'Anthony asked me to marry him because he wanted half of Grace's inheritance,' I said firmly. 'That's all. And after everything I've done, I'm the last person you want to ask for advice on relationships.'

'Not the *last* person,' Helen said, attempting a smile. 'But maybe you've got a point. Maybe you're not the perfect person to turn to for guidance. But you're the only person here, so you'll have to do. Do you think I should trust John or not?'

'I don't know,' I said with a sigh. 'Hel, I've never even met the guy. What does your gut tell you?'

I hadn't trusted Hugh. Not initially, anyway. And I'd been right.

'It tells me he's probably telling the truth,' Helen said, sitting back despondently.

'So why the long face?' I asked, curious. 'It's almost as if you'd prefer there to be some deep dark secret.'

'No!' Helen shook her head vehemently. 'No, I wouldn't. No, not at all.'

I studied her face for a few seconds, then took a slurp of coffee. 'Come on, then. What do you think makes the ideal husband? The ideal wife?' I asked.

Helen frowned. 'The whole idea of marriage freaks me out a bit,' she said, shuddering.

'Boyfriend, then,' I said. 'If you could design the perfect partner, what would he be like?'

'God knows.'

'At least try. Once you know what you want, you can see if John measures up.'

Helen nodded thoughtfully. 'Okay, if you put it like that. But let me state for the record that I categorically do not believe that perfection exists. If it did, we'd all give up now, because we're so completely lacking. So, let me think. Obviously he'd have to be completely in love with me,' she said, pausing briefly. 'Yes, absolutely smitten. And he'd also have to be gorgeous. Tall. Rich, definitely. He'd have a sports car. And maybe a private jet. He'd whisk me off to Barbados on holiday when I'd had a bad day at work. Not that I'd have to work because . . . well, why would I? He'd be loaded.'

I shook my head in exasperation. 'That's it? You want someone rich and handsome who has a jet?'

'And who's crazy about me,' Helen reminded me. 'That's the crucial piece of the jigsaw. C-R-A-Z-Y.'

I laughed. 'Fair enough.'

'Talking about crazy,' Helen said, leaning forward suddenly, 'have you heard from Ivana lately?'

Ivana was a friend of ours. More Helen's, actually, but I'd gotten to know her pretty well during the whole Project Marriage thing, when she'd coached me in the art of flirtation. Ivana was a kind of stripper or lap dancer – none of us was entirely sure exactly what she did for a living, and to be honest we didn't really want to. She was Russian, beautiful in a voluptuous leather-wearing kind of way, very domineering, and married to a guy from Manchester called Sean, who absolutely adored her. Helen had met her a few years before when she was making a documentary about strip clubs, and somehow Ivana had become a firm fixture.

Except now things had changed slightly.

'Not since—' I said tentatively.

'The baby?' Helen interrupted, an amused expression on her face. 'No, I didn't think so. You know, I went round there a week or so ago and she made me take off my shoes.'

I stared at her in confusion. 'She what?'

'She said she didn't want me bringing germs into the house.'

'Ivana? Ivana said that?'

I'd been to Ivana's studio flat only once; it was on Old Compton Street in Soho, and it stank of bodily fluids mixed with heady perfume and didn't look as if cleaning products had ever made their way through the door.

'She wouldn't even let me see Giorgio, either. He was asleep, and she said that he didn't like having his routine disturbed.'

'Giorgio?'

'As in Armani. Apparently the baby looks just like Ivana.'

I met Helen's eyes and suppressed a giggle. 'Seriously?'

She was giggling, too, holding a hand over her mouth to try to make out that she wasn't. 'That's what Sean said.'

I nodded seriously, trying to get the image out of my head of a baby boy dressed in leather hot pants with thick black eyeliner scrawled on his face. It was too much. I snorted.

'We should go round together,' Helen said suddenly, leaning forward. 'We should go this week.'

'Good idea,' I agreed.

'Great.' Helen sat back in her chair. 'So, look, do you think I should call John to catch him off guard, or do you think I should leave it up to him to call me?'

'I think I'd leave it a day or two,' I said.

'Yeah, good idea. I won't obsess. I'll just relax. Not think about it.'

'Exactly,' I said. 'Think you can do it?'

Helen nodded firmly, then shook her head, grinning. 'Not in a million years. But I'll give it a go.'

Chapter 3

❧

ON MONDAY MORNING, I found myself studying Max as he indicated right and pulled into the Milton Advertising car park. He was so handsome, I thought. So noble and good, and funny, and clever . . .

'You all right?' Max asked. 'You haven't said a word all morning.'

I nodded vaguely. 'I'm fine.'

Someone that amazing deserved someone better than me. Someone who really *was* perfect.

'Jess?' Max looked at me worriedly.

I shook myself and forced a smile. 'I'm really fine,' I assured him. 'Honestly.' Someone who didn't lie to him all the time, too, I was thinking.

'Well, okay, then,' Max said, getting out of the car. 'If you say so.'

'I do,' I said quietly, as I followed him into the office, my shoulders slumped. Was Helen right? Could I *never* tell Max? Did that mean I was beholden to Hugh forever? Did that mean that my marriage was, for all intents and purposes, a sham?

I sighed despondently. There was no way out of this – no *good* way, anyway. If only . . . I frowned suddenly, as something occurred to me.

'Jess?' I looked up to see Max peering at me.

'Sorry,' I said. 'I was . . . just thinking about something.'

'Evidently,' Max said, raising an eyebrow. 'Listen, you remember that ethical-audit idea Chester had?'

I nodded uncertainly. 'Yes?'

'Well, it's definitely happening. And the great news is, we're being audited first. Chester said it would be a test case.'

The way Max said it suggested he didn't think it was great news at all.

'But the other night,' I said cautiously, 'you said it was a good idea. A chance to show ourselves off a bit.'

Max sighed. 'But that was in front of Chester. The reality is it's going to absorb all our time, alienate our staff, and use up valuable resources.'

'So tell Chester that,' I said, frowning. 'Tell him we're not going to do it.'

Max stopped walking. 'And risk losing his business?' He shook his head. 'Jess, I know that Chester is your future stepfather and all warm and cuddly, but he is also a powerful businessman who likes to get his way. As his advertising agency and, lest we forget, an agency that in these troubled times is entirely reliant on his business to keep our heads above water, it is not for us to put obstacles in his way or to say no. Remember the old adage that the client is always right?'

'But we're also here to advise him,' I protested. 'Advise him that it's a terrible idea if you think it is.'

'I don't. Not necessarily,' Max said wearily. 'I can totally see the logic. I can just see a whole lot of potential problems that I could do without. And it's Chester's idea. He's the client.'

'So if he says jump, we jump?' I asked. I loved Chester, but I loved Max more, and I hated seeing him like this.

'In this economic climate, yes, we jump,' Max said flatly.

'We can't afford to lose Chester. And that's the end of the matter.'

I nodded thoughtfully. 'If you *do* want to say no,' I said tentatively, 'and if Chester did pull his business, we could always use my money to keep things afloat for a while. I mean, I've still got nearly four million pounds sitting in the bank and nothing to do with it, so . . .'

'No,' Max said firmly, as I'd known he would. 'Your money is your money, Jess. I don't want bailouts. I want a successful business. So we're going to meet this auditor and we're going to play nicely and we're going to keep our fingers crossed that it all goes smoothly. Okay? Now, look, I'd better run. I've got a million and one things to do before this guy arrives.'

He marched off to his office, BlackBerry in hand; I turned to my desk, where Caroline was standing, eagerly waving at me. Caroline was my assistant. Actually, she was more than just an assistant – she'd turned out to be a confidante, a rock, when everything seemed to be crumbling around me because of Hugh and his plan to totally ruin Max. Plus, she seemed to know everyone who mattered in London, whether they were minor celebrities, huge pop stars, or even royalty. But right now even she couldn't really raise my spirits.

'Hi, Caroline,' I said heavily. 'How's it going? Nice weekend?'

'Oh my God,' she said, handing me a coffee, her eyes dancing and her free hand waggling at the side of her head. 'You'll never believe what's just happened.'

I took the coffee gratefully. 'Um, has Prince William asked you out?' I joked.

Caroline's forehead creased in confusion. 'No!' she exclaimed. 'God, that would be awful. I mean, Kate's lovely.

There's no way— ' She caught my eye and realized I wasn't serious, then flushed a deep red. 'Oh, right. You were joking.'

I giggled. 'So come on, then, what did happen?'

Her eyes lit up again.

'Someone made an offer on my Chloe bag. Two hundred pounds! And that's just an opening bid!'

'Your what?' I asked, slightly nonplussed.

'My Chloe bag! I'm selling it on eBay.'

'Ah!' I said, understanding now. 'But why? It's a lovely bag. I mean, you love it, don't you?'

Caroline nodded seriously. 'Yes, but I don't need it, do I?'

'No, I suppose not,' I agreed, turning on my computer and immediately clicking my *Project Plan* icon. 'So you're still into that book, then?'

The book had appeared on Caroline's desk a few weeks back. *Do You Need It?* by Jerome D. Rutter was a self-help tome that, according to its cover, enabled anyone who read it to de-junk their life, free themselves from the shackles of consumerism, find love, find fulfillment, and generally feel loads happier. It was on the bestseller list because the credit crunch had made everyone rethink their spending and finances. Caroline, though, saw it in an entirely different light – she had read it cover to cover and announced the next day that it had spoken to her at a fundamental, even spiritual level. She'd realized, she told me sagely, that her life was too full and that she'd never achieve a Zen-like existence without radical change.

And she hadn't messed around in following the book's recommendations. Each week she appeared to be clearing out a different section of her wardrobe – shoes, scarves, skirts, trousers, tops, dresses, coats, miscellaneous accessories, and now bags – with huge black sacks destined for the charity shop. Friends who, according to the book, *exerted a toxic influence on her life* were told in no uncertain terms that she wouldn't be seeing them for a while, if ever, and all the poor boys who constantly called her to ask her out had been given a polite but firm no. 'Because you have to clear the decks if you're going to find yourself,' Caroline had explained to me knowingly.

'Yes, of course I'm still into the book,' Caroline said now, as though surprised by the question. 'It's not a fad, Jess. It's a way of life. You really should try it.'

I smiled. 'A book that is entirely made up of platitudes.'

'Oh, no,' Caroline sighed. 'It's full of wisdom. You just can't see it because you're completely fulfilled already. You don't need to de-junk anything.'

'De-junk? Who's de-junking?' I turned quickly to see Anthony appear between my desk and Caroline's. Anthony, who I'd almost married. Anthony, who had left the firm for Max to run so that he could jet around the world and then, when he'd run out of money, had come back again, cap in hand. He had somehow convinced Max to let him have his old office back, but, as far as I could see, he never seemed to do any work at all. He grinned laconically at me. 'You're not finally getting rid of poor Maxy, are you, Jess?'

My eyes narrowed. 'If I was de-junking, Max wouldn't come into it, Anthony,' I said levelly. 'You, on the other hand . . .'

'Ah, touché.' Anthony turned to Caroline and winked at her. 'Excuse our banter, Caro. Jess here never really got over me.'

'As I recall, Anthony, I was never really—'

'Under me?' Anthony's grin deepened, and my cheeks went a deep crimson.

'Never in love with you,' I said, trying to regain my composure. 'Or even slightly interested in you, actually.'

'Jess, you cut me deep,' Anthony said, affecting a sad look. Then he turned back to Caroline.

'So, Caro, what are you up to? Ah, you're on eBay. Pitching for their account, are you? Didn't know it was up, myself. You must have great industry sources.'

Caroline looked up at him worriedly. 'No. I mean . . . I was just selling something. But I was only having a quick look. Not using company resources to . . . I mean, I . . .'

'Leave her alone,' I said firmly. 'Caroline can check eBay if she wants to.'

'Of course she can,' Anthony said indulgently, putting his arm around her. 'I was only teasing.'

I rolled my eyes at him as my computer flickered to life. I was far too busy to listen to Anthony's rubbish. Back in the car I'd had an idea. An idea that might just save me and save my marriage. And I needed to think about it. Anthony, unfortunately, showed no signs of leaving. 'Anthony, do you actually want anything, or are you hanging around here because you haven't got anything better to do?' I asked irritably.

Anthony's eyebrows shot up. 'Dear me, can I not spend some time with two of my colleagues without being accused of time-wasting?' he asked, shaking his head sadly.

I opened my project-planning software, my heart thudding in my chest, not with fear this time but with hope.

Project Ideal Wife.

I couldn't believe I hadn't thought of it before. Max thought I was perfect; I knew I wasn't. Not at all. So I would make myself perfect. I would learn to cook; I would work in soup kitchens; I would be the most thoughtful, considerate, devoted person in the whole wide world. And maybe, just maybe, if I could be perfect in every single way apart from what had happened with Hugh, then that sordid incident would be so insignificant in the scheme of perfection that it would barely even exist anymore. It would be like one drop of poison in a whole sea of freshwater; it would disappear, would be diluted into oblivion. And when I told Max about it, he would think it was insignificant, too.

The more I thought about it, the more I knew I had to do it. I owed it to Max, owed it to us. And I was hardly a stranger to self-improvement plans – or, rather, self-reinvention plans. When I'd thought that marrying Anthony Milton was the only option open to me, I'd been about the least likely candidate for his attentions: a mousy workaholic who had no experience with (or interest in) men. And Helen and Ivana had whipped me up into a total fox who knew how to dress, how to wear her hair, and, importantly, how to flirt. Of course, the one person my transformation hadn't impressed was Max, but that was one of the reasons I loved him so much – he loved me for who I was, not because I'd learned how to do a flicky thing with my hair. But that wasn't the point. The point was that I'd transformed from workaholic mouse to flirtatious vamp in the space of about three days. So I could totally transform myself into the perfect wife. And it would be much easier, because I *wanted* to do it. This time I would be doing it for the person I loved more than anything else in the whole wide world.

'Jess, you do know that creating a dynamic atmosphere is as much about building relationships as it is about' – Anthony peered over at my computer – 'project-planning computer programs.'

'There's nothing wrong with project plans,' I said, turning

my screen slightly so he couldn't see it. 'They help organize things.'

'Do you like project planning, Caro?' Anthony asked, leaning over her like a boa constrictor evaluating its prey.

'Yes, actually, I . . .' Caroline said, but Anthony wasn't listening.

'Never could understand them, myself,' he continued, 'but then again, when you're creative, things like project plans just fence you in, put up walls where you don't need them.'

I counted to ten. 'Creative people also use them,' I said tightly.

'Do they?' Anthony asked innocently, then looked at me, wide-eyed. 'Oh, I see. You mean you? You think you're creative? Really?'

'Jess is very creative,' Caroline said immediately, rushing to my defense.

'That's one word for it,' Anthony said silkily.

I stared at him impatiently. 'Anthony, is there something you want? Because if there isn't, I'd appreciate it if you'd bugger off.'

He laughed. 'Matter of fact, there is. Do you know anything about an ethical audit? Max was blathering about it earlier, and I have to confess I stopped listening after about a second – you know what he's like when he gets going . . .' I met his eyes stonily. 'No, maybe you don't,' he said, grinning to himself. 'Anyway, suffice it to say I didn't catch what it's all about and was hoping you could fill me in. He wants to hold a company meeting or something, and I really can't be bothered listening to him talk about it again.'

'You should,' I said, turning back to my computer un-comfortably as I remembered the audit. 'Because you could be in trouble. Chester wants to head up the perfect company full of perfect people. And that includes his partner companies, like us. So we're going to be audited. He wants to check that everyone who works for him is whiter than white. You know, trustworthy.' I looked up at him meaningfully, telling myself that the auditor wouldn't be interested in kisses in bars but in important stuff like fraud and embezzlement. And, anyway, Anthony was way worse than me. He didn't even know the meaning of the word 'ethical.' 'If I were you, I'd start looking for somewhere else to pretend to work. I think the idea is that we have a blemish-free workforce.'

'Blemish-free?' Anthony raised an eyebrow. 'Sounds terribly dull.'

'I think that sounds amazing,' Caroline said, her eyes widening. 'Jerome D. Rutter says that trust is the foundation of everything. He says paring back to the basics makes you realize whom and what you can trust.'

'Well, there you go,' I said.

'Don't worry about me,' Anthony said, straightening up, his eyes twinkling now. 'It'll be a questionnaire, I bet. I'm very good at questionnaires. By the time I'm finished with mine, they'll be nominating me for the Nobel Prize. Or at least offering me a commendation.'

'Sure they will,' I said, rolling my eyes. His confidence was shocking.

Anthony winked. 'Just you wait,' he said, looking back over his shoulder as he walked toward his office.

'Is it true that clients really like Anthony?' Caroline asked, once he was out of earshot.

I shrugged. That's what Max always said. And he was right – Anthony's charm knew no bounds, could convince the hardest cynic to give business to Milton Advertising. But he still infuriated me. 'He basically gets paid for flirting,' I said with a sigh. 'And everyone else has to do the work.'

I turned back to my computer. Peace at last. Now my work could begin.

'Darling?'

I frowned. That sounded like . . .

'Darling! You shouldn't hunch over your computer like that.'

'Mum?' I said incredulously. 'Mum, what are you doing here? I'm working. And you're meant to be in Wiltshire.' Mum was staying in my house in Wiltshire. The one Grace had left me in her will. Chester had asked her to move in several times but Mum insisted she needed her 'own space' until they were actually married, not seeming to notice that Wiltshire wasn't her 'own' at all. I didn't mind – at least my lovely house was being used by someone.

'I'm on my way to do the wedding list. Of course, Chester should be coming with me, but naturally he's too busy. So if he doesn't like the dinner service I choose, then it's really his own fault and he's going to have to live with it.'

'You know,' Caroline said, leaning over, 'Jerome D. Rutter says that wedding lists can hold a negative force over you, because you feel like you've got to keep everything you're given even though your life and tastes may change. He says that you should ask people to give to charity instead. That way you improve the world and don't weigh yourself down.'

Mum looked at Caroline and smiled tightly. 'Well, Jerome D. Rutter obviously hasn't seen the dinner service from Royal Doulton that I've got my eye on,' she said.

'Mum, look, I'm kind of busy here. Is there something specific that you want?'

She frowned. 'You know, I've come all the way from

Wiltshire. I don't expect a welcome party, . manners, darling.'

'I'm sorry,' I said, embarrassed. 'It's just Monday . ing. You know. Can I get you a cup of tea?'

'Tea would be nice; thank you, darling,' Mum said, looking slightly mollified. 'One sugar, if it isn't too much trouble.'

'I'll make it, if you like,' Caroline offered immediately, but I waved her away. I wanted a couple of minutes to myself to turn my idea around in my head a bit before it got lost behind all my mother's chatter. Max believed in perfection, I thought, as I wandered to the small office kitchen and found a vaguely clean mug. He thought I was perfect and the ideal wife. I knew I wasn't. What we had was a gap between perception and reality. So . . . wouldn't the obvious solution be to close that gap? Maybe not completely but as far as possible?

I took a tea bag from the box and switched on the kettle. So what if perfection didn't actually exist? That didn't mean aiming high was a bad idea. Just like Chester with his audit. He wanted his company to be the ideal against which others would measure themselves; surely I could aim at being the ideal wife?

I finished making my mother's tea, then wandered back to my desk and handed her the mug. She was sitting at Caroline's desk now, opposite mine, with her mouth wide open. 'And you can buy things just like that?'

Caroline nodded. 'You bid, you see. It's an auction.' She shot me a little smile. 'Your mother was interested in eBay,' she said by way of explanation.

'It's amazing,' Mum said. 'I'd heard about it, but never actually . . . Now, what else is there on the Internet? Chester bought me a computer, you see. He thought it would help

...ne with the wedding. What about networking? Everyone networks on their computers, don't they?'

I found myself laughing. 'Mum, you sound like a dinosaur. Have you seriously never been on eBay before?'

Mum looked at me haughtily. 'Dinosaurs would still be roaming about if it hadn't been for the meteorite that hit earth,' she said. 'And, anyway, I've never had my own computer before. But now I'm connected to the World Wide Web. So, come on, Caroline, how do I network?'

Caroline looked at me helplessly. 'I don't know. Um, Facebook, maybe?'

'Facebook?' Mum looked at her uncertainly. 'Is that a book of faces?'

'Kind of,' Caroline said. 'Look, let me show you.'

'Is this what you wanted to see me about?' I asked. 'Getting online?'

'Yes, darling,' Mum said airily. 'But you get on with your work. Caroline and I will be fine. Won't we, Caroline?'

Caroline smiled sweetly, and I rolled my eyes, then turned back to my own computer.

PROJECT IDEAL WIFE

Mission: To be the perfect wife.
Objectives:

I frowned, trying to remember what Max had said on the subject, trying to remember what Chester, Mum, and even Helen had said.

1. To be honest.

I squirmed slightly as I thought about Hugh.
As far as possible, I added.

2. To learn to cook fabulous food and to cook a lovely meal
~~every night. Some nights.~~ on occasion.

Sure, Max had said he didn't mind that I couldn't cook, but what man didn't like it when his wife went the extra mile and baked him something delicious? No, I was going to learn to cook, and I was going to do it soon. Max wouldn't know what had hit him.

I thought for a moment. What else? Then I remembered what Chester had said.

3. To make sure Max's shirts are always dry-cleaned.

I frowned. Were shirts dry-cleaned? That didn't sound right.

Or just laundered. Beautifully. And ironed.

4. To learn to iron.

I reviewed the list, then sighed. It was pathetic. Cooking and ironing? Was I trying to be the perfect wife or a housekeeper? I started to delete, then changed my mind. They weren't bad things in themselves; I just needed more. I thought for a moment about what I loved about Max and what he did that made me feel so happy, so special. And then I started to type again.

5. To listen to Max, to hear what he actually says instead of hearing what I think he says or, worse, what I want him to have said.

6. To be a better person generally. To give my time to others. Soup kitchen, maybe?

7. To make life easy for him, not run to him every time I have a problem and expect him to sort things out.

8. To pay him little compliments every day, so he knows how loved he is.

9. To be supportive. Always. Unwaveringly. To be on his side no matter what.

10. ???

'Jess? Jess, what are you doing?' I looked up and reddened when I saw Max walking toward me, a perplexed expression on his face. 'Didn't you get my email? Oh, hello, Esther. I didn't know you were coming in today.'

'I just stopped by,' Mum said, standing up. 'Actually, I have to go now. Got an appointment at Harrods. Lovely to see you, though. And, Caroline, thank you so much. I'm going to Facebook myself later this evening. I'll look you up, shall I?'

'Definitely.' Caroline beamed as I closed my project-planning program guiltily. Sure enough, when I checked my email in-box, there were three new ones from Max.

'The partner from the auditing firm is here,' he said. 'He's going to brief us on the process.'

'Oh, great!' I stood up quickly. Too quickly: I spilled the rest of my forgotten coffee all over my desk. Caroline immediately started to mop it up with tissues.

'You're sure everything's all right, Jess? You're acting kind of weird today.'

'Me? No, I'm fine. Completely fine,' I said, trying to sound as supportive as I possibly could. 'So the partner's here. Let's go and see him!'

'Yes,' Max said, looking rather unconvinced. 'Let's.'

The partner from the auditing firm was waiting in Max's office and smiled pleasantly when I walked in.

'Name's Joshua,' he said, smiling broadly. 'Hope I didn't pull you away from anything important.'

I smiled brightly. 'No. Not at all.'

'Great. Well, as I said to Max, this is really just a form-ality, just a quick visit to run through the process.'

'Yes,' Max said seriously. 'Yes, of course. Very good of you to spare the time. So . . .'

'So,' Joshua said, pulling out a file, 'this has got every-thing you need in it. Chap who's going to be auditing you is called Eric. Eric Sandler. He'll be here a week from Tuesday and he'll get right to it. He may need some help pulling together an interview schedule and he might want to go through some of your paperwork, but essentially you should barely know he's here.'

'Interviews,' I said earnestly. 'He'll be interviewing . . . everyone?'

Joshua smiled reassuringly. 'Probably not. He might just pick some random names from your staff list. Then he'll be doing his own research, of course. Different auditors have different ways of doing things, although Eric is one of our more thorough people. Chester said he wanted a fine comb!'

'Thorough,' I said, trying my best to sound enthusiastic. 'Well, that's good. Isn't it, Max?'

Max looked at me quizzically. 'Absolutely. And thank you, Josh, for making the time to come see us.'

'No problem at all. Here's a pack of information that should cover everything. And here's my card – any prob-lems, give me a call. It's a painless process, though – basically we want to work with you, identify anything that we think you need to know about, and then we report back to Chester.'

I nodded weakly. 'It sounds great,' I said. 'I'm sure everyone will be, you know, excited about it.'

'Let's hope so,' Josh said. 'Some people get a bit funny about audits like this. They think we're out to catch them.'

'Well, I doubt there's anything to catch here,' Max said firmly. 'Fortunately, I know my workforce and we are a loyal, hardworking bunch. I'll have to work out a way of selling this idea to them, but I'm sure we'll pass with flying colors.'

'Glad to hear it,' Josh said. 'Anyway, I'll be off, don't want to hold you up. Great to meet you both, and I look forward to seeing the report!'

'Likewise,' Max said, reaching his hand out to shake Joshua's before showing him to the door. 'And thanks again.'

'Yes, thank you,' I said uncomfortably, and reminded myself to breathe. It was going to be fine. And, anyway, I had a plan. Project Ideal Wife. I had it all mapped out. Now I just had to find a soup kitchen. And learn to cook. Soup, ideally. And be supportive. And learn to iron. And . . .

Chapter 4

'AND . . . WHAT?' I sighed. 'I need help, Helen. What makes the perfect wife?'

'You're really serious about this?' Helen looked at me cautiously. It was Monday evening, and Helen and I, along with our friend Giles, were on our way to Ivana's to meet Giorgio.

'Very,' I said. 'I have to be the best wife ever. It's the only solution. So you have to help me.'

'But . . . why? If it ain't broke, don't fix it, I say. And it isn't broken, is it?'

'Not right now,' I admitted. 'But there has to be only a hairline crack and then one knock and it's smashed.'

'And you think Hugh Barter is a hairline crack?'

I looked at her uncomfortably. 'I'd say he's a bit more than that, actually.'

Helen nodded slowly. 'Yeah, I guess. Still, at least you've got a relationship to worry about.'

I frowned. 'What about John?'

'Well, sure, yes, there's John,' Helen said vaguely. 'Anyway, we're not talking about me, we're talking about you. Oh, look, there's Giles.'

Giles, my former wedding planner and the campest man in London, was waiting for us outside the café opposite Ivana's flat. In front of him was a huge box. 'Hello!' he said

41

excitedly. 'Oh, I can't wait to see Giorgio. Look. I got him a music station.'

'A music station?' I frowned. 'What's that?'

Giles rolled his eyes. 'What isn't it, you mean. It's amazing. It starts off as a play mat with surround-sound nursery rhymes. Then, when little Giorgio can sit up, it becomes an activity center, complete with keyboard – can you imagine? He'll be able to play the piano before he can walk!'

'You're serious? You got that for Giorgio?' Helen asked.

Giles nodded worriedly. 'Why? Has he already got one?'

'No, dummy,' Helen sighed. 'It's just that I only got him a Babygro. I'm going to look really stingy now. I mean, you hardly even know Ivana.'

'I know her well enough,' Giles said defensively. 'Anyway, I don't mind. Say you went in halves with me.'

'Really?' Helen asked. 'You don't mind?'

'Not if you give me fifty pounds.' Giles grinned.

There was a sharp intake of breath from Helen. 'Look, I'm freelancing,' she said. 'I can't go round spending fifty pounds on someone who can't even thank me for it.'

'I'll chip in your half,' I said quickly, putting my arm around her. 'Consider it payment for the advice you're going to give me.'

'Seriously?' Helen asked delightedly.

'Seriously,' I said. 'What else am I going to do with my money, anyway?'

It was a flippant comment, but the truth was that I had no idea what to do with all the money I had sitting in the bank. When Grace had named me her beneficiary, I'd been so focused on saving the house that she'd grown up in – the house she was determined to see go into the right hands instead of into the hands of developers, who'd turn it into lots of flats – that I hadn't even thought about the money.

Not much, anyway. And the longer I left it, the less confident I felt deciding what to do with it. No one ever wanted to talk about it – Max always told me it was my money to do what I wanted with, and my friends mentioned it only in jest, probably because they felt as awkward about it as I did. Every so often, Helen would tell me to buy a yacht or go mad in Chanel, but only because that's what she thought she'd do if she had £4 million sitting in the bank. I knew differently. It was one thing to spend a figurative £4 million, quite another to spend the real thing. You could blow £400 on something nice; £400,000 would buy a lovely flat in London. But £4 million? It was too much to splurge, too much to squander. That kind of money had to be spent well, had to make a difference. But a difference to whom? A difference to what? I didn't know, couldn't decide. So instead I pushed it from my mind and tried to pretend it didn't exist. Rather like Hugh Barter. Funnily enough, he was the only person who didn't seem to mind talking about my money.

'Oh, Jess, you're an angel,' Helen was saying. 'So what did you get Giorgio, anyway?'

I smiled secretively. 'You'll have to wait and see,' I said.

'Ooh, sounds exciting,' Giles said with a big smile. 'But what advice? What's going on?'

'Jess wants to become the ideal wife,' Helen said, rolling her eyes. 'Whatever that means.'

'The ideal wife? What is that, a reality show or something?' Giles asked interestedly.

Suddenly Helen's eyes lit up. 'Ooh, now you're talking,' she said excitedly. 'You know, come to think about it, that would make great telly. Put couples on an island somewhere with backup partners trying to outdo them . . . Make them do tasks, get people to vote them off if they don't do them properly—'

'Helen,' I said sternly, 'this is not about a television program.' I turned to Giles with a pained expression. 'This is serious. I want to . . .' I thought for a moment. Then I bit my lip. 'I want to be the best wife I can possibly be. I want to make Max really happy. There's nothing wrong with that, is there?'

'So, what, a whore in the bedroom, a chef in the kitchen, and a hostess in the living room?'

I pulled a face. 'You really think that constitutes an ideal wife? Shouldn't there be more to it than that?'

'Depends if you're talking ideal wife or ideal person,' Giles said thoughtfully. 'I mean, an ideal person probably wouldn't be a whore in the bedroom. Would they?'

'They would be appropriately whorish when it was required of them, I reckon,' Helen said with a glint in her eye.

'Are there degrees of whorishness?' Giles asked.

I sighed. 'Can we maybe move on from that particular aspect of the ideal wife?' I suggested. 'I want ideas. I want input.'

'Depends what kind of ideal wife you want to be,' Giles said. 'Depends why you're doing it.'

'She's doing it because of Hugh Barter,' Helen said wearily. 'Because she's trying to sweeten Max up so he won't dump her when he finds out she – shock, horror – kissed someone.'

Giles's eyes widened. 'Hugh? He's been in touch again?'

I nodded. Giles had been with me when Hugh's first call came through, bright and breezy, just wondering if I might help him out with some additional funding. And as Giles had said at the time, once I started this, there was never going to be an end in sight. If Hugh thought he had money on tap, he'd drink from it as long as he possibly could. 'He asked for ten grand this time,' I said quietly.

'Blimey. You're going to tell Max?'

'I don't know,' I said miserably. 'If I don't, I'm a terrible person, and if I do, Max might . . . He might decide he doesn't love me anymore.'

'Because of one kiss?' Helen screwed up her nose.

'Not one kiss.' I shook my head. 'It's the lying he wouldn't be able to take. The fact I've kept it from him for so long. He's so moral. He'd never lie to me. Never.'

Giles nodded slowly. 'So you want to be perfect to, what, make it up to him?'

I shrugged uncomfortably. 'I want to live up to his expectations. He thinks I'm perfect. He actually said that. And he deserves perfect, too. He's made me so happy. Happier than I ever expected to be. You know, I grew up thinking that men were selfish people who would use me and leave me if I gave them half a chance. Grandma told me I should never trust a man, never rely on one for anything. And then I met Max, and I trust him completely and rely on him hugely and . . . and . . .' I felt tears pricking at my eyes. '. . . and it turns out that it's me who's the untrust-worthy one. I have to be better, Giles. I have to be better than that.'

'You know,' Giles said thoughtfully, 'there was something about trying to be perfect in *Psychologies* this month, about the problem with being a perfectionist. The article said it's more important to feel good about yourself, to feel fulfilled, than to be perfect. And maybe it has a point. Maybe you need to stop beating yourself up.'

Helen raised an eyebrow. 'That's what I said. Get over it.'

'I prefer the way Giles said it,' I said.

'Seriously? He sounded like something off *The Oprah Winfrey Show* to me,' Helen said dismissively.

'And what's wrong with *Oprah*?' I asked. 'I like *Oprah*.'

'Oh, so you'll watch *Oprah,* but you're dismissing *Reality Wives: The Race to Perfection*?' Helen said, shaking her head in disappointment.

I looked at Helen uncertainly. '*Reality Wives: The Race to Perfection*? What's that? Have I missed something?'

'My new television pitch, of course!' Helen said, as if it was the most obvious thing in the world. 'The television show about couples who go to a desert island and have to compete for their other halves all over again.'

'It's a television show now?' I said, feeling a little smile edge its way onto my face. 'You had the idea only a minute ago.'

'Sometimes a minute is all it takes to create something fantastic,' Helen said, evidently very pleased with herself.

'But what would the winner get?' Giles asked uncertainly. 'Would they be competing for their husband? Who are they competing against? Would it be a fight between the wife and the mistress or something?'

Helen grinned. 'Ooh, I like that! I love it, actually. Giles, you're a genius. I may just employ you on the show.'

He looked at her excitedly. 'Really? I could be on television?'

'Not on. Behind the scenes,' Helen said quickly, then looked at Giles reassuringly when his face fell. 'But that's the best place to be, believe me.'

I sighed. 'Enough already. We're here to talk about my project plan. Will no one take it seriously?'

'I took it seriously,' Giles complained. 'I said you needed to be fulfilled.'

'I will be fulfilled when I know that I am as near to the

ideal wife as it is possible to be,' I said pointedly. 'Are you going to help or not?'

'Of course I will,' Giles agreed. 'We both will. Won't we, Helen?'

'Sure we will,' Helen said, as we approached Ivana's building.

I smiled gratefully. 'Thanks, guys. So are we ready to meet Giorgio?'

'More than ready,' Helen said with a grin as she pressed Ivana's doorbell. 'I can't wait!'

The door buzzed open, and we started the climb up the staircase to Ivana's apartment, with Helen helping Giles to lug the music station.

Ivana was waiting for us at the top, her front door propped open with her outstretched toe. She gave Helen and Giles a look of distinct disdain when they deposited the music station in her tiny hallway, but, after embracing her with kisses of hello, we all trooped inside.

And then my mouth fell open.

'Oh my God,' Giles said uncertainly. 'It's amazing.'

'Oh my word,' I said, my eyes like saucers.

We looked around, trying to take in the scene in front of us and exchanging expressions of incredulity.

'Vat?' Ivana demanded. 'Vat is wrong?'

'I . . . You . . . We . . .' Giles stammered, seemingly unable to string a sentence together. 'I . . .'

'Vat?' Ivana asked, her hands on her hips and her dark eyes flashing. 'Vat is it?'

I looked at her in amazement. 'Nothing,' I said, shaking my head in bewilderment. 'Nothing's wrong. It's just that . . . It's so . . . I don't—'

'Recognize the place,' Helen finished for me, looking

triumphant at being able to finally talk properly. 'See? I told you.'

'Is a bit different.' Ivana shrugged. 'Is clin.'

'Clean?' I asked. 'You call this clean?'

The truth was, it was like a hospital. A good hospital. It smelled of disinfectant; everywhere you looked were pastel colors and soft fabrics. I couldn't believe it was the same apartment I'd been to in the past. It looked bigger, better, like a completely new place.

'This is beyond clean,' Giles breathed. 'It's—'

'Bebe is asleep,' Ivana cut in, rolling her eyes. 'You vant tea? Coffee? Drink hot drinks now. Once bebe is awake, you not have anymore. Okay?'

We nodded in unison. 'Tea,' Helen said. 'Tea would be lovely.'

Ivana disappeared into the kitchenette; we walked into the main room of the flat – a bedroom-cum-sitting room-cum-general reception area. The last time I was here, there'd been a heavy veil of smoke over the place, a smell of incense, of . . . well, not to put too fine a point on it, of sex. Now it smelled of pine. Of tea tree oil. The whole place was bathed in a white glow, bottles were neatly stacked up on the side, and a bright-colored rug lay on the floor. In the corner, looking angelic in a little Moses basket, was a baby.

Ivana appeared again, carrying a tray with three cups of tea and some biscuits, along with a glass of water.

'This is for me,' she said, placing the tray carefully on the rug and swiping the water, gulping it down. 'You sit. Here. Here. Here.'

We duly sat where Ivana pointed.

'You look amazing,' I said. 'And this place, it's . . .'

'Yes,' Ivana said with a shrug. 'I chenge a few things.

Now, drink, plis. Bebe wek up in ten minutes. Then feed, then play. Then I heff washing to do. Ironing.'

'Ironing?' Helen arched an eyebrow but was met by a stony glare.

'Ironing,' Ivana confirmed. 'Good mother is ironing clotheses, no?'

'Sure,' I agreed immediately. 'I mean, definitely. I guess there must be a lot more of it to do now.'

Ivana stood up. 'I get muslin and bottle ready. You stay, plis.'

We nodded silently and watched in astonishment as Ivana disappeared back into the kitchenette. Doors began to clank.

'I nid tumble dryer,' she said, emerging again a few seconds later. 'But is no room in flet.' She eyed Giles's present, which was taking up almost the entire hallway – which wasn't really a hallway, more a gap between doors. 'And vat is thet?' she asked darkly.

Giles attempted a smile. 'It's for the baby,' he said. I could see that his hands were shaking slightly; he was terrified of Ivana, always had been.

'Is very big.' Ivana's voice was flat.

'Yes, it is,' Giles said. 'But it has to be big. It's a music station.'

'A vat?' Ivana's eyes narrowed.

'A music station. Look!' He jumped up and opened the box, transporting the contents into the sitting room, where he quickly set it up. 'I had a practice run at home,' he said with a nervous smile. 'There. What do you think? Giorgio goes here; he can kick his legs, and look what happens!' Giles pressed the side of the station, and immediately the flat was full of the sound of nursery rhymes. 'So what do you think?' he asked.

We all looked at Ivana; to our shock and surprise, she started to cry.

'Oh God, it's not what you wanted,' Giles said immediately. 'You hate it. Oh, I should have known. I should have asked someone. What do I know about babies?'

'No.' Ivana shook her head miserably. 'No, I do not hate it. I em loving it. Is just . . . I should be buying this for Giorgio. I no work, I heff no money. Giorgio no heff best toys.'

'Don't be silly,' Giles said with a soothing voice. 'He has you, and that's better than any toy. Anyway, that's the point of presents, isn't it? Getting other people to buy stuff for you?'

He was grinning, but Ivana didn't raise a smile. 'Sean no like other people buy stuff.'

'He doesn't?' I asked, curious. 'What, he doesn't like presents?'

'He no like presents from my friends,' Ivana said.

'So he's not going to like the music center?' Giles sounded worried. 'Should I pack it up again?'

'Not you,' Ivana said dismissively. 'Other friends. Friends I use work with. He say they Mefia. He say we no nid they money.'

None of us said anything for a few seconds.

'The . . . Mafia?' I asked tentatively.

Ivana rolled her eyes. 'Russian Mefia, not Italian. And I don' know. Mebe they Mefia, mebe not. They use come to club, use pay me money to be friendly, to be sexy. Sometime I do them favor. Special favor. Now Sean say no more do favors for them, no more working for money. I heff ask him for money instead. I no like.'

I cleared my throat uncertainly. She'd been doing special favors for the Russian Mafia? No wonder Sean wasn't keen on her working. 'Ivana, do you want to borrow some money?' I asked. 'I mean, I've got loads just sitting around doing nothing if you—'

'No!' Ivana snapped, her eyes blazing. 'I no borrow. I em not cherity. I vant work for my money. Is better. Independent.'

'You . . . you want to go back to work?' Giles sounded incredulous. 'Do the . . . I mean, would the hours work?'

Ivana shrugged. 'Sean say escort stripper no job for mother. He no think is *appropriate*.' She said the word with distaste.

'Still,' Giles said quickly. 'You're obviously brilliant at this motherhood lark. Isn't she, Helen?'

'God, yes.' Helen was nodding furiously. 'Amazing. The best.'

Ivana contemplated this for a few seconds, then nodded. 'Is true. I em best mother. End I like music station. Giorgio will be very good musician, I think. He will be very good everything.'

I took out a little parcel from my pocket. 'This is for Giorgio, too,' I said. 'From Max and me.'

Ivana took it and unwrapped it. Then she looked at me, a frown on her face.

'It's a frame,' I said. 'An antique silver one. It was one of Grace's. I thought you could put a photograph of Giorgio in it.'

She didn't say anything for a moment, then she rushed over to me and threw her arms around me. A few seconds later she released me and walked over to her ironing board as though nothing had happened. 'So, I heff ironing to do,' she said, matter-of-fact. 'You talk, plis.'

'You really do have this under control, don't you?' Giles said in amazement as she took out an ironing board and started to iron T-shirts as if her life depended on it. One by one they were laid flat, ironed, folded, ironed again, then placed on a pile of equally neat, precisely folded white garments. 'I mean, usually when people have babies, they're in a mess for months. I can't believe how organized you are. How on top of everything.'

Ivana nodded. 'Yes,' she said flatly. 'Yes, I em very good mother. I heff book.'

She took a book off the shelf; it had been sitting between a large dildo and an Ann Summers catalog. 'Meking heppy bebe,' she said, handing it to us. 'It tell vat to do.'

I took the book interestedly. Inside were chapters on sleeping, feeding, washing, playtime; there were pages and pages of routines.

'*Ten A.M.: Have a piece of toast and some water,*' I read. '*Baby should sleep for no more than one hour.*'

Ivana looked at her watch immediately. 'Thet mins twenty T-shirts ironed.'

'You can iron twenty T-shirts an hour?' Giles asked in amazement.

Ivana shot him an incredulous look. 'Of course. Now, talk. I no heff talking very much. You tell me about things. I nid hear things other than waahhh. Yes?'

'Jess wants to learn how to iron,' Helen said, sitting back in her chair. 'You should teach her.'

Ivana looked at me closely. 'You no iron?'

I reddened. 'Not really,' I admitted.

'And you want learn?'

I nodded firmly. To be honest, I was pretty sure that ironing came pretty far down the list of attributes of the perfect wife, but at least it was something tangible. Being a good listener was so much more difficult to measure.

'She thinks it's going to save her marriage,' Helen said,

grabbing a magazine from a neat pile, then putting it down again when she saw that the title was *Mother and Baby*.

'Merriage? Vat is wrong with your merriage?' Ivana asked, her eyes narrowing.

'Nothing!' I said, shooting Helen a meaningful look, because the last thing I wanted was for yet more people to know what was going on. 'I mean, not specifically with our marriage. It's more that—'

'Hugh Barter,' Helen cut in. 'And don't look at me like that, Jess. Ivana knows already. She was in the bar when you went off with him, remember?'

Ivana looked at me curiously. 'You still feel guilty about kiss gay boy?' she asked. 'You no boom-boom, no?'

'No,' I said wearily. 'We didn't boom-boom, so to speak. But I never told Max the truth about it. And now Hugh's . . . He's . . .' I didn't want to say the word, didn't want to accept what it was he was doing.

'He's blackmailing her.' Helen's voice was serious. 'Fifteen grand so far.'

Ivana's eyes darkened. 'He bleckmail you? You vant me get rid of problem? I do it. I do it now for you.'

I shook my head and cleared my throat. It wasn't the first time Ivana had made such an offer, but Ivana's way of 'getting rid of the problem' involved making a call to people I really didn't want to know existed. People who wouldn't just get rid of the problem but would get rid of Hugh himself. 'I appreciate the offer,' I said carefully. 'But I don't think that's quite what I had in mind.'

'So you learn how to iron instead?' Ivana folded her arms and stared at me, incredulous. 'This will help?'

'No,' I sighed. 'It isn't going to help. Not really. I just thought that if I could be the ideal wife in every way, then when Max does find out – or even if he doesn't – it'll kind of make up for it. Does that make sense?'

'Perrrfect,' Ivana said dismissively, rolling her R dramatically. 'You vant feel better. You learn to iron, so no feel guilty. Yes?'

I looked uncertain. 'No, it's not about me. It's about being more worthy of Max.'

'If you say so,' Ivana said.

'I do.'

'Okay.' It was a stalemate; Ivana had returned to her ironing, evidently not at all convinced. Then she looked up. 'So vat else on plen?'

I frowned. 'On what?'

'Your plen,' Ivana said irritably. 'Your plen be perrrfect wife.'

'Oh, right. The plan.' I dug out my list, slightly embarrassed. Helen grabbed it and started to read it out.

'1. To be honest. As far as possible.'

'Why only as far as possible?' Giles asked.

I cleared my throat uncomfortably.

'Because she's not going to actually tell him about Hugh,' Helen said knowingly. 'Are you, Jess?'

I didn't say anything.

'Ah,' Giles said carefully. 'Good point. And, anyway, white lies are the fundamentals of most relationships. Tell people what they want to hear, that's what I say.'

'You don't really think that,' I complained. 'And what if Hugh tells him?'

'He won't. If he tells, he's got nothing on you,' Giles said firmly. 'So, what next?'

Helen continued:

'2. To learn to cook fabulous food and to cook a lovely meal ~~every night. Some nights.~~ on occasion.

3. To make sure Max's shirts are always dry-cleaned. Or just laundered. Beautifully. And ironed.

4. To learn to iron.

5. To listen to Max, to hear what he actually says instead of hearing what I think he says or, worse, what I want him to have said.

6. To be a better person generally. To give my time to others. Soup kitchen, maybe?

7. To make life easy for him, not run to him every time I have a problem and expect him to sort things out.'

Helen raised an eyebrow.

'Like if something's broken,' I explained. 'Or if my car tax is up for renewal.' The truth was that before I'd met Max, I'd done everything myself, had been so independent I didn't know how a boyfriend, let alone a husband, would offer me anything I didn't have already. But bit by bit, Max had started to do little things – take the rubbish out, change lightbulbs, take my clothes to the dry cleaner with his stuff – and I discovered how lovely it was being looked after, having someone else there to turn to every so often. He knew more about cars, so he'd started to check my oil on a regular basis; he liked shopping, so he regularly went to the supermarket on Saturday mornings to stock up the kitchen. The trouble was, I'd gotten used to it. He did loads of things, all the time, and I'd begun to let him. 'I don't want to take him for granted. Don't want him to feel as if he does everything.'

'If you say so,' Helen said, looking back at the list.

'**8.** To pay him little compliments every day, so he knows how loved he is.

9. To be supportive. Always. Unwaveringly. To be on his side no matter what.

10. ???'

Then Helen cleared her throat. 'Okay, I'm beginning to see why your marriage needs help.'

'You think my marriage needs help?' I asked worriedly.

'Of course. There's nothing in there about sex.'

'Sex isn't the problem,' I said immediately. 'I mean, everything's great on that front. It's the . . . other fronts that I think I need to improve on.'

'Sex good, no nid improve anything else,' Ivana cut in.

'Exactly,' Helen agreed. 'And look at what you've got in there instead! Ironing! Cooking! What are you trying to be, a Stepford Wife?' She shook her head wearily.

'You think is bed thing to iron? To cook?' Ivana said suddenly.

Helen looked up in alarm, met Ivana's steely glare, and immediately shook her head. 'No. God, no. I just meant that Jess has to, you know, consider her priorities . . .'

'Ironing and cooking still important,' Ivana said authoritatively. 'For bebe. And most men are like bebe. Yes?'

Giles giggled. 'You're absolutely right, as always, Ivana.'

'Yes,' Ivana said, looking pleased. 'Yes. Em always right.'

'Fine.' Helen frowned. 'But aren't we forgetting something here? Jess has a few million quid in her bank account. She can employ a cook and a housekeeper to do all this stuff.'

'I don't want a cook and a housekeeper,' I said uncomfortably. 'I want to be able to cook a meal without burning it or giving him food poisoning. Or . . . or . . .'

56

Helen smirked. 'Or making custard that's completely solid?'

I met her eyes and giggled. 'Exactly.'

'Solid custard? What do you mean?' Giles asked curiously.

Helen looked at me and grinned. 'Shall I tell the story?'

I nodded, and she started to giggle, too. 'I made an apple pie,' she explained. 'And I asked Jess to make the custard.'

'I didn't even make it properly – I used the instant stuff,' I admitted ruefully, 'and I still screwed it up. It seemed to be too watery, so I added more powder and . . .'

'Five minutes later, custard cake,' Helen spluttered.

'So you admit I need help?' I pleaded.

'Oh God, you really do,' Helen laughed.

'I'm so pleased you agree!' I said happily. 'Because I've found a one-day cookery course and I want you to come with me.'

Helen stared at me. 'Come with you? Are you serious?'

'Yes,' I said, shooting her an imploring smile. 'I can't go on my own. I'll be too embarrassed.'

'But I don't want to learn how to cook,' Helen complained. 'I like eating out.'

'Just because you can cook doesn't mean you have to do it,' I begged. 'It's in Kensington, so you can shop afterward. And you get to take home the food you've made. You could invite John round for dinner. He'll love it. Please?'

Helen looked at me for a moment. 'Oh God, all right,' she said eventually. 'So long as you're paying.'

'End I tich iron,' Ivana said flatly. 'I tich sexy-sexy, too, if you vant be better boom-boom. I tich together. Save time.'

'Great,' I said, a rather strange image flitting into my mind – an image I immediately tried to get rid of.

'And what about me?' Giles asked, looking a bit left out. 'What can I do?'

'You are going to provide me with weekly flower deliveries to make the apartment look beautiful,' I responded.

Giles grinned. 'Oh, that's a fabulous idea. Ooh, yes, I'm going to start thinking about it now. Flowers that bring romance, flowers that boost your mood.'

'Yes, definitely those ones,' I said, rubbing my eyes. I hadn't been sleeping well, ever since Hugh's latest demand, and it was beginning to catch up with me. 'And de-stressing ones would be good. You know, for relaxation—'

'And mind-blowing sex,' Helen giggled. 'I know it's not on your list, but, trust me, you'll soon realize it's the only thing that matters.'

'Flowers that encourage mind-blowing sex,' Giles said seriously. 'Okay, I can't make any promises, but I'll see what I can do . . .'

Chapter 5

❧

'SO HE CAN RIFLE THROUGH our bins? And you want us all to sign a waiver? Are you serious?'

It was the next day, and the company meeting announcing the ethical audit had not gone quite as well as we'd hoped. Max had set out Chester's idea as enthusiastically as he could, selling it as a chance for us to show just what a great set of people we were, and not everyone was buying it. But if Project Ideal Company was suffering a temporary setback, Project Ideal Wife was steaming ahead. The cookery course was booked. I had been listening, supporting, and complimenting Max so much that he'd asked me several times if I was okay. I'd taken my car for its inspection without even mentioning it to Max, had renewed our television warranty, and had filled the kitchen cupboards with all of Max's favorite food. I'd even given his feet a rub during *Top Gear* the night before, although it didn't entirely fulfill its aims of relaxing Max: I hadn't realized how ticklish his feet were, and he'd howled in agony rather than sitting back and enjoying it. Hey, at least now I knew, so it was a learning opportunity.

But despite all my efforts, I still felt like something was missing. I just wasn't sure that being an ideal wife was about car inspections, complimenting your husband, and learning to cook. Sure, they might be factors, but were they enough? They felt more like a job description for a personal assistant or housekeeper than the ingredients for true love.

Max turned to Sarah, one of the designers, and shook his head. 'I'm sure he won't be going through our rubbish.'

'But you said he might do research. What kind of research?'

Max looked down at the notes Joshua had left him. 'Well,' he said, 'it says here that the auditor can undertake any reasonable research to confirm that the information interviewees supply him with is correct.'

'And is rummaging through bins reasonable?'

'Tell you what,' Max said uncertainly. 'I'll let him know that it isn't. How about that?'

Sarah shrugged. 'I still don't like it.'

'Why? Got something to hide?' someone said under their breath. I thought it was our receptionist, Gillie, but I couldn't be sure. Max's eyes flickered slightly, and I felt my stomach turn. I hated watching him sell something that he patently didn't believe in. I wished he had the courage of his convictions to stand up to Chester like he used to.

'So,' Max continued, 'the parameters for the audit include five key values against which we're going to be measured. They are loyalty, care, goodness, appreciation, and honesty. And these have been broken down for us. Loyalty: Are we loyal to our staff, to our clients, to our values? Care: Do we care for our clients and staff; do we make a difference in the community around us? Goodness: Do we recycle; do we work with charities; do we try to make a difference? Appreciation: That's whether our clients value us. I think they send out a questionnaire or something. And honesty speaks for itself, but I think we can be pretty proud on that one. We don't lie or even exaggerate things to our clients, and we don't lie on behalf of them, either. That's something we've always been very sure about at Milton Advertising.'

'Then why is our biggest client checking us out with

an audit?' Simon, one of the market researchers, asked defensively. 'Why don't they trust us?'

Max looked at him blankly, and I realized that he didn't have an answer. He probably wanted to ask Chester the same question. But he was right – we should be proud. And not just of being honest. We were all the things he'd said – those were the values Max believed in.

'Look,' I said, standing up. 'No one likes to be tested, we get that. But the fact is that business is tough – for us as well as for the banks. We'll pass this audit with flying colors, I know we will. And when we do, what a great selling point! We'll trounce the competition because we can legitimately say we're the only agency clients can truly trust. Because we are trustworthy, like Max said. And we're also loyal. So let's show some of that loyalty. Okay?'

'What if we fail?' Sarah said, scowling. 'Then we'll be known as the agency no one can trust.'

'We're not going to fail,' I said tersely. 'There's no reason on earth we would. And, anyway, we can't. This audit is important. We pass, we retain Jarvis Private Banking and steal a march on our competitors. We fail . . .' I looked at Max nervously.

'We fail, and everything goes tits up,' he said, with a little smile that didn't reach his eyes. 'Whether we like it or not, we are going to pass this audit with no moaning or being difficult. Jarvis Private Banking wants us to do this, and Jarvis is not just an important client; it is keeping us in business. So we're going to play nicely, okay?'

Simon stood up. 'I still don't like it,' he complained. 'I mean, what are they going to ask us? Our political views? Our sexual preferences?'

'Absolutely not,' Max said quickly. 'We are clear that this audit is about ethics – about work-relevant ethics – and not about personal choices. If you've been caught shoplifting, that's relevant. Shagging a sheep isn't.'

There was a ripple of laughter. 'That's a relief, huh, Simon?' one of his colleagues joked.

'Yeah, funny,' he retorted, but sat down anyway.

'So can we support this?' Max asked. 'Not everyone will be interviewed. And anyone who is interviewed can stop the interview if they are uncomfortable with the questions.'

'Without penalty?' Sarah asked, suspicious.

Max scrutinized the notes again. 'It doesn't say,' he said eventually. 'But that doesn't really matter. This is not a witch hunt.'

'Exactly. It's an opportunity,' I said firmly.

'An opportunity? I love an opportunity!' Everyone turned to see Chester walking through the door; he seemed slightly bemused to see the entire workforce in reception, but it was the only place big enough to hold a meeting.

'Chester. How are you?' Max said, looking slightly taken aback to see him. 'We're just briefing everyone on the audit. And it's . . . uh . . . going down really well. Isn't it, guys?' He gazed around the room meaningfully, and everyone duly murmured vaguely supportive things.

Chester beamed. 'I'm real excited about this. Folks at the bank don't seem too pleased at the moment, but they'll come around. So everyone here is psyched?'

No one said anything. 'They're very psyched,' Max replied.

'Well, that's great. I'm sorry to interrupt. You just carry on, Max. I'll wait in your office, shall I?'

'Actually, we're pretty much done,' Max said. He turned back to the floor. 'Audit starts next Tuesday. Any questions, ask me. And I believe that Caroline is going to be coordinating the interviews. Right, Caroline?'

Caroline nodded seriously; a few minutes before the

meeting I'd asked her if she'd do the organization, and she'd been almost tearful that I trusted her with such an important job. 'Absolutely,' she said.

'Good. In that case, meeting adjourned. Thanks, everyone.'

Everyone filed back to their workstations; I followed Max to his office, where Chester was waiting.

'You were great,' I whispered. 'You really sold it.'

'You think?' Max asked dubiously.

I nodded and gave his hand a squeeze. The truth was, he had sold it. Perhaps not to everyone, but to me. And not the audit itself but the values. I'd been looking at the ideal-wife thing from the completely wrong angle, I decided. A checklist didn't make a person perfect, and it wouldn't make Max happy. But values? They were something I could work toward. Loyalty, care, goodness, appreciation, and honesty. If I could exhibit all of those things, surely that would make me a great wife. To be loyal to Max, to care for him, to be a good person, to be completely honest. And to be appreciated. To be loved. That was really the reward, wasn't it? The measure of success. If Max loved me, then I was doing an okay job. If he still loved me when I was completely honest about Hugh, then . . . then . . . then everything would be okay. Everything would be good again.

'So, Chester,' Max said warmly. 'What can we do for you?'

'Actually,' Chester said, 'I was hoping you might do me a favor. Jess, I mean.'

'Of course,' I said immediately. 'Anything.'

'Great,' Chester said vaguely, then wandered over to the window. Max and I looked at each other curiously.

'Chester, is everything okay?' Max asked uncertainly.

'Of course!' Chester said, clasping his hands together. 'And how're things with you guys?'

'Um, good. They're good,' I said hesitantly. 'And . . . you? You're sure everything is okay with you?'

'Me? Sure. Great. Real great. Very excited about the ethical audit . . . It's going to be great!'

'Great!' I said. 'So then everything's great?'

'It sure is!'

I nodded.

'You know, Chester,' Max said carefully, 'there's something about using the word "great" about fifteen times in two sentences that makes me think that perhaps things aren't actually that great.'

Chester took a deep breath and exhaled loudly. 'That's an interesting theory.'

'Interesting and accurate?' I asked. 'Is there something you want to talk to me about? Is there a problem?'

Chester looked at me for a few seconds.

'Okay, you got me,' he said.

I took a deep breath and tried not to panic. 'All right, just tell me,' I said. 'Is it about the account?' I looked over at Max, whose eyes were serious. This couldn't be bad news, I told myself. If anything happened to Jarvis, if we lost Chester's business, things would be desperate for the agency. And the agency meant everything to Max – it was his way of proving to the world that he was a success, that he was worthwhile. Before we were married, when my stupid mistake nearly cost him the firm, I'd offered to bail him out with Grace's millions and he'd steadfastly refused; he'd even wanted to postpone the wedding because he felt like a failure. I couldn't see him go through a crisis of confidence like that again.

'Not the account, Jess, no,' Chester said, and Max's expression lightened a hundredfold.

'Okay,' I said, confused. 'Then . . . what is it?'

Chester looked at me with a pained expression on his face. 'It's about your mother. I have to confess I'm a bit worried.'

'Worried?' I asked uncertainly.

'Yes,' Chester said carefully. 'I'm worried because I have to go away on a business trip, and I don't think she's going to be very happy about it. I was hoping you might keep an eye on her while I'm gone. Stop her from getting silly ideas in her head and—'

'Stop her from getting cross with you?' I asked, my whole body flooding with relief. 'Because you're going to miss a whole load more wedding meetings? Oh, that's no problem. No problem at all. Stop worrying right now.'

Chester raised an eyebrow. 'Jessica, if you only knew – I worry more about your mother's volatile temper than I do about volatile stock markets.' He grinned wickedly, and I laughed.

'She can be quite formidable,' I conceded.

He nodded seriously. 'She can make a grown man weep,' he said, his eyes twinkling. 'But that's what I love about her, too. She's unpredictable. Difficult. But she keeps me on my toes. So you'll keep an eye on her? Make sure she doesn't get lonely?'

'Of course I will,' I promised.

'I appreciate it, Jess. Funny, we'll be family soon. Although, you know, it's always felt a bit like family with you. Ever since your first pitch when you convinced me that we should launch a fund for women by convincing them that finance would be as desirable as handbags.' He grinned again, and I felt a warm glow rise up within me.

'So when do you go?' Max asked.

'This afternoon.'

The warm glow stopped in its tracks, and I looked at him with trepidation. 'And she knows that?'

Chester said awkwardly, 'Okay, here's the thing.'

'The thing?' I asked, narrowing my eyes. 'She does know you're going? Right?'

'The thing' – Chester paused briefly – 'is that with your mother I've learned that the best strategy is a swoop.'

'A swoop,' I said. 'And that is?'

'It's when you see a company you want and you go for it quickly – buying up stock, forcing a takeover, whatever. As opposed to a circle, where you spend longer developing a deal, flirting with the board and shareholders, launching a long-term charm offensive.'

I frowned. 'I still don't see how—'

'The longer she knows something, the longer she has to stew over it. It never works in my favor,' Chester explained. 'Believe me, I've tried charm offensives and your mother sees through them every time. Far better to give her the news with minutes to spare and hope that by the time I'm back she's forgiven me.'

'You're a brave man, Chester,' Max said, shaking his head.

'Brave?' I was incredulous. 'He's . . .' I turned to Chester. 'You're . . .' I wanted to tell him he was an idiot. But I wanted to say that to my prospective stepfather; I still didn't dare talk to Chester the client that way. Instead, I just looked at him with my mouth open. 'You're going to have a very difficult conversation,' I said eventually. 'And she's going to be pretty angry with you.'

'Which is where you come in.' Chester was smiling again. I found myself wondering if this was how he did all his deals; certainly it was hard to say no to him.

He caught my expression and pulled a puppy-dog face.

'I know. I screwed up. But I'll be gone only a couple of weeks.'

'Two whole weeks?' Max whistled. 'You couldn't take her with you?'

'I thought about that,' Chester said with a shrug, 'but I'm going to be too busy. And two weeks isn't so long. I've just got some ends to tie up, you know? I never saw myself living here permanently, and now that I'm getting married, well, there are things to do.'

Max and I nodded; Chester beamed at us. 'So you'll go and see her? Keep her occupied so she forgets how pissed she is? Talk me up all the time?'

'Sure,' I gulped. 'But you'd better go and tell her now. And you'd better wear some armor.'

Chester nodded quickly. 'I know. I will. And thanks, Jess. I appreciate it. Max, you're a lucky man, you know.'

Max grinned. 'Don't I know it. And don't worry about Esther. We'll keep an eye on her. You go on your business trip and leave her to Jess.'

'Yes,' I agreed, trying to sound as certain. 'Everything will be fine. Don't worry at all.'

Of course, things weren't fine. They weren't fine at all.

'He didn't tell me until this afternoon,' my mother said, incandescent with rage when I called up to see how she was that evening. 'An hour before his flight left. He called me from the airport. From the bloody airport, Jess.'

I bit my lip. My mother very rarely swore; I got the feeling that Chester hadn't managed his departure particularly well.

'Maybe he was just nervous about telling you,' I said tentatively.

'Well, he should have been nervous. He's gone away for two weeks. Leaving me to organize everything. And who knows what he'll be up to over in the States. Chatting up women, out partying every night . . .'

I frowned. I had never seen Chester chatting up a woman, and the idea of him being out partying was simply . . . well, if not inconceivable, then certainly un-likely. 'Mum, I don't think he's really a party animal,' I said. 'And he's gone out there to tie up loose ends so that he can marry you. It's quite romantic when you think about it. And he'll be back soon enough—'

'The point is, he doesn't appreciate me. That is absolutely clear. And I don't appreciate being unappreciated, Jess. I don't, it's as simple as that.'

'Of course he appreciates you,' I said quickly. 'It's obvious he's mad about you.'

Mum paused. 'Maybe,' she said a moment later. 'But love doesn't stop us from taking others for granted, darling. And I won't be taken for granted. I won't. Chester needs to realize that.'

'I'm sure he does realize that,' I said uncertainly.

'Does he? Then why is he abandoning me?'

I sighed. 'I wouldn't call a two-week trip abandoning you. And, anyway, isn't that a bit rich coming from you? After all, you did leave me with Grandma and fake your own death to escape from some debts, didn't you?'

There was silence for a second or two. 'That,' Mum said eventually, 'was different. Very different. I'd have thought you knew that, Jessica.'

I could tell I'd upset her; she used my full name only when she was cross with me.

'I do know that,' I amended. 'But I think you should maybe give Chester a break. Cut him some slack. He's gone for two weeks, so enjoy it. Plan the wedding, get everything organized, go and have a few facials.'

'Facials?' Mum said, sounding incredulous. 'I don't have time for facials. No, I shall be networking. You know I'm a Facebook now?'

I suppressed a giggle. 'You're a Facebook? You mean you're on the site?'

'Yes, and I have lots of friends,' Mum said triumphantly. 'Chester had better watch out.'

'I'm sure he's quaking in his boots,' I said indulgently. 'Just be careful, will you? There are all sorts of loons on the Internet.'

'There are loons all over the world,' Mum replied in a patronizing tone. 'I'm well aware of that.'

'Good,' I said with a smile. 'And the two weeks will pass in a flash, I promise.'

'Perhaps,' Mum said archly. 'But a lot can happen in two weeks. An awful lot.'

Chapter 6

MUM WAS RIGHT, of course. Lots could happen in two weeks; in fact, I had my own two-week schedule all mapped out to get Project Ideal Wife off the ground. I had devised a new plan, setting out the values with key objectives associated with them. So under *Goodness* I had *Doing charitable works,* and under *Care* I had *Looking after Max,* and for each of these objectives I had a list of things to do each week. Already this week I had run Max a bath (care), spent all day Thursday talking to as many people as I could at work about the audit to convince them it was a good thing (loyalty), and had contacted a local soup kitchen to offer my services (goodness). I hadn't worked out how or when I was going to tackle the whole Hugh business (honesty), but I figured that if I did the other things well, then telling Max the truth would somehow fall into place.

In fact, as Helen and I made our way to the cookery course the following Saturday (care), I had a little spring in my step for the first time in what felt like ages. I might not be perfect, but I was on my way.

'Is this it?' Helen asked, peering at a sign outside a small house. 'The Mary Armstrong Cookery School?'

'Yes!' I said, and pressed the buzzer, then felt Helen's hand on my shoulder.

'We're really doing this?' she asked incredulously. 'I mean, seriously? Because we can still leave. There's still time to run.'

'We're not running anywhere,' I said firmly. 'We're going to learn to cook.'

'And remind me again why? You used to tell me that cooking was just a form of enslavement, that the trick was to work hard and earn enough to employ a cook.'

I frowned; she was right, I did say that. I'd meant it, too. 'Helen, I'm not saying I want either of us to be chained to the kitchen,' I said, shrugging. 'But cooking is a basic skill. Everyone should be able to cook.'

'They should?'

'Yes, they should . . .' I caught her expression: She was laughing at me.

I sighed. 'Oh, please, Hel. You know why we're here. I want to do something for Max. He's so stressed out at the moment. We've got this bloody audit at work, we're losing business every day, and I swear Max has started to go prematurely gray with the stress of it all. Even if you don't care about cooking, at least be supportive.'

'Of your transformation into Bree Van de Kamp?' Helen raised an eyebrow.

'No,' I said, trying not to smile. 'Not Bree.'

'Then who? I mean, do you have any evidence that Max wants you to be able to cook?'

I frowned. 'Well, no, but—'

'Look, I know that he teases you,' Helen said, 'but I don't think I've ever heard him actually criticize you. Or even suggest that he cares at all that you're a total idiot in the kitchen. It's one of your charms.'

'One of my charms? So I do have some?'

'One or two. Maybe.' Helen grinned. 'Do you really want to do this?'

'Yes.' I nodded. 'I want to be able to cook. Anyway, food is the best way to a man's heart. Everyone knows that.'

'No, everyone knows that's a myth,' Helen corrected me. 'Blow jobs are far better, as I discovered last night . . .'

'Hello?'

Helen looked up and reddened. A woman had opened the door and was standing in front of us, looking slightly confused.

'Hello!' I said hurriedly. 'Hello, we're here for the class. We're late, I'm afraid. We were just . . . um . . . um . . .'

'Just discussing the use of blowtorches when making crème brûlée,' Helen said, smiling. 'Versus the broiler.'

'Ah,' the woman said knowingly. 'Well, we all have our favorite methods, don't we?'

I nodded and tried not to giggle when Helen nudged me in the ribs. 'We certainly do,' she said seriously.

'So you're quite an accomplished cook?' the woman asked, leading us inside. 'I'm Mary Armstrong, by the way.'

'The eponymous Mary Armstrong?' Helen asked, rushing after her and purposefully sidestepping the question.

'That's right.' Mary smiled. 'Now, we're in here.' She opened the door to a room made up of ten workstations. 'Why don't you two take that one?' she suggested, pointing to one toward the back.

'Great!' I said enthusiastically.

'And grab a coffee. We're going to start in five minutes.'

She pointed toward a filter coffee machine, around which people were gathered.

'Coffee,' Helen said brightly, as Mary walked away. 'Great idea,' and she promptly collapsed into a fit of giggles.

The others, it turned out, were made up of two sorts of people: gap-year students who needed to learn to cook so that they could get jobs as chalet assistants for the winter season, and middle-aged divorced men who had realized that they couldn't live on takeaway and toast for the rest of their lives.

'Looking forward to getting your apron on?' a man said, coming over to talk to me. 'So what's someone like you doing here?'

I blushed. 'Oh, you know,' I said. 'I want to learn to cook so I can produce nice meals at home.'

He nodded sagely. 'Nice,' he said. 'Very nice.'

'And you?' I asked.

He shrugged. 'Got to face facts, haven't you? Got to accept that life has changed, that it's time to move on. There's no one cooking meals for me anymore.'

'Oh,' I said. 'Sorry.'

'Yeah, that makes two of us,' he said, evidently relishing the chance to talk. 'Divorce came through six months ago, and I still wake up sometimes thinking that maybe she'll come back.'

'But?' I asked gently.

'She's not coming back,' he said sadly. 'She's getting married soon. Apparently the kids love him.'

I didn't know what to say. 'Well, maybe you'll meet someone, too,' I said eventually, deciding that he could probably do with a little positivity. 'I mean, if she left you, then you have to think good riddance, don't you?'

He shook his head. 'Not really,' he said. 'I miss her every day. I don't want to meet anyone else.'

'Ah,' I said, biting my lip and wondering where Helen had got to. She was way better at this kind of stuff than I was.

'And the worst thing is that it was all my fault.'

'What was your fault?' Helen asked, appearing at my side. I looked at her in relief.

'This is . . .' I started to say, then realized that I didn't know who this man was.

'Andrew,' the man said.

'This is Helen,' I said. 'And I'm Jessica.'

'We were just talking about . . . about . . .' I looked at Andrew awkwardly. Was it good taste to say we were talking about his divorce? About the fact that his wife had left him, plunging him into a pit of despair? 'About marriage,' I finally said.

'Divorce, actually,' Andrew said. 'That's why I'm here. Got to learn to stand on my own two feet.'

'That's the spirit,' Helen said encouragingly. 'We're here because Jess wants to become a Stepford Wife.'

'No, I don't,' I said crossly. 'Learning to cook doesn't make me a man-pleasing clone.'

'My wife's cooking was amazing,' Andrew said balefully. 'Whenever we went out to a restaurant, I always said to her that her cooking was better.'

'And she still left you?' Helen asked, apparently serious, but I could see the twinkle in her eye.

Andrew didn't notice it. He nodded gravely. 'And it was all my fault,' he said again.

'Oh, don't say that. Takes two to tango,' Helen said briskly.

'Okay, people,' Mary called out suddenly. 'We're going to start in just a minute, so please make your way to your workstations, where you'll find some ingredients in glass bowls laid out for you. We're going to start by cooking a nice simple lasagna, followed by a yummy chocolate pudding.'

I looked at Andrew uncertainly. 'So what happened?' I asked him, as Helen ran off to bag a workstation right at the back of the room.

74

He laughed, a low, bitter little laugh that sent shivers down my spine. 'I cheated. One stupid drunken night. Same story as every guy here, I imagine.'

'And she left you right away?' My heart was thudding in my chest.

He nodded. 'Said it was too much of a betrayal. That I wasn't the person she thought I was. And the thing was, the night I did it . . . all I was thinking about was her. Wishing I was at home. Stupid, right?'

I suddenly remembered being in the bar with Hugh, feeling so angry with Max, feeling betrayed and hurt but still wanting him so badly.

'Pretty stupid,' I agreed, my voice catching slightly. 'Pretty bloody insane, actually.'

'So,' Mary said, as I nipped over to the workstation Helen had saved for me, on which were two carefully laid-out steaks and various bowls. 'Making lasagna is really quite straightforward. But first we need to get our prep done. Which means mincing our beef and making our pasta. Has anyone here made pasta before?'

One of the gap-year students and one of the middle-aged divorcés put up their hands.

'Wonderful.' Mary beamed. 'The rest of you, just follow my instructions and you'll find that it's the easiest thing in the world.'

It wasn't the easiest thing in the world. It wasn't *at all* the easiest thing in the world. I did my best to concentrate, but Mary kept shouting out instructions and I didn't even hear her because I was still trying to complete my first task – making a pasta dough and turning it into sheets of lasagna.

'Helen,' I said tentatively, 'how do I—'

'Look!' she said triumphantly, not hearing me because

she was too preoccupied with her pasta maker, out of which perfect, square lasagna sheets were emerging. 'Look, I made that!'

'Great,' I muttered unenthusiastically. 'Just great.'

'Oh dear,' Helen said, noticing the lumpy and misshapen sheets that I had produced. 'Are you maybe putting too much in at a time?'

'Maybe,' I sighed, as I put my lumpen dough back on the workbench, where it immediately stuck.

'And I think your mixture has got too much water in it. It's not meant to be that sticky. See?'

Helen put more of her mixture through and smiled happily as another perfect sheet emerged.

'You're a natural,' a guy at the next workbench said, grinning at her. 'Are you sure you aren't a great cook who's come here to make the rest of us look bad?'

Helen smiled flirtatiously. 'Make you look bad?' she asked. 'Impossible. I'm Helen, by the way.'

'Will,' the man said. 'Nice to meet you.'

I looked at Helen in frustration. 'I didn't put too much in. I put in the same amount of water as you,' I said, trying to stay calm. 'We were given the same exact amounts in our bowls.'

'Yeah, you're right,' Helen said, shaking her head in bemusement. 'So why is mine coming out okay and yours is . . . is . . .'

'Is crap?' I asked, surprising myself with the anger in my voice.

'Not crap,' she said quickly. 'Try it again, okay? And I'll help you.'

'If you help me, then I'm not learning, am I?' I said hotly. 'Just leave me alone. Let me get on with it, okay? Because actually it's quite distracting having you talking at me all the time.'

'Fine,' Helen said defensively. 'I was only trying to help.' I watched as she picked up her perfect squares of lasagna and placed them, as Mary had instructed, under a piece of muslin on the cool stainless-steel counter. 'I'll get on with the beef, shall I?'

I nodded and went back to my pasta-making. It was no big deal, I told myself. So pasta-making wasn't going to be my forte – there were other things, right? Maybe my sauce would be spectacular. Maybe my chocolate pudding would be the best ever.

'Right, so your pasta squares should be ready and waiting and your beef should be gently frying with your onions,' Mary called out. 'Now, simply add the fresh tomatoes that you've squished, along with the herbs, and leave that to simmer on a low temperature. Meanwhile, we're going to turn our attentions to our chocolate pudding.'

I looked up in alarm. I hadn't even started to fry my beef. Quickly, I grabbed a frying pan and shoved my minced beef, onion, and a few other things in it before turning the hob on high to make up some lost time. Remembering the tomatoes just in time (not squished – I hadn't got round to that – so I grabbed a knife and roughly chopped them as they went in), I looked up quickly as Mary was telling us to decant the white powder in the blue bowl into the large clear bowl and to add the eggs. Hurriedly, I did as she suggested. I could do this. I was a grade-A student – always had been at school and university. But there I'd had more time. If I'd slipped behind, there was always the evening to catch up. Not like this. Mary and her instructions were relentless. There was no time to think. No time to . . .

'So now beat gently and add the milk, which is in the red

dish in front of you. Add it gradually so that you create a nice, smooth paste . . .'

I grabbed the red dish. Okay. Milk. Slowly add milk. Gently, carefully, I poured it into the bowl. Then I started to mix. I sneaked a quick peek at Helen's – her bowl was definitely full of a nice, smooth paste, as Mary had promised. So there was no reason why mine wouldn't turn out like that, too. I just had to mix it. Slowly. No, the pouring was slow, not the mixing. The mixing could be any speed. At least, I guessed it could. I looked over at Helen again. She'd stopped mixing; she was checking on her beef again.

Despondently, I turned back to my bowl.

'Everything all right over here?' I looked up to see Mary hovering at my side, a bright smile on her face. 'How are we doing?'

I managed to smile back. 'Well,' I said uncertainly, 'I'm trying to get my paste working . . .'

She nodded reassuringly and looked in my bowl. Her face fell slightly. 'Ah. Now, what have we here?'

'We have the ingredients ready to be mixed,' I said, trying to keep my voice calm.

'So we have flour? Eggs? Milk?'

I nodded.

Mary nodded, too, then proceeded to stir the contents of the bowl, her expression becoming increasingly vexed. 'You're sure you . . .' she started to say, then her eyes scanned my side of the workstation.

'Your flour is here,' she said, pointing to a purple bowl.

'No,' I said. 'The flour is in the blue bowl. Here.'

'Oh,' Mary said, her smile faltering slightly. 'That's the lilac one. This is the blue one.' She held up the purple bowl.

'That's purple,' I said.

'Oh.' Mary looked taken aback. 'You think? I'm not

78

sure . . . I mean, I don't think anyone's confused the two before. Perhaps it is a little on the purple side . . .'

I swallowed uncomfortably. 'So what was in that bowl? The one I used?'

'Parmesan,' Mary said weakly.

I nodded slowly. 'So that'll be why my mixture isn't really turning into a paste,' I said.

'And this!' Mary grabbed another bowl, her face taking on an increasingly worried expression. 'This should be in your pasta!'

'It should?' I hadn't even noticed that one – a small ceramic bowl with something white and powdery in it.

'Yes, it should.' Mary looked around helplessly. 'Perhaps we should start – no, there's no time. I'll get you some more flour, though. For the chocolate pudding.'

'Thanks,' I said. But just as she was walking away, there was a bang and a fizz, and we both turned to see the lid flying off the saucepan on my hob. Meat and tomato spewed out of it, as Mary desperately grabbed a tea towel and turned down the flame.

'Simmer gently,' she managed to say, as she pulled the saucepan away. 'Not set fire to.'

I felt my lip begin to quiver. 'So that's ruined, too?'

'Ruined?' She looked down at the saucepan and gingerly stirred the contents before looking back at me unhappily. 'Well, I think perhaps this lasagna sauce has . . . I think perhaps we should focus on the pudding. Don't you?'

'The pudding I put Parmesan in?' I could feel myself choking up, could feel everyone's eyes on me. I felt hot. I wanted to get out.

There was a snigger from the other side of the room and I glared over, catching the eye of one of the gap-year students, who hurriedly looked down.

'The pudding we can start again with,' Mary was saying. 'With flour this time?'

She meant it nicely – I knew she did. She wasn't laughing at me; she wanted to help. But I wasn't sure she could help anymore. I could barely remember why I was even here. 'Actually, I think I'll go,' I said, my voice slightly brittle.

'Go? Oh, no. No, don't do that. There's nothing here that can't be fixed,' Mary assured me. 'We could turn this into a soufflé. We could take this . . . this mince and . . . and . . .' Her brow furrowed as she tried to come up with something.

'And make golf balls?' Helen grinned. 'Or cat food?'

'Cat food,' I said quietly. 'Well, I guess that wouldn't be a complete waste. Although I don't have a cat.'

'I used to have a cat,' Andrew said. 'But my ex-wife took her.'

I sighed heavily, and Helen put her am around me. 'Oh, come on, Jess. So you aren't a great cook. So what? No big deal. I mean, who cares, anyway?'

'I do,' I said, the words sticking in my throat. 'I thought this would be an easy one; I wanted to surprise him with a really lovely meal, to show him how much I love him.'

Helen shook her head. 'I'll tell you what. If Max finds you naked on the bed with a rose between your teeth when he gets home, that'll go down way better than a stupid lasagna.'

She caught Mary's eye and reddened. 'No offense, Mary.'

'None taken.' Mary shrugged. 'It's only lasagna.'

'Your friend's right,' Will said earnestly. 'Sex beats cooking every time.'

'We never had sex after the kids were born,' Andrew said dolefully. 'I think that's why I cheated—'

'Okay, enough,' I said, holding up my hands. 'Mary, tell me seriously: Is it worth me staying?'

'Of course it is,' Mary said firmly. 'We all have to start somewhere. Rome wasn't built in a day, after all!'

'No, but I bet they didn't put the bricks in all the wrong places on day one,' I said, allowing myself a little smile.

'I bet they did,' Will said. 'And if they didn't, they were just stupid show-offs. Like your friend here.' He winked at Helen. 'I mean, come on, no one likes a goody two-shoes, do they?'

Helen grinned. 'Exactly. And, anyway, you should see this as an opportunity, Jess. You've never been bottom of the class, so this is a great new experience for you.'

I felt a little smile creep onto my lips. 'I'm really bottom of the class?'

Mary looked as if she was trying to suppress a grin of her own. 'You're not top,' she admitted.

'So the only way is up?' I asked tentatively.

'Undoubtedly,' Mary said, matter-of-factly. 'That's the spirit. Shall I get you some more flour?'

I nodded. 'And everything else, if that's okay,' I said. 'I think I'd like to start from the beginning, if it's all right with you.'

Chapter 7

❧

I DID IT: I actually cooked lasagna and chocolate pudding for Max. Okay, so I had a bit of help from Mary Armstrong. Sure, she kept an eagle eye on me at all times, and she didn't let me add any ingredients until she'd checked them first. But that didn't matter. What mattered was that I was on my way home, clutching an entire home-cooked meal in various plastic boxes (packed by Mary and Helen, neither of whom trusted me with the job), with very clear instructions on how to heat them up (I overheard Helen telling Mary that they couldn't leave anything to chance with me, and I didn't even get offended). I could cook. Sort of. And although I could see now that being able to cook was hardly on a par with betrayal, that they hardly canceled each other out, it made me feel a little bit better. At least I'd tried.

Anyway, I got home as quickly as I could, called Max to find out what time he'd be home, decanted the food (as detailed in my instructions) into cooking implements (Mary had thoughtfully drawn them for me so that I didn't have to distinguish a cassoulet from a casserole dish), and put them in the oven. Then I retired to the bedroom, where I showered, smothered myself in body oil, and lay on the bed, covering myself in the roses that Giles had sent over. Those guys at the class had better be right, I thought as I put the last rose between my teeth. If this went poorly, I was never going to talk to Helen again. Well, not for a day or two. I heard the key in the door and froze.

'Hello? Jess, are you here?'

'In here,' I called, in what I hoped was a seductive voice.

'Something smells good. Did you pick up some food? Listen, I know it's Sunday tomorrow, but I think I'm going in to work, if that's okay. I've got a million and one things to do and we've got the audit starting on Tuesday . . .' He wandered into the bedroom, then stopped, his eyes wide. 'Hello!' he said, a twinkle in his eye. 'What's going on here?'

'I cooked,' I said.

'You cooked? Really?'

'I took a class,' I said, with a little smile. 'I . . . We cooked lasagna and chocolate pudding.'

'I see,' Max said, taking off his jacket. 'And then did some gardening?'

I nodded, then winced as a rose stabbed my arm. 'Something like that.' I felt faintly ridiculous, was sure that Max was going to laugh, but he hadn't so far. 'So, are you hungry?'

He grinned back. 'Famished. But you know what they say – the hungrier you are, the better the food tastes. I think I can still work up a bit more of an appetite.'

'You're saying you think my food isn't going to be that great? That you need to work up an appetite to enjoy it?' I teased. 'Because I'll have you know that—'

'Stop talking,' Max said softly, removing the roses one by one.

'Fine,' I said, giggling as he took the last remaining stem and used it to stroke my leg.

'What brought this about?' he asked, as the rose moved steadily upward.

'I just thought it would make a nice change,' I said. 'Better than takeaway.'

He nodded seriously. 'Very nice change,' he agreed, taking off his shirt. He leaned down to kiss me, and, one by one, all his clothes were discarded onto the floor.

'And change is good, right?' I said. 'You know, spicing things up.'

'I love spice,' Max said, pulling me toward him. He looked so happy. 'You're full of surprises, Jess, you know that? I love that about you.'

'You do?' I looked at him tentatively.

'Yes, I do,' he murmured. 'God, you're gorgeous. I love you, Jess.'

'And I love you,' I said, and then closed my eyes. If I loved him, I would tell him the truth and let him decide if he still loved me. That would be the right thing to do. That's what the truly ideal wife would do, wouldn't she? I took a deep breath. Then I opened my eyes again. 'Max,' I said hesitantly, 'there's something I have to tell you.'

I moved forward just as he was leaning in toward me and ended up cracking him on the head. 'Oh God. Oh, I'm sorry,' I said desperately, pulling my legs out from underneath him so I could see if I'd done any damage. But as I moved, I yelped; something was jabbing into my knee. Quickly, I moved back, flinging my leg away from the rose that was embedded in it and catching Max in the groin. He groaned in agony, rolling off the bed and onto the wooden floor with a huge crash, pulling me down on top of him. I landed heavily on something: his leg, I realized when I looked down. His leg, which looked kind of weird.

'Oh shit! Max, I am so sorry,' I said, leaning down over him. 'God, I am such an idiot. Such a klutz. Max?'

I looked at him uncertainly. He'd gone white.

'My . . . leg,' he gasped. 'You're on . . . my—'

'Your leg?' I asked, jumping up. 'Sorry, did you hurt it when you fell? I'm so sorry – it was this thorn in my knee. I knelt on it and—' I frowned. 'Max, your leg looks really funny.'

He nodded.

And then I realized why he was so pale.

'It's broken, isn't it?' Max managed to say.

I nodded dismally. He had landed on his leg, twisting it under him; when I landed on top of it, I'd bloody well broken it. It wasn't a crash I'd heard; it was a crunch. And now his leg was bent the wrong way, his foot looking completely out of place, facing inward instead of outward.

'What was it you wanted to tell me?' he asked through gritted teeth, then fell back on the floor, passed out.

'It can wait,' I whispered, as I dashed out of the room to call an ambulance.

'So tell me how this happened?' It was two hours later and we were in the hospital; Max's leg had been X-rayed several times, and he was lying on a bed in a hospital gown. The doctor had come in a few minutes before to tell us what the prognosis was.

We looked at each other. 'You want the long version or the short version?' Max asked. He'd been given some really strong painkillers, which had done something to his head; he was being cheeky and flirtatious and acting like he was drunk.

'How long is long?' the doctor asked.

Max looked at me with a raised eyebrow, and I reddened. 'We were . . . I mean, I was . . .' I said hesitantly.

'My wife,' Max said seriously, 'decided to try something new.'

'Don't tell me – a new sport?' The doctor sighed. 'If you knew how many people end up here with broken limbs because they've embarked on a health kick, you'd be amazed. So what was it? Rollerblading? Squash?'

Max winked at me. 'Why don't you tell the doctor, darling?' he suggested.

I cleared my throat. 'Well . . .'

'I got home to find her on the bed, naked but for some roses.' Max grinned. 'And then she kicked me in the groin and threw me off the bed. Women, huh? They just can't make up their minds.'

I looked at him incredulously. 'I was going to say that I took a cookery class.'

'Yes!' Max said excitedly. 'She cooked, too! What an amazing woman.' Then he looked at me sadly. 'And we never got to eat it.'

'Oh God,' I said, clapping my hand to my mouth. 'I didn't turn the oven off. I put the food in to heat and I didn't turn it off before we left to come here!'

'Then it's probably a little on the charred side,' Max said. 'Oh well, not to worry.'

The doctor patted him on the shoulder. 'You've had some bad luck today,' he said. 'Your food's burned and your leg's broken.'

'It's definitely broken?' Max asked, not looking particularly concerned. 'It couldn't be a twist? Or a sprain?'

'Definitely broken,' the doctor said. 'I can show you the X ray if you like.'

Max shook his head and sighed. 'So, what, I go home in a wheelchair?'

'Home? No, Mr. Wainwright, I'm afraid you're not going home for a little while yet.'

'Well, obviously not right now,' I said quickly. 'I suppose you've got to put plaster on it first—'

'Hey, slow down. I'm afraid your husband is going to be in here for at least a week,' the doctor said gently.

'A week?' Max looked up at him with a goofy smile on his face. 'No, that's impossible. I'm a very busy man. I've got an ethical audit starting on Tuesday. A business to run. Tell him, Jess.'

'It's true,' I said seriously. 'He can't be in the hospital for a week.'

'And yet you're going to be.' The doctor shrugged. 'You'll need some serious pain relief, and we'll need to keep an eye on you for a while. Your break is nasty. Usually a fall off a bed would result in a twist or a sprain, but it seems you landed badly, and the additional' – he looked at me with a half-smile – 'weight that landed on top of it . . .'

'You can say it,' I said dismally. 'I broke his leg.'

'You helped him break it,' the doctor said diplomatically, then turned back to Max. 'You'll need to be off your feet for a few weeks, I'm afraid. We can get you some crutches, a wheelchair, eventually, but you're in a lot of pain, even if you can't feel it now. I think it would be sensible to stay here for a few days. You'll need some physical therapy as you start to recover, too.'

Max nodded sagely. 'Why don't you start the physio now?' he suggested. 'Then we can all go home.'

The doctor turned to me. 'Seems the painkillers are doing their stuff,' he said, with a wry smile.

I smiled back uncertainly. It was great seeing Max so relaxed, so unconcerned about the business. But I knew the moment the painkillers wore off he'd go into panic mode. 'So there's really no way of speeding this up?'

The doctor shook his head. 'Bones don't generally work

to our timetable,' he said. 'I'll leave you two alone, and the nurse will be in shortly. Press this buzzer if you need anything.'

He pointed to a red button on the side of Max's bed; Max pressed it immediately. 'Room service,' he said, grinning.

'I am so sorry,' I said desperately, as soon as the doctor had left. 'I can't believe this happened.'

'Is there a menu anywhere?' Max asked.

'A menu?' I looked at him carefully. 'Max, were you listening to what the doctor said? You're going to be in here for a while. Are you really okay about it?'

'Maybe they'll have lasagna,' Max said, as a nurse walked in. She was pretty, with dark hair and olive skin.

'Hi,' she said, smiling warmly. 'I'm Emily. How can I help?'

'I'd like some lasagna,' Max said. 'And chocolate pudding.'

Emily laughed. 'Well, I'm not sure we have either of those things, but I'll see what I can rustle up, shall I?'

'You are a gem,' Max said happily. 'My wife cooked, but then she kicked me out of bed and broke my leg.'

'Poor you,' Emily said, puffing up Max's pillow. 'I'm sure she didn't mean to.'

'Maybe,' Max said conspiratorially. 'But maybe she did. Who knows?'

I watched Emily uncertainly. I wasn't wild about some pretty nurse tucking in his sheets like that. Then I kicked myself. She was a nurse. That was her job. She'd go off shift soon and there'd be some much older, less attractive woman looking after him. Or a man. Maybe I'd ask specifically for a male nurse . . .

'You left the oven on, remember,' Max said. Then he smiled at Emily. 'She left the oven on. The lasagna's probably burned.'

88

'Probably,' Emily agreed.

'Well, I can always make another one,' I said quickly, forcing a bright smile. 'So, look, darling, is there anything I can do?'

'Actually,' Emily said, 'it's quite late, and visiting hours are over. It's best if you come back tomorrow.'

'Best,' Max echoed.

'Oh,' I said uncertainly. 'Oh, right. Well, if you're sure, Max?'

Max looked at me vaguely, then smiled again. 'Remember to turn the oven off. Don't want the apartment burning down on top of everything else.'

'No,' I said, wondering how our perfect evening had ended up so crappily. 'No, we wouldn't want that.'

Chapter 8

∾

VISITING HOURS, I LEARNED BEFORE leaving the hospital, started at 10:00 A.M., after the doctors had done their rounds. The following day, at 10:01 A.M., I stepped through the door to Max's room, clutching a large bouquet of flowers courtesy of Giles, a newspaper, a latte with one sugar, and a croissant. Breaking Max's leg had not exactly been part of the whole being-perfect plan, but it was, I told myself, just a minor setback, an opportunity to demonstrate my ability to not bother him with anything, to listen to him, to be supportive. I was going to be a pillar of strength, I'd decided. I was going to ensure that Max didn't have to worry about a thing while he was in the hospital. It would be the holiday he kept promising he'd take and never did – we didn't even take a honeymoon. Who knows, he might get a taste for leisure, I found myself thinking. Maybe I'd get him away for a proper holiday when he was better.

Max took the coffee gratefully and watched as I arranged the flowers on the little cabinet to the side of his bed.

'They're saying a week,' he said grimly.

'Yeah,' I said, turning to give him a kiss. 'The doctor said that last night.'

'A week. I can't be here for a week. I can't.'

'Max,' I chided, 'don't worry. It'll be okay. I'm going to look after everything for you.'

90

'Jess, do you know what looking after everything entails?' Max asked.

'Yes,' I said quickly. 'I mean, no, not really. But I'll check with you before making any decisions. Come on, chief execs go on holiday and companies don't all grind to a halt. I don't expect Jarvis Private Banking is falling apart because Chester's gone to the States.'

'Chester's business isn't in the fragile state we're in,' Max said flatly.

'Fragile? We're not that fragile, are we?' I asked, frowning.

Max looked away. 'We're okay,' he said. 'I just can't be away. Not for a week. Salaries go out this week. The audit's starting. We've got two important pitches. I simply cannot be laid up in the hospital. It isn't an option.'

'It is an option,' I said impatiently, then checked myself because the ideal wife would be understanding, not impatient. 'Look, I do know why you're worrying, but let it go. You don't have a choice, so enjoy it.'

'Enjoy it,' Max said tersely. 'Enjoy being in agony? Enjoy being stuck here, unable to work?' He looked at me, then let out a long breath. 'This is just a really bad time.'

'I know,' I said quietly. 'And I know it's my fault.'

Max shook his head. 'I didn't mean that. I don't blame you. I wish it hadn't happened, that's all. I appreciate your help, but I need to be there. We've got some big invoices to pay next week, and I need to keep on top of cash flow, make sure we've got the funds to pay. We're still chasing payment from Anix for the campaign we did last month, and without it we could be in trouble for a week or two until Jarvis's monthly payment lands.'

'So I'll loan the company some money in the short term,' I said exasperatedly.

'No,' Max said immediately. He looked at me irritably.

'Sometimes I wonder if that money has made you forget what the real world is like. I don't want a short-term loan; I want to manage my business.'

'I'm sorry.' I stared at him, bewildered. 'I know exactly what the real world is like. I only meant that—'

'I know what you meant,' Max interjected. 'And I'm sorry. I didn't mean that. My leg hurts and . . . I didn't mean it. Forget I said it. Just . . .'

'Just what?' I asked uncomfortably.

Max sighed. 'Look, Jess, we're really leveraged up at the moment. We took on more staff to service Chester's Internet bank account, which is fine but only if we keep on top of everything. Only if nothing goes wrong.'

'Nothing's going to go wrong,' I said.

'The audit,' Max replied. 'Chester's little ethical audit. *That* can't go wrong. I know Chester is virtually family now, but he's still a client and a crucial one. We can't afford to make any mistakes, okay?'

I nodded firmly. 'Okay,' I said. 'I'll make sure it goes perfectly. I promise.'

'Thanks, Jess,' Max said, managing a half-smile.

I smiled back. 'So, look, here's a newspaper. And a croissant.'

'You're a star,' Max said, as I placed them on the small table in front of him. 'Have you heard from Chester?'

'Since last night?' I raised an eyebrow. 'No, Max. It's the weekend, remember?'

'Right. Of course. I feel like I've been here longer than one night. Right. Good.' He looked at me quizzically. 'You're really going to run things for me while I'm here?'

'Absolutely,' I said with confidence. 'You tell me what to do and I'll do it. I don't want you worrying about a thing.

92

Now, can I fluff up your pillows? Adjust the volume on your television?'

Max smiled wryly. 'I haven't watched it, to be honest. They don't have the news channel.'

'There are other channels,' I pointed out.

'Other channels worth watching?' Max asked. His jaw was clenched, and I noticed him gripping the newspaper rather too tightly.

'Max,' I said, concerned. 'Max, are you—'

'Ah, here we are. Sorry I'm a bit late. Got delayed by the last patient having a bit of a hissy fit. Oh, hello!'

It was Emily. I smiled brightly. 'Hi! How are you?'

She didn't reply; instead, she went straight to Max with a syringe. 'Roll over. That's right. Just a little scratch and . . . there we are.'

Max let out a huge sigh, and Emily smiled at me. 'Pain relief,' she said. 'Poor Maxy should have had that half an hour ago.'

'Maxy?' I asked, a rather frozen smile on my face.

'He's lovely, isn't he? Such a poppet.'

I cleared my throat. I could think of many words to describe Max: energetic, dynamic, serious, substantial, honorable, generous, funny, intense. But a poppet? Was she kidding?

'So, look,' I said, turning back to Max. 'Is your schedule for next week emailable? Anything you want to talk me through?'

'Talk you through?' Max said goofily. 'I can talk you through it. Talk you through it all. Lots of meetings. Yes, meetings and other things.'

'Other things?' I asked.

'Other things,' Max confirmed, grinning at Emily. 'My wife doesn't want me to worry about a thing,' he said.

'Very sensible,' Emily said.

'I'm guessing the pain relief has kicked in?' I asked her.

She smiled. 'It's pretty quick when it's injected.' Then she turned back to Max. 'Maxy, shall we put the television on?'

'I tried that.' I rolled my eyes. 'He only wants the news channel, and you don't have it here.'

'Television?' Max's eyes lit up. 'Yes. I think television is a good idea. Don't you, Jess? You don't want me to worry about a thing, do you?'

'No, darling,' I said, watching disconcertedly as Emily flicked on his bedside TV and received a rapturous smile from Max for doing so. 'Not a single thing.'

The City soup kitchen was about a twenty-minute walk away from the offices of Milton Advertising. It was an uninspiring gray building that had been built as a municipal center in the 1970s and had apparently been neglected since then.

'Although, of course, we don't call ourselves a soup kitchen,' intoned Christina, the woman who ran the place, as she showed me around.

'You don't?' I asked curiously.

'No,' she said, smiling and shaking her head. 'We prefer to call ourselves a resource center. The people who come here call us RES.'

'RES?'

'Rest and Eat in Safety,' she explained. 'They're all equally important. Soup is just a small part of what we offer. And most days it isn't even soup. Do you cook?'

I smiled weakly. 'Um, sort of. I mean, I've taken a class, but I'm not really—'

'You've taken a class? Oh well, you're streets ahead of the rest of us. So, this is the kitchen.'

She led me into a tiny, dark back room and switched on the lights; immediately I was hit by the glare of stainless steel and aluminum. It smelled like a school canteen, but there was barely room to swing a cat, let alone cook for large numbers. 'We try to be inventive with the food. Stretch the budget, you know. It's vegetables that cost the most, but sometimes the local supermarkets give us the stuff they're about to chuck out. It's a terrible waste, you know, and we can make good use of it.'

'Absolutely,' I agreed.

'This is the living area. A lot of people come here during the day for some peace and quiet or to get out of the cold in the winter.' I looked around the room she'd led me to – this one had a different smell, one I vaguely recognized as the musty scent of the unwashed. It was laid out a bit like a doctor's waiting room, with chairs along the wall and a few sofas in the middle, and there were about fifteen men and women crammed into it – reading, playing cards, or sitting silently on their own. One woman stared at me, her eyes hostile. She was wearing several layers of clothing, and her feet were bulbous, squeezed into a pair of sandals. As I walked toward her, she bristled visibly, then stood up and held out her arms as though to fend me off.

'That's Greta,' Christina said with a smile. 'She likes to be left alone. Hello, Greta!'

Greta muttered something under her breath and sat down again.

'And this' – Christina opened another door – 'is the resting room. If you can just look through the door, we won't disturb anyone.'

I squeezed past her to peek inside – the room had mattresses on the floor, on which people were curled up to sleep; a loud snore could be heard from the far corner. 'If you sleep on the street,' Christina said, 'there's always a chance someone will steal from you. You're very vulnerable. Here, people can sleep in peace. Apart from Alan's snoring, of course.' She smiled again. 'Now, why don't we go to my office?'

I followed her back through the living room to a door past the kitchen. Inside, there was barely enough room to sit down; Christina's desk was piled high with paperwork, and every other surface was covered in stacks of paper and books.

'Do excuse the mess,' she said with a little shrug. 'I keep meaning to tidy up, but the problem is that there's nowhere to put anything. I need a bigger office, really, but we're so tight for space as it is.'

'You couldn't move somewhere bigger?' I asked.

Christina laughed. 'Oh, we could. If we could raise a ridiculously large sum of money. Do you know how much property costs around here? No, I'm afraid it's impossible.'

I persisted. 'What about if you got some of the big banks around here to help out?'

'Funnily enough, we did,' she said with a sigh. 'Two years ago we came close to securing a large sum of money from one of the big banks. Enough to buy somewhere twice the size of this place. But then the credit crunch happened and, well, you know the rest. Still, this place is fine for our purposes. We're very lucky to have it. You know it was going to be demolished? Fortunately it's in a conservation area and no property developer could get permission to build anything else. So it hung around empty for a few years, and then we came along and the council sold it to us for virtually nothing on the proviso that we maintain the building. But I digress. Now, let me just find your email.

Here we are. So, Jessica Wild Wainwright. You want to help us?'

I nodded firmly. 'Yes, that's right.'

'Well, that's great,' Christina said happily. 'We can always use more hands on deck. You cook, you say?'

I bit my lip. 'Not really.'

'But you've done a class?'

'I did a class because I wanted to cook my husband a meal. You know, one that didn't involve opening a packet and putting it in the microwave. Only . . .' I looked down.

'Only?' Christina prompted me.

'I wasn't very good. The instructor ended up cooking most of the meal for me.'

'Ah,' Christina said sagely. 'Still, I'm sure your husband appreciated the sentiment.'

'He broke his leg, actually,' I said, pulling a face.

'The food was that bad?' Her eyebrows shot up. 'I've never heard of food attacking limbs like that.'

I giggled. 'He didn't even get to eat the food. He broke his leg before we got round to that. I was . . . well . . .' I went red, mentally kicking myself for bringing up the episode at all.

'You were treating your husband, were you?' Christina evidently understood exactly what we'd been doing. 'Was it his birthday?'

I shook my head. 'No. I just, you know, wanted to be a better wife, to be a better person generally. That's kind of why I'm here.'

'I see,' Christina said seriously. 'Well, let's see what you can offer. I'll say no to cooking, shall I? What about DIY? Putting up shelves, changing plugs, that sort of thing?'

I grimaced. Helen and I had once tried to put some shelves up in the kitchen; we'd managed to fix them to the wall, put all our cooking equipment on them, and two minutes later they'd fallen down again. 'I'm probably not the most handy person around,' I confessed. 'I'm willing to try, but . . .'

'But you may not be able to meet the stringent health and safety measures?' Christina asked. 'Okay, then. What can you do?'

I took a deep breath. I'd already had an idea of what I could do, how I could really help. 'Well, actually,' I said, leaning in toward her, 'I work in advertising. I help to leverage brands to build awareness in the marketplace and embed them in the public consciousness.'

'Gosh,' Christina said. 'Well, I'm not sure we have any brand to leverage, but—'

'You do,' I cut in. 'And I was thinking that maybe I could help you build that brand to raise funds. For the new premises you need.'

Christina frowned. 'I'm sorry?'

'Strategic partnerships,' I said seriously. 'Your brand offers a warm, fuzzy good feeling. Financial institutions love that stuff. One of our clients, for instance, is Jarvis Private Banking. A partnership would give you money and make them look good for helping out.'

Christina looked at me uncertainly. 'That's very nice, but I think we prefer not to have strategic . . . partnerships, was it? The thing is, we're a small charity and we like to do things our own way.'

'But you could!' I enthused. 'I mean, there might be a photo shoot or something to publicize the partnership, maybe a press conference, but that would be great for you, as well. Publicity's great for raising funds, right?'

'It can be,' Christina said tentatively, 'but—'

'But what?' I asked excitedly. 'Look, I could really make a

98

difference here. We leverage the great stuff you're doing and turn it into an irresistible offering.'

Christina took a deep breath and exhaled slowly. 'Jessica,' she said, looking at me warmly, 'I can see that you're brimming with ideas. And I'm sure that you're a wonderful advertising professional. But what we're about here is providing a place of refuge for the homeless, somewhere they can come without fear, without any questions, and without any demands on them. We feed them, we let them rest. We don't leverage them. We don't package them up as an offering, irresistible or otherwise. I know you mean well, but it's not what we're about. We leave that to the bigger charities. Us? We just provide soup and shelter.'

'And not always soup,' I said quietly. 'I get that. But—'

'No buts,' Christina said gently. 'So let's think of something else that you can do, shall we?'

'Sure,' I said, trying not to feel too disappointed. 'Whatever I can do to help. Really.'

Christina leaned forward. 'You know, with the skills that you have, I think the best job for you is that of companion.'

'Companion?' I frowned.

'Talking. Listening.' Christina shrugged. 'Many of the people who come here barely speak to anyone for weeks at a time. Except to ask for money, of course. Some of them ramble constantly, but most of them hardly recognize their own voices anymore. They like being read to, which I'm sure you can do very well, and sometimes they like to talk. Your job is then to listen. What do you think?'

'Listen? That's it?' I asked.

'It's harder than you think,' Christina said seriously. 'But it's worth it. You'll hear all sorts of interesting stories. Some true, some absolute fiction, but fascinating all the same.'

'Okay.' I tried not to sound disappointed. I'd wanted to do something significant, to really make a difference; instead, I'd proved myself to be completely useless and was obviously being given a non-job because Christina felt sorry for me. 'Sounds great. When do I start?'

'You can start now if you like,' she said warmly.

'So, what, I just go in and . . . and what?' I asked uncertainly.

'Just go in. Sit down. See if anyone wants to talk to you,' Christina said. 'And when you want to go home, you leave. It's as simple as that.'

'Okay, then,' I said, standing up. 'I'll . . . Well, I guess I'll go to work.'

I waited for her to say something, but she was already looking down at one of the piles on her desk, so I walked out and made my way to the living room. Greta was still there with her hostile expression. I made my way to the other side of the room, where two men were sitting side by side.

I sat opposite them. 'Hello!' I said.

One of them ignored me; the other grunted, then looked blankly ahead. I smiled as brightly as I could. 'You want to talk?' I asked. 'Because if you do, I'm here to listen. Whatever you want to say, you go right ahead.'

Neither man said a word.

'Or I could read, if you want?' I looked around for a book or a magazine but found nothing. 'Maybe next time I'll bring a book,' I said. 'Is there anything you particularly like? Any favorite authors?'

I was met by a wall of silence, and I sighed inwardly. This wasn't a job. This was nothing. Christina had simply taken pity on me. I was useless. Completely useless.

'Maybe a thriller,' I said to no one in particular. 'Or

maybe a romance. Or, you know, we could just sit here.'
I crossed my legs and tried not to think of all the other
more useful things I could be doing – developing strategic
alliances with supermarkets or lobbying city firms for funds
to buy new premises. Instead, I was sitting around in a
waiting room, achieving nothing. 'Yes, sitting here sounds
like the best plan. Just sitting here and not saying a thing,' I
said miserably. And two hours later, having listened to no
one and read zip to anyone, I picked up my bag and made
my way home.

Chapter 9

◌◍

THE FOLLOWING MORNING I got out of bed, had breakfast, and got dressed, as if everything was fine. Sure, Max was in the hospital, my attempts to be the perfect wife having backfired spectacularly; sure, I was going to have to somehow cover Max's work while he was out; and, sure, I'd had a horrible dream in which Nurse Emily had barred me from the hospital so she could seduce 'Maxy.' But, apart from that, everything was just hunky-dory.

I sighed as I printed out Max's schedule for the day. He was right about having a million and one things to do: *9:00 A.M., go through accounts and get salaries processed; 9:30 A.M., call Chester to get update on Internet-bank advertising campaign; 10:00 A.M., prepare desk for Eric Sandler (arrives Tuesday, 10:00 A.M.); 10:30 A.M., discussion with HR manager about pensions; 11:30 A.M. . . .* I folded the schedule and put it in my bag. That was enough for now. I'd find out what 11:30 A.M. held for me once I got through the first few things.

I wouldn't let Max down, I thought firmly. I may have burned the lasagna, but business I could do; business was what I was good at.

As I got into my car to drive to the office, my phone rang and I flipped it open immediately. It would be Max, I figured; he'd have woken up, the painkillers would have worn off again, and he'd be worrying about work. I would tell him calmly that everything was under control and that all he had to do was concentrate on getting better.

'Darling! It's me.'

'Oh, Mum, hi,' I said, trying not to sound disappointed. 'How are you?'

'You mean, how am I coping with desertion by my fiancé?'

'He hasn't deserted you, Mum. He just had to go to the United States.'

'You always take his side, Jessica, when it's absolutely clear that he's been very unreasonable. But that's not why I called. I need to talk to you, darling. It's about my Face-booking.'

'Facebook isn't a verb, Mum,' I said tersely. 'To be honest, now isn't a great time to talk, I'm afraid. Max had a—'

'It's never a good time with you,' Mum interrupted. 'And this is really very important. I was hoping we might have coffee this morning. I could take the nine-thirty train and be in London by eleven.'

'This morning?' I sighed; I was fairly sure that my idea of important and her idea of important were probably a long way apart. 'No, Mum, this morning isn't going to be possible at all.'

'Well, then, maybe you could come down to the house this evening?'

'This evening? No,' I said, exasperated. 'I mean, I'd love to, but I can't see you today. Or this week, actually. You see, Max is—'

'You're busy *all week*?'

'Yes, Mum. If you'd just listen to me? Max had a—'

'Max, Max, Max. Darling, there is more to your life than your husband. There is more to all of us than our husbands. Or fiancés. We have to be independent, you know. But I do

103

need to talk to you. You're going to have to make some time in your busy week, I'm afraid.'

I rolled my eyes. 'If it's to do with the bridesmaid dresses, don't worry,' I said. 'I'll wear whatever you want me to.'

'It's not the bridesmaid dresses,' Mum said. 'I told you. It's about my Facebook . . .'

Facebook? I took a deep breath. No doubt she needed help uploading some photographs or something equally ridiculous. 'Fine. I'll help with whatever it is,' I said quickly. 'Just not now. I've really got to go, okay?'

I didn't wait for her response. I knew she'd be angry, but right now Mum was not my priority. I shut my phone, then started the engine. Immediately my phone started to ring again. Irritably, I looked at the number, then blanched and flipped it open.

'Chester!' I exclaimed. 'How are you? How's it going in the States?'

'Hey, Jess. Things are great. I was just wondering how your mother is. We weren't on very good terms after I told her about my trip.'

'Mum? Oh, she's . . . fine,' I lied.

'You're sure? Well, that's a relief, because I haven't heard from her since I left. I keep leaving messages, but she hasn't called back. So you say she's okay? She's not mad?'

I bit my lip awkwardly. 'Well, maybe a little,' I said. 'But—'

'But nothing you can't handle. Right?'

'Right,' I said immediately, then smiled to myself. God, he was good, I thought. Delegating his dirty work and then making you feel grateful that he thought you could handle it. No wonder he was running a huge bank.

'I knew I could rely on you, Jess. You know your mother

listens to you, don't you? She really values your opinions on things.'

'She does?' I asked, feeling slightly guilty about cutting her off so harshly. 'I'm going to call her later,' I said. Then I remembered something. 'Actually, I was going to call you later, too. Max wanted to talk to you about the Internet-bank campaign. Getting some dates in the diary for the launch, that sort of thing.'

'Okay, I'll call him later, shall I?'

'Well, he's had an accident,' I said soberly.

'An accident?' Chester sounded concerned. 'What kind of accident?'

'He broke his leg.' I sighed. 'He's in the hospital.'

'Jeez. Poor Max.'

'Yeah. So, look, about this campaign? Max'll be bugging me for information later, I know he will.'

'You tell him to focus on getting better. I think we're going to hold off on any new campaigns until this ethical audit is done. It'll give us something new to shout about, wouldn't you say?'

I bit my lip, harder this time. 'But . . . you're going to do it, anyway, aren't you? So shouldn't we—'

'I'd feel better if the audit is done first. So when we launch we can talk up the audit as well as everything else,' Chester cut in. 'Don't you agree?'

'Of course,' I said hesitantly, realizing that Max had been right about the significance of the audit. We couldn't afford for there to be any problems. 'I mean, yes. It makes perfect sense.'

'Great. Well, send my best to Max.'

'I will,' I said. 'See you, Chester.'

*

I shut off my phone and reversed out of the garage, driving just over the speed limit all the way to work.

'Excuse me?' As I walked toward my desk, a tall, thin man approached me. I looked over at Gillie's desk but it was empty – our receptionist often arrived late on Monday.

'Hi,' I said distractedly, wondering if I could palm him off on someone else. 'What can I do for you?'

'I'm here to see Max Wainwright,' the man said.

I dug out the schedule – there was nothing about a 9:30 A.M. meeting. If I didn't get the salaries confirmed by 10:00 A.M., they wouldn't hit everyone's bank accounts in time, and there was nothing like not getting paid to create a mutiny.

'Um, well, I'm afraid he won't be in today,' I apologized. 'Perhaps you could come back another time, or give me your card, or . . .'

The man nodded interestedly and took out a notebook, then started to scribble. 'There appears to be no one at this reception desk,' he said.

'No,' I said, smiling. 'That's Gillie, our receptionist, for you. She's a bit of a party girl, so Monday mornings aren't really her best time, I'm afraid.' I hoped that my friendly approach would be reciprocated and that he would leave me to get on with Max's long to-do list.

'Party girl?' the man said, his forehead creasing as he continued to scribble. 'That's interesting. That's very interesting.'

'Is it?' I said, then shook myself. 'I'm sorry, I didn't catch your name. I'm sorry about Max. He's broken his leg, you see. But if you'll just—'

'Sandler,' the man said, holding out his hand, a thin smile on his lips. 'Eric Sandler.'

I looked at him for a few seconds. The name rang a bell. A very loud bell. Then I felt the blood drain from my face.

'Eric Sandler? The auditor? But you're not meant to be here until tomorrow.'

Eric looked very pleased with himself. 'Yes, I like to arrive earlier than planned. See things as they really are, not as you'd have us see them,' he said, his beady eyes shining.

'Oh, right!' I said, reminding myself to breathe. 'What a . . . great idea. Well, very nice to meet you, Mr. Sandler. I'm Jessica Wild. Max's wife. He's . . . really sorry he isn't here, but I'm going to be deputizing for him, so anything I can do . . .'

'You can get me an office,' Eric said. 'I'll need somewhere to work.'

'Of course,' I said quickly, gulping as I looked around. The only empty office was Max's, and there was no way I was putting him in there. My eyes rested on the door next to Max's. It was risky, but . . .

'I'll put you in Anthony's office. I'm sure he won't mind,' I said, knowing that he would mind very much. 'Although I'll have to clear it out first. If you could wait just a few minutes?' I had a smile fixed on my face, and my cheeks were beginning to hurt. 'And, in the meantime, can I get you anything? Coffee? Tea? Muffin? There's a great café around the corner that does the best muffins this side of the river.'

Eric shook his head. 'We don't accept anything but water from our auditees,' he said. 'Otherwise we could be accused of accepting bribes.'

'Muffins as bribes? I thought bribes involved suitcases of cash,' I joked, immediately regretting it when Eric looked at me suspiciously. 'Or maybe this is post-credit-crunch bribery,' I found myself saying. What was I, a comedian all of a sudden?

Eric didn't smile back. 'I'll wait here,' he said pointedly, and looked at his watch. 'Let me know when my office is ready.'

He sat down, and I turned away in relief. Okay. This was not a disaster. Not yet. Things were going to be fine. They had to be. I rushed into Anthony's office and started to clear things into piles – then, when I realized that most of the stuff in there wasn't in any way work-related, I opened his cupboard and chucked the whole lot in. For good measure, I grabbed a spare laptop computer that was used for pitches and put it on the desk.

'It's ready,' I panted, rushing back out to Eric. 'There's a computer on the desk if you need it. Anything else, just let me know.'

'Thank you,' Eric said curtly, and disappeared into the office. 'I think my time here is going to be very productive. Very productive indeed.'

'Who's that?' Caroline whispered as I collapsed at my desk twenty minutes later. I'd just told everyone about Max's accident (being pretty vague about how it had happened, of course) and reassured them that everything was perfectly under control.

Caroline was referring to Eric, who was standing in the doorway to Anthony's office, looking around. I shuddered. 'He's the ethical auditor,' I said, trying not to make eye contact with him. He kept doing that – coming out and looking around. And whenever I asked him if he needed anything, he just shot me his supercilious smile and told me that he'd let me know in due course.

Caroline's eyes widened. 'Gosh. The ethical auditor. I've

never met an ethical auditor before. He must be really interesting.'

I opened my mouth to say that frankly I thought he was the least interesting person I'd met in a long time, then decided against it. 'I guess,' I said instead. 'Anyway, it means we have to all be on our best behavior. Let's knock him dead with the intensity of our ethics, shall we?'

Caroline nodded again. 'Intensive ethics,' she said thoughtfully. 'That sounds like a pitch for a campaign.'

I found myself grinning. 'Nice idea,' I said. 'Look, can you keep an eye on him? Eric, I mean?'

'Of course,' Caroline said seriously. 'It would be an honor. So are you, like, the chief executive until Max gets back?'

I laughed. 'Me? Chief exec? No. No, I'm just filling in. You know, steering the ship.'

'Then you're the captain?' Caroline asked, uncertain.

'Think of me as an account director,' I said sagely.

'An account director,' Caroline mused. Then she frowned. 'But that's what you are. Were, I mean.'

'Exactly. And now, if you'll excuse me, I've got a to-do list to get back to,' I said, standing up so I could finally get into Max's office. Before I could, though, Anthony appeared at my desk, his face furious.

'What the hell is some bloke doing in my office?' he demanded. 'And what's this I hear about Max?'

'Max has broken his leg,' I said, looking at my watch and raising my eyebrows. 'The bloke in your office is the ethical auditor. And have you ever heard of getting in to work before ten A.M.?'

'I decide my own hours,' Anthony said dismissively. 'And why isn't the auditor in Max's office if Max can't be bothered to come in? Anyway, I thought he was starting tomorrow.'

'He likes to surprise auditees,' I said tightly. 'And Max *can* be bothered; he can't physically get in. He's in the hospital.'

'So who's running the place in his absence?' Anthony asked curiously. 'Me, presumably. This used to be my firm, after all.'

'Yes, and Max bought it from you when you plunged it into debt,' I reminded him. 'Thanks for the offer, but I think I'll just keep on top of everything, if it's all right with you.'

'It's all right with me.' Anthony shrugged. 'But does Max really want you in charge? Particularly if we've got an ethics audit going on? Bit risky, isn't it?'

I looked at him uncertainly. 'I'm not sure what you mean. To be honest, I was thinking about asking you to stay away for a week until it's all over. If anyone poses a risk, it's you.'

Anthony smiled sweetly. 'How thoughtful,' he said. 'But, lest we forget, it was you who thought it was perfectly reasonable to marry for money. To jilt me at the altar. To seduce an old lady into leaving her entire inheritance to you instead of her own family. Frankly, you're a liability.'

My eyes narrowed. 'You are totally twisting the facts, Anthony, and you know it. I didn't get Grace's entire inheritance. You got your money,' I said levelly. 'If you blew it, that's not my problem.'

'And the audit is apparently not my problem,' Anthony retorted. 'Luckily for me.' He was looking at something behind me; I turned to see what it was and gasped. Eric was standing a few feet away, scribbling furiously in his notebook. How long had he been listening? What was he writing?

'Eric!' I said, as cheerfully as I could manage. 'Um, this is Anthony Milton. The Anthony whose office you're using.

He and I were just . . . um . . . joshing. You know, office banter.'

Eric smiled thinly. 'Indeed.'

'Yes,' I continued, seemingly unable to stop talking. 'Yes. We do all like to joke around here. Don't we, Anthony?'

Anthony rolled his eyes, then walked over toward Eric. 'So how long are you going to need my office?' he asked. 'A day? Two?'

Eric finished scribbling in his notebook, then looked at Anthony, his face giving nothing away. 'I think I could be here for a little longer than that,' he said. 'Quite a bit longer, in fact.'

'Quite a bit longer?' I asked, swallowing uncomfortably. 'How much longer? I thought you only needed to interview a selection of our—'

'I take my job very seriously,' Eric said. His voice had a horrible nasal twang to it that made me recoil. 'And where I feel there is evidence of . . . how shall I put this . . . unethical tendencies, then it is my duty to root them out, to explore them, to analyze how they fit into the organization's culture.'

'Unethical tendencies?' I gulped. 'But there's nothing like that here. I mean, there really isn't . . .'

'No?' Eric looked at his notebook, flicking back through the pages. He smiled silkily. 'Let me see,' he said, licking his lips. 'We have nepotism—'

'Nepotism?' I asked.

'Your husband is Mr. Wainwright, is he not? And you are an account director?'

I nodded.

'And it is you whom he left in charge?'

I nodded again.

'I see,' Eric said thoughtfully. 'The account-director job was advertised externally, was it?'

'No, I was promoted,' I said uncomfortably.

'It was advertised internally, at least?'

'No,' I said, feeling rather hot all of a sudden. 'But—'

'And your current role, deputizing for Mr. Wainwright. Was that role advertised?'

'No, but he only broke his leg on Saturday, so . . .'

'Indeed,' Eric said smugly. 'What about drinking? Drugs?'

'What about them?' I said, my voice catching slightly.

'There is no drinking or drug-taking here,' Anthony said with a sigh. 'Disappointing, I know, but—'

'Perhaps not on the premises,' Eric said curtly. 'But your receptionist is a party girl, I understand. Is regularly late on Mondays. Have you looked into this? Have you offered her rehabilitation for her habits? Counseling?'

Anthony shrugged and looked at me with a grin. 'I don't know. Do you offer counseling, Jess?'

I shook my head in confusion. 'Counseling? Because she goes out on Saturday night?'

Anthony winked at me and wandered off. Eric was tutting to himself. 'Saturday night does not usually lead to a Monday hangover,' he said. 'No, I can see that you are oblivious to the cries for help from your staff. As for the root cause, I will need to assess the stress that your employees are under, Ms. Wild Wainwright. If your company culture is driving them to alcohol dependency, to drug addiction, then that is a very serious matter.'

'Driving people to drugs?' I asked incredulously. 'But . . . but—'

'And Anthony Milton,' Eric said before I could finish. 'Is that the Milton in the company name?'

I nodded. 'It used to be Anthony's firm,' I said stiffly. 'But Max bought it and—'

'Yet he is back here working. I'd like to see the details of the financial settlement,' Eric said, closing his notebook. 'The tax accounts. We don't like to see sales of businesses used as tax-avoidance schemes.'

'There wasn't any tax avoidance; Max just bought the business, end of story,' I said, irritated now. 'This is a good company, and Max has worked really hard to make it the best advertising firm in London.'

'Well, we'll see about that,' Eric said smoothly. 'We'll certainly get to the truth of the matter. I just hope for your sake that there aren't any real problems.'

I took a deep breath as I imagined what would happen if we failed the audit. It would be all over the press, we'd lose our clients, and the business would be ruined. I wanted to kick that horrible man out onto the street, never allow him to return. But I knew it wasn't going to happen. Instead, I had to make sure we didn't fail. For Max's sake. 'Mr. Sandler,' I said, forcing myself to calm down. 'Look, I think maybe we got off on the wrong foot here. What you're doing is important, and we want to help you in any way we can. So why doesn't Caroline here help you to set up some interviews, then in a couple of days – when you've spoken to people and gotten a better feel of the place – you can assess how long you need to stay?'

Eric looked at me suspiciously, as though I'd asked him to let a hardened criminal out of prison or something. 'Well,' he said, after a pause, 'I suppose that would be acceptable.'

'Great,' I said, sighing with relief. 'That's great.'

He walked off and I turned to Caroline anxiously. 'Keep

Anthony away from him,' I said. 'Millie's on holiday for two weeks. Give Anthony her desk upstairs. Okay?'

Caroline nodded quickly and jumped up. 'Okay,' she said, in that earnest way of hers that made me want to hug her. 'I'll tell him right away.'

Chapter 10

'YOU'VE REALLY NEVER watched *Doctors*? It's genius. It's about these doctors, you see. Isn't it, Emily?'

I cleared my throat. I was at the hospital, exhausted; I wanted to talk to Max about the audit, about the hideous day I'd had, about how I only just got the salaries off in time and nearly missed an important meeting at 11:30 A.M. because I hadn't even looked that far into his schedule. I wanted to tell him all the crappy things that had happened, the snide remarks from Eric, the trouble I'd had trying to figure out the company's pension scheme, the fact that I hadn't eaten a thing all day because I'd been so rushed off my feet. But I couldn't; I didn't want to bother Max with any of it. And, anyway, he was still away with the fairies. I'd never seen him so relaxed. Me, I was a bundle of nerves. There was so much adrenaline coursing through my veins, I felt like I'd drunk ten cups of coffee; I was almost tempted to ask for a shot of Max's painkillers for myself.

'No, I've never watched it,' I said, attempting a relaxed smile, which was easier said than done. For one thing, I didn't feel remotely relaxed, and for another, Emily was sitting on the chair next to Max's bed, forcing me to perch on the bed, and there wasn't much room what with Max and his broken leg taking up most of it.

'Max loves it, don't you, Max?' Emily said, grinning.

'Actually, what Max really loves is current affairs,' I said. 'News, mostly.'

'News?' Max shook his head. 'Too depressing. What's that other one I like, Emily? The one with the woman.'

'*Murder, She Wrote,*' Emily enthused.

Max nodded happily. 'That's the one. Brilliant. Sheer genius.' Then his face clouded over slightly. 'You got here very late,' he said. 'There's only an hour of visiting time left.'

'I know. I'm sorry. It's just been a really long day, and I didn't manage to leave the office until about half an hour ago,' I said. 'But I'm here now!'

'Yes,' Max said. 'Anyway, it's okay, because Emily has been here to look after me.' He smiled at her goofily, and she smiled right back at him. I shifted uncomfortably on the bed, telling myself to relax and stop being so paranoid. Emily was a nurse; of course she was looking after him. I should be pleased that she was keeping him occupied, pleased that he wasn't stressed out or worried about work. And I was pleased. Sort of. If she'd only get off that chair . . .

'Well, thank you, Emily,' I said brightly. 'You're obviously doing a great job. Max is looking much better already.'

Emily turned her attention to me. 'Oh, that's what I'm here for. And I enjoy what I do. Max has been in a lot of pain,' she said. 'It's not easy being stuck in a hospital bed all day on your own.'

I looked at her steadily. Was she suggesting that I should have been here earlier? No, of course she wasn't, I chided myself. 'I know,' I said, forcing myself to be pleasant. 'It must be awful. But at least I'm keeping everything at work on track so he doesn't have to worry about that.'

'Well, that's good,' Emily said. 'Isn't it, Max?'

Max smiled dopily. 'Jess is quite brilliant,' he said.

'Oh, I don't know,' I said, reddening with pleasure and shooting a little triumphant smile at Emily. 'I'm not really.'

'Yes, you are,' Max said, nodding vigorously. Then he grinned. 'At work, I mean.' He turned to Emily. 'She can't cook very well. Burns everything. Don't you, Jess?'

My smile faltered slightly. 'I'm not the greatest cook,' I admitted.

'Not the greatest?' Max laughed. 'You went on a cookery course and still burned the lasagna!' He carried on laughing, evidently pleased with his joke.

I, on the other hand, was failing to see the funny side. 'Cooking isn't really my forte,' I said tightly.

'Emily cooks,' Max said. 'She brought me in homemade biscuits this afternoon. What were they again?' He turned to Emily, who winked.

'Ginger snaps. And you'd better not eat too many, you know. With your leg like that, you can't exercise, and we don't want you getting tubby.'

I stared at her indignantly. 'Max can eat what he wants,' I said. 'He's not going to get tubby. And even if he did, I wouldn't care.'

'She would.' Max winked conspiratorially. 'That's why she doesn't cook: Doesn't want me turning into a tubby tubster. Did you bring me anything to eat, Jess?' I shook my head uncomfortably. I'd been planning to bring flowers, biscuits, a selection of books by Max's favorite authors. But I hadn't had time to get anything. 'See?' Max said to Emily. 'Case closed.'

He was grinning and I knew he was joking, knew he thought he was being really funny. But it didn't feel funny. It felt awful, like I was just one big letdown. I didn't want him teasing me about my cooking and highlighting my failures. I was meant to be the ideal wife, and instead I was an abject failure. Unlike bloody Emily, who could do everything. She probably made great soup, too.

I looked at her disconcertedly. 'So, look, Emily. Thanks so much for looking after Max so well. But you must have other patients to see,' I said. 'I can take things from here.'

'Oh, of course,' Emily said, quickly standing up. 'I'm so sorry – you want time alone. I'm awful like that. I'm really very sorry.'

'Don't be sorry,' Max said, frowning. 'Jess didn't mean she wants you to go, did you, Jess?'

I cleared my throat. 'No, of course not,' I lied. 'I was just saying that there's no need for her to stay if . . . you know, if she's got other people to look after.'

'To be honest, my shift ended an hour ago.' Emily shrugged. 'But Max here looked so lonely I thought I'd stay.'

'You're not even working at the moment?'

'Going beyond the call of duty is what she's doing,' Max said, shaking his head in admiration. 'And people moan about the NHS. Incredible, isn't it?'

'Incredible,' I agreed. Max opened his mouth to say something, then appeared to change his mind. His eyes started to close and I wanted to lean over and kiss him, but I couldn't. Not with her in the room. Not when I was perching so awkwardly on the bed. 'Emily,' I asked instead, 'do you have a boyfriend? A husband?'

She rolled her eyes. 'With this job? Not likely, the hours I work. Haven't got time to meet men.'

'What a shame,' I said.

'Travesty,' Max said, his eyes opening again. 'Jess works long hours, too. That's how we met. At work.'

'Is it?' Emily asked interestedly. 'That's nice.'

'Very nice,' agreed Max. 'Jess is very, very nice.'

I blushed happily. 'Well, I'm sure you'll meet some-one eventually,' I said to Emily, feeling a sudden surge of warmth toward her. If she was looking after him, who was I to complain? After all, I wanted him to be happy. That's all that mattered.

'I hope so,' Emily said dreamily. 'So what work do you do?'

'We're in advertising,' I said. 'Max is the chief executive of an advertising agency, and I'm an account director.'

'Sounds very glamorous,' Emily said.

I shrugged. 'It can be. Most of the time it's just work, though. Like any job.'

Emily nodded. 'That's what I love about my job,' she said. 'It's so fulfilling.'

'So's advertising,' I said quickly. 'You know, devising a campaign that really fits with a company's strategy, that moves their brand forward.'

Emily laughed. 'Oh, I wouldn't know about that. I'm not into strategy myself, only into looking after people. The managers here talk about strategy, but what they mean is cutting costs, spending all the money on audits instead of care. Crazy, isn't it?'

Max's eyes opened wide. 'Audit,' he said, looking at me. 'Tomorrow.'

I shook my head. 'Today,' I said with an uncomfortable smile.

'No, tomorrow,' Max said.

'He turned up early. Said he likes to surprise people.'

Max frowned. 'Really? That's not very friendly.'

'Not really,' I agreed. His brow creased; he looked as if he was having trouble formulating a complex sentence. 'Don't worry, Max. It was fine. It's going to be fine. It's all under control,' I said quickly.

A look of relief crossed his face. 'So grateful, Jess,' he said, his eyes closing again. 'Depending on you. Can't screw up. Can't.'

'We won't,' I said gently.

'Have to pass,' Max said dreamily, then started to snore.

'I guess that's my cue to leave,' I said, looking at my watch. It was 9:00 P.M.; visitors' hours had just ended.

'Guess so,' Emily said. 'We'll see you tomorrow, will we?'

'Of course,' I said, trying not to be bothered by her use of the word 'we.' And by the fact that she was still here in Max's room.

'I'll let him know.' Emily smiled. 'Bye, Jessica.'

'Bye, Emily,' I said, then took one last look at my sleeping Max before leaving the room.

I didn't feel like going home – not right away. All that waited at home for me was yet another microwave meal and a big empty bed that didn't have Max in it. Instead, I found myself stopping by RES. I might not be the perfect wife, I decided – not yet, at least – but I could at least try to be a good Samaritan.

The place was buzzing when I got there. If it had seemed on the small side the day before, tonight it seemed tiny. People were everywhere – sitting down, shuffling around, spooning food into hungry-looking mouths.

I saw Christina standing by the entrance to the kitchen and waved; she shot me a big smile.

'Hi!' I said, as I made my way toward her. 'Busy tonight?'

'Every night,' she said. 'This is our busiest time – people wanting to sleep here, others looking for a hot meal before they brave the streets again. Come to hear some stories, have you?'

120

I smiled. 'Absolutely.' Then I looked at her seriously. 'The truth is, I've been thinking.'

'Oh, Bernard, be careful with that, will you? It's very hot. Sorry, Jess, what were you saying?'

I cleared my throat. 'I was thinking that I could help you. More than just being a companion, I mean. I get that you're not interested in a strategic alliance with any financial institutions or anything that might require press attention. But how about I try to work up some kind of official agreement with a major supermarket? They would probably be happy to supply you with food if we can sell it to them as a corporate-responsibility initiative. They love putting that kind of stuff in their annual reports, and you could get all the vegetables you need. What do you think?'

Christina didn't say anything for a moment, then she smiled at me. 'You know,' she said, 'being a companion is really important.'

'Oh, I know that,' I said quickly. 'I mean, obviously it's a very significant role. And it's not that I don't want to do it. I do. Definitely. I just want to, you know, add some real value. And this is what I'm good at. I could set up a meeting and we could see what comes out of it and—'

'Thanks, Jess,' Christina said, putting her hand on mine. 'I appreciate it, truly. But the thing is, I don't think we're interested in being some supermarket's corporate-responsibility initiative, you know? We have to think long term. We have to protect the people here.'

'But they'd be protected; they'd just have more vegetables!' I said enthusiastically. 'I could put in a call—'

'Bernard! I told you that was hot . . .' Christina's face fell as Bernard, an old stooped man, spilled coffee on his hand; she rushed to help him. 'Thanks, Jess. But, honestly, where you can add value is in being a companion. If that's okay?

Now, Bernard, we need to get your hand under a cold tap. You have to be careful, do you hear me? Your arthritis isn't getting better, and you can't go picking up hot cups of coffee like that . . .'

'Sure. That's fine,' I said, my shoulders slumping slightly. 'No problem at all.'

I wandered into the living room and sat down on a chair. No one even looked at me; they certainly didn't try to talk to me. I felt very heavy all of a sudden. I wasn't looking after Max properly and I'd totally screwed up the audit at work. Now I couldn't even be a good companion – and that wasn't a proper volunteer job, anyway; it was just a consolation prize to make me feel better about the fact that I couldn't cook or put up shelves. I sighed. Maybe I should go home after all, I thought. Maybe the best place for me was my big, empty bed.

I yawned and stood up.

'You look tired.'

I frowned. I hadn't noticed the man sitting two seats away from me – he was slight, with a full head of dark hair and a scrawny face that looked as if it had over-ripened in the sun.

'I am,' I said with a little smile. 'I think I'm going to be off now.'

'You can . . . you can have my bed if you want,' he said. 'I've got one tonight. You don't want to be out on the streets, a nice girl like you.'

I reddened awkwardly. 'The streets? Me? Oh, no. I'm not . . . I'm helping out here. I . . . I have a home.'

'Oh,' the man said, looking embarrassed. 'Right. Well, that's good, then. That's really good.' He looked down at the floor studiously.

'It is good, yes,' I said, biting my lip. 'You . . . enjoy your bed, okay? And thanks for the offer.'

'Yeah,' the man said, not meeting my eyes.

I slowly made my way out of the center. It *was* good, I thought, chastened. And it wasn't a bad idea to remember that sometimes.

Chapter 11

THE NEXT MORNING I arrived at work to find Eric waiting for me with a long list in his hand.

'It's a checklist,' he said, handing it to me. 'A checklist of all the information I need.'

'Right,' I replied uncertainly. I hadn't even had my coffee yet; I wasn't ready to review a checklist. 'Well, I'll just take a look at it, shall I, and get back to you?'

Looking slightly disappointed that I wasn't reviewing it then and there, Eric shrugged. 'I'll need all that information by close of business today,' he said, hovering over me. 'So don't delay too long.'

I took a deep breath and walked to my desk. The problem with Eric Sandler, I'd already decided, was that he was a lurker. And I hated lurking. I couldn't bear the way he skulked around the place, listening in on conversations, lying in wait like a panther – or like a weasel pretending to be a panther, since there was absolutely nothing panther-like about him. It was as if he was determined to find something untoward that someone, somewhere, was doing. And when I say someone, I really mean me. Call me para-noid, but every time I looked up, he was there. He always had a cast-iron excuse – liaising with Caroline over the interview schedule, checking his database against the one on Caroline's system, asking her how the coffee machine worked, when it was obvious that you just pressed the

124

button that said *Coffee*. But those eyes of his – furtive and gloating, all at once, which you'd think was impossible but, believe me, isn't – were always staring beadily at me, his ears pricked up to listen in on my telephone conversations and to watch my every move.

Sitting down, I took a gulp of coffee and did a quick survey of the list. As I read, I found myself getting hotter and hotter. He needed health and safety records going back five years, accounts to demonstrate positive cash flow, policies on everything from charitable giving to staff counseling, evidence of involvement in the local community, evidence that our campaigns did not exploit anyone, and evidence that all our clients were assessed ethically before we agreed to work for them.

It was insane. I got up and half ran to Eric's office. 'This list,' I said.

He smiled; evidently he'd been expecting me. 'Yes?'

'We don't have half this stuff. I mean, we do a lot of it – like, this year we sponsored the local street fair, and Max always encourages charitable giving via the payroll, and we don't work for any tobacco companies or anything. But we just do that stuff; we don't have policies on it. And Max has all the health and safety stuff, but he's in the hospital. Can I talk you through everything instead?'

'Talk me through it?' There was a little smile on his lips; I realized Eric was enjoying this.

'Or maybe if I had a bit more time we could pull some of this stuff together?'

Eric shook his head slowly. 'I'm afraid that's impossible. Our client, Chester Rydall, has set the timeline. I can't alter it.'

'So you really need all this by . . . by the end of today?' I asked incredulously.

'Close of business, that's right,' Eric said. 'Is there anything else?'

I took a deep breath. Was there anything else? You betcha. But I couldn't say what I wanted to say. I'd promised Max the audit would go without a hitch, and telling Eric that he was the most horrible man I'd ever met wasn't going to help achieve that objective. 'No,' I said tightly. 'That's all.'

I wandered back to my desk, miserable. There was no way we'd be able to meet Eric's deadline. I picked up the phone. Maybe Max had some policies kicking around that I didn't know about – maybe he'd prepared for this stuff without me knowing. I dialed his number, and after a couple of rings he picked up.

'Hello?'

'Hi, darling. How are you?'

'Jess! Hi! I'm watching *Heir Hunters*. These people track down beneficiaries of wills. It's a fascinating world. Grubby but fascinating. You should put it on.'

'I'd love to,' I said, trying not to sound as stressed as I felt. 'Maybe later. I'm calling about work, actually. About the audit. I just wondered—'

'The audit? It's going okay, isn't it? There aren't any problems?' Max cut in urgently.

I bit my lip. 'No. No problems,' I said quickly. 'Listen, are there any policies I don't know about on things like charitable giving, community alliances, that sort of thing?'

There was a pause. 'No, we don't have any policies. But we got involved in the fair. Tell him about that. We promoted it for free and manned a stand and—'

'Yes, I know,' I said. 'I only wondered if there was any paperwork. You know what these guys are like. If it isn't written down, it doesn't exist.'

126

There was a pause, then Max said, 'I need to come in, don't I? I knew it. Look, I'm feeling much better. I'll just – owwwwwwww.'

Apparently Max was trying to move. 'Max? No. Stop it. Don't move. Don't be ridiculous.'

'Bugger, that hurt,' Max grunted. 'Look, I'll ask the doctors to help me.'

'You'll do no such thing,' I said crossly. 'Max, don't be so silly. We don't need policies; I wanted to check if there was anything extra I could give the auditor, that's all. Everything's completely under control.'

'It is?' Max asked dubiously. 'But you said he wanted everything written down.'

'No, I said that's what these guys are like. Actually, our auditor is really nice. Very flexible and understanding. Don't worry at all. I'm sorry I even mentioned it.'

I was, too. Hadn't I told myself I wouldn't trouble Max with anything?

'Oh, that's a relief. So it's all going well?'

'Couldn't be better,' I lied. 'I'll tell you more when I see you later. But I'd better go. You know, lots to do.'

'Thanks, Jess. I appreciate this.'

'It's the least I can do,' I assured him. 'After all, it's my fault you're in the hospital in the first place.'

'Don't be silly. But you're coming by later? Could you bring some muffins if you get a chance? The food here is dreadful.'

'Muffins. Definitely. No problem,' I said. 'Bye, Max. Enjoy *Heir Hunters*.'

'Bye, gorgeous.'

I put the phone down and sighed heavily. Okay, time for Plan B. Tentatively, I picked up the phone again and dialed Chester's mobile.

'Jess! Hi!' he said warmly. I felt better already. Chester would understand. We were almost family, after all.

'Hi, Chester,' I said. 'Listen, I was just calling to ask a little favor of you. It's about the—'

'Have you spoken to her? She's still giving me the silent treatment.'

'What?' I asked, slightly thrown. 'Oh, right, Mum. Yes. I mean, no, not since—'

'Please call her, Jess. You have to make her see sense.'

'I will,' I said quickly. 'But, look, I was wondering if we might delay the—'

'It's not like I'm on vacation. I've told her a million times I'm out here so that we can get married. Clearing the decks, tying up loose ends. She's acting as if I'm with some fancy woman or something.'

'I'm sure she doesn't think that,' I said patiently. 'So, look, Chester, about this audit . . .'

'Audit? It's started, has it? That's just great. Keep me posted, won't you? I've been telling all the folks over here about it. They're waiting with bated breath to see what happens. You're our test case, Jess. Now, look, I'd love to talk with you some more, but I'm kind of in the middle of something right now. I'll call you tomorrow, okay? And give that mother of yours a kiss from me. Tell her I love her, even if she's driving me crazy.'

'Of course I will,' I said with a sigh. 'Bye, Chester.'

'Bye, Jess.'

The line went dead, and I let my head fall onto the desk in front of me. So much for Plan B. I'd have initiated Plan C, only I didn't have one.

'Jess, are you okay?' I heard Caroline's voice and looked up toward her desk, then my face fell. Eric was sitting next to her. Which meant he'd seen me collapse onto my desk.

No doubt he'd have read into it and decided that I was a drug addict or a manic depressive or . . . or . . .

'I'm fine,' I said, in as business-like a tone as I could muster. 'I was just . . . thinking, that's all. I find it easier to think with my head on my desk.'

'Right,' Caroline said seriously. Then she turned back to Eric. 'So have you ever come across anything awful in one of your audits? You know, anything really bad?'

Eric nodded slowly, as if he were a gunslinger sharing stories of his dangerous exploits. I rolled my eyes and brought up a spreadsheet that I'd emailed myself from Max's computer – I had to pay some bills and needed to check our cash flow first, but it was proving rather harder than I'd expected. 'Oh, I've come across some terrible things in my time,' he said, as if he was really enjoying it. I huffed in irritation at his pomposity, at his obvious delight in catching people out, and he stopped. 'Sorry, did you say something?' he said, his eyes narrowing in my direction.

'Nope, nothing,' I said, smiling brightly.

'I'm sure I heard something,' Eric said pointedly.

'I was just clearing my throat,' I said. 'Sorry. Got a cold coming.'

'Poor you,' Caroline said, shaking her head. 'Eric, you were saying?' She turned back to Eric, all wide-eyed, and I slumped back behind my computer screen.

'We come across all sorts,' Eric said, pausing for dramatic effect. 'People always think they can hide things from me. But they can't.'

'It must be so exciting, going through those spreadsheets,' I muttered before I could stop myself.

Eric's eyes fell on me again. 'Paperwork is an important part of the job,' he said, his voice becoming extra nasal. 'But I also have other tactics.'

129

Like snooping on people, I thought crossly.

'Well, you won't find anything here,' Caroline said earnestly. 'Max is, like, the best boss, and Jess always makes sure everything is perfect. If it isn't, we have to totally redo it.'

Eric nodded slowly. 'You're the one who named a campaign after a handbag, aren't you?' he asked me.

'Yes.' I nodded back, uncertain.

'I see,' he said, as if he were Sherlock Holmes and I'd just given him a clue. Any minute now he'd start stroking an imaginary beard.

'Anyway,' I said curtly, 'I hope you're not too bored here. As Caroline has said, I don't think you're going to find anything untoward going on within these four walls.'

'Maybe not.' Eric smiled. 'But who knows? Things often turn up.'

'Jerome D. Rutter says that bad things always make themselves known eventually, because they infect the air around them,' Caroline said seriously. 'They produce negative energy. And I can't feel any negative energy around here, so I think Jess is right.'

Eric looked at her uncertainly. 'Jerome D. Rutter?' he asked.

'It's this book I'm reading,' Caroline explained. 'How to—'

'I know who Jerome D. Rutter is,' Eric cut in, his eyes wide now. 'But I didn't know you were a fan, too.'

'Oh, I think he's amazing,' Caroline said fervently. 'He's the reason I'm selling so much stuff on eBay.'

Eric nodded vigorously. 'Material goods are just baggage that we drag around with us. Freeing ourselves gives us the energy to run instead of walk!'

'Exactly!' Caroline enthused. 'I feel better already, you

know. I've gotten rid of loads of stuff, and I feel so energ-ized!'

'Although,' Eric said seriously, 'really you should have given the stuff to charity rather than selling it on eBay. Spread the good energy around.'

Caroline smiled. 'Yes, I thought of that. But then I decided that I'd make more money on eBay than the chari-ties would in their shops. So I'm selling my stuff, then giving the money to charity.'

Eric's mouth fell open. 'That's inspired,' he said. 'You should email Rutter about it. You might be featured as one of the tip-givers in his next edition.'

'No!' Caroline gasped. 'Do you think so?'

'I think it's worth a try,' Eric said with a nod.

'You like Rutter, too?' I asked him.

'Oh, yes,' he said, his eyes shining. 'The man is a genius. He changes lives.'

'Really?' I asked dubiously.

'Jess thinks that his book is full of platitudes,' Caroline said quietly. 'And she's probably right, but—'

'She is not right!' Eric said, looking at me as though Caroline had told him that I thought Father Christmas was a child molester. 'Jerome D. Rutter does not speak in platitudes. He speaks right from the heart.'

'I'm sure he does,' I concurred. 'I'm just, you know, not entirely convinced by his philosophy.'

'Until you give away the possessions that are weighing you down, you won't understand his philosophy,' he said, his eyes narrowing again.

'Okay,' I said uncomfortably. 'Well, maybe you're right.'

'Definitely,' Eric said, bearing down on me now. 'Abso-lutely definitely.'

'Definitely, then,' I said. 'Now, I hope you don't mind,

but I've got to make a phone call. I promised to give Chester some figures.'

'Chester? Chester Rydall?' Eric asked, and I nodded.

The lie worked; as I'd expected, he blanched slightly at the name and stood up. 'Yes, well, as it happens, I should be getting back to my work, too,' he said, scurrying back to his office.

I picked up the phone and took a deep breath. I'd realized there was a Plan C; I just didn't relish initiating it. However, I didn't have a choice. I was going to have to call my mother.

I dialed her number; sure enough, one ring later, she answered.

'Hi, Mum.'

'Jessica! Finally. Now, darling, I need to talk to you, but I think it would be better if you came down in person. What are you doing this evening?'

'Hi, Mum. Look, actually, I was calling about Chester. I was hoping you might do me a favor and get him to delay the—'

'Chester? Darling, Chester is in America, as you well know, and frankly I don't intend to talk to him until he says he's sorry for abandoning me like this.'

'He said he's sorry,' I sighed. 'And this audit is a complete nightmare. I just need another week or so to pull together the paperwork. I tried calling him, but all he wanted to talk about was you, and . . .' Caroline was waving at me, and I looked at her questioningly.

'Well, he can talk *about* me all he wants,' Mum was saying. 'Talking *to* me isn't going to be so easy. So, he's got you working for him, has he? Typical. You're my daughter, but he's got you taking his side.' Caroline was standing up now and pointing to something behind me. Reluctantly, I turned around.

'I'm not on any side, Mum,' I said, then my mouth fell open. Standing in reception, wearing a tight black mini-skirt and a low-cut top, balancing precariously on five-inch stilettos with Giorgio clamped in her right arm, was Ivana. 'Mum, I've got to go,' I said, my eyes widening.

'Go? But I need to talk to you, darling. I need to—'

'I'll call you back,' I said quickly, then hung up and rushed over to Ivana. Eric had come out of his office and was looking at her with his eyes hanging out on stalks, and I wanted to get her as far away from him as possible.

'Ivana! What a . . . surprise! What are you doing here?' I asked, ushering her over to one of the leather sofas in the reception area. She sat down and smiled, two gold teeth glinting under the overhead lights.

'I do you fevor, yes?'

I frowned. 'You do? I mean, you are? You will? What favor? Sorry, Ivana, um, what?'

She rolled her eyes. 'I do you fevor. I tich iron, yes?'

'Oh, right!' I said, realizing what she was on about. 'Yes. I mean, that would be great. But . . . not now. Not here. I'll give you a call. To be honest, I'm really busy here, because Max broke his leg and—'

'Yes, yes. I tich when is better time,' Ivana said dismissively. 'But is good for me do fevor for you, and you do fevor for me. Yes?'

'I guess,' I said uncertainly. I looked up, briefly caught Eric's eye, and immediately looked away again. He was probably going to start scribbling in his notebook any second now, I thought irritably.

'Good,' Ivana said, looking very pleased with herself. 'So, I heff trunk outside. You look after for me, yes?'

'Trunk? What, you've got it here now? Where?' I asked in alarm.

'In taxi,' she said, as though it was absolutely obvious. 'I heff it brought in, yes?'

'Yes? No! Ivana, you can't just turn up at my office with a trunk. Where am I going to put it?'

Her eyes widened and her nose flared. 'You put in big house in country,' she snarled. 'I do you fevor. Meny fevor. Make man want merry you. Help when you boom-boom with gay man. Now I nid fevor from you. Hide trunk for me.'

'I didn't boom-boom,' I said, lowering my voice and hoping Ivana would do the same. Her voice was bouncing around the open reception area, and already people were beginning to look up from their desks, trying to listen in. Eric, meanwhile, was now standing at Gillie's desk, probably on the pretext of checking up on something, but I knew full well he was doing his usual thing and listening in on my conversation. 'I just kissed . . .' I whispered, then decided that now was not the time to explain yet again that boom-boom hadn't come into it. 'Oh, it doesn't matter. And I'm sorry. I really appreciate everything you've done. It's just, you know, a bit of a surprise, that's all. If you'd called ahead, I could have cleared some—'

'If I call ahead, you find reason I no come.' Ivana shrugged. 'I em here. With trunk. You tek, plis.'

'Okay,' I said dubiously. I'd only just clocked something she'd said earlier. Hide trunk. Not *store* it; *hide* it. What did she mean by that?

'So . . . what's in it?' I asked in as casual a tone as I was able to adopt, bearing in mind that the entire office was now staring right at me, mouths open, ears pricked up.

Ivana's eyes narrowed. 'Is not important. You no ask, I no tell. Vat important is you tek.'

I did ask, I wanted to point out but decided against it. Ivana was a formidable opponent. Not that I'd ever dared find out, and Helen had told me stories about her that made me very glad I hadn't. 'But why?' I persisted. 'Why do you want me to look after it?'

She looked me in the eye for a couple of seconds and I felt myself falter; then she said lightly, 'Nid more room. Heff bebe, need room. For music center.'

'Oh, I see,' I said, relieved.

'Now you tek trunk, so heff more room,' Ivana said, looking very pleased with herself. 'I heff taxi men bring in.'

'But . . . but . . .' I stammered.

'Ven you tek to house?' she demanded, looking around. 'Tek soon, I think.'

Eric was staring at me intently, so I forced a smile.

'I'll tell you what,' I said, standing up and encouraging Ivana to do the same. 'You bring the trunk to the car park.' I put my arm around Ivana and steered her toward the main doors. 'We'll put it in my car.'

Ivana considered this, then nodded. 'Yes. Car park,' she agreed. 'Is good idea. You show me, plis.'

'Sure.' I quickly bundled her and Giorgio out of the office. 'It's right this way.'

I offered to help carry the trunk but was dismissed by Ivana, who handed me Giorgio to carry instead. She looked pretty dubious that I'd even manage that okay.

'There,' she said, when she and the taxi driver – who didn't look very pleased with his role as removal man – had wedged the trunk into my car boot a few minutes later.

135

'There,' I agreed.

She took Giorgio from me and inspected him as if he were a rental car that had been brought back by a customer. Satisfied that he wasn't broken or damaged in any way, she nodded.

'I call you ven nid trunk again,' she said over her shoulder. 'And I ready to tich iron. You come to house. Sean tell you, I best ironer. Better ironer than stripper, and I very good stripper.'

'Great,' I managed to say as she strode out of the car park. After making sure my car was locked, I went back to the office and sat down heavily at my desk. I was out of plans. I was out of ideas. And now I had a trunk to look after.

My mobile started to vibrate, and I pulled it out of my pocket – it was a text message. As soon as I looked at it, my heart sank. It was from Hugh Barter. *Sweetie, wonder if we can catch up sometime? I've got a favor I need to ask you. Call me, H.*

I stared at it for a few seconds, my heart sinking. Now? Hugh was texting me now? What next? What else could possibly go wrong?

'Ah, Ms. Wild Wainwright, was that a friend of yours? Or was that part of your work in the community?' I looked up to see Eric bearing down on me, a snide expression on his face.

'Ivana?' I asked in a slightly strangled voice. 'No, she's a friend.' I swallowed uncomfortably. 'Listen, Eric, about this paperwork. I know you said you need it by the end of today, but is there any way at all that I could maybe have an extension?'

'I'm sorry, but no,' he said, evidently not sorry at all. 'We all have to work within our relative timetables. I'm sure you don't miss your clients' deadlines, do you?'

'No,' I said tightly. 'No, I don't suppose I do.' I felt tired. Exhausted. I felt like running away and pretending he didn't exist. But instead, I made a decision. Plan D. I was going to Wiltshire.

Chapter 12

∞

IT WASN'T THAT I WANTED to go all the way down to Wiltshire. I had plenty of better things to do, not least of which was visiting Max in the hospital. But it was, as far as I could make out, the only way open to me. In one fell swoop I would talk Mum into calling Chester, making up with him, and getting him to delay the audit, and I could stash Ivana's trunk somewhere. Of course, I would also have to listen to Mum tell me all about her new friends on Facebook, complain about Chester, and ask my opinion on the minutiae of her wedding arrangements, but I figured that was a small price to pay. As Max said, the audit had to go well, and for it to go well, I needed time to put together a file of policies. In a week, I could get the paperwork together, Max would be out of the hospital, and everything would be okay again.

I picked up my phone to call Mum and give her the good news, then saw Eric approaching and put it down again. Quickly, I darted over to the reception desk, where Gillie was eating a packet of Maltesers.

'Want one?' she offered.

'No, thanks,' I said, scrutinizing her face briefly for signs of alcohol or drug addiction, then shaking myself. 'I just need to use the phone, if that's okay?'

'Sure,' Gillie said, frowning. 'But why not use . . .' Her eyes flickered over to my desk; Eric was right next to it, leaning over Caroline's desk and shooting me furtive glances. 'Ah, I see what you mean,' she said quickly. 'Here, go right ahead.'

I took the phone and dialed my mother's number. Or, rather, my number. It rang a few times. 'Hello?'

I started slightly. It wasn't Mum. It was a man. A man whose voice I didn't recognize. 'Hello?' he repeated.

'Who's this?' I asked cautiously.

'Who's this?' the man replied, equally suspiciously.

I frowned uncertainly. 'Is Esther there?' I asked.

'Who's asking?' the man responded.

'Her daughter is asking,' I said, my voice taking on a rather shrill tone. 'And the owner of the house. Can you tell me to whom I am speaking, please?'

'Her daughter—?' The line went dead, and I stared at the phone uncertainly.

'That was weird,' I said, to no one in particular.

'What was?' Gillie asked.

'There was a . . . a man.'

'A man?' Gillie's eyes lit up. 'Where? What man?'

Ignoring her question, I frowned and pressed redial. The phone rang for some time, then Mum picked up.

'Mum?' I said, relieved. 'I called just a second ago and this man picked up and was really weird. Who was it?'

'Darling!' She sounded strange. 'Darling, I—'

'He hung up on me. Is he doing some work for you or something? Because you shouldn't let people answer the phone unless they—'

'I . . . Actually, I can't really talk now,' Mum cut in. She sounded nervous. Worried.

'What do you mean, you can't talk?'

'I mean . . . darling, I have to go.'

'You have to go? Where? You're scaring me, Mum.'

139

'Really?' Mum said, her voice shaking slightly. 'Well, there's no reason to . . . No reason at all . . .'

'No reason to what?' I asked, my hand gripping the receiver rather more tightly than before.

'Well, lovely talking to you, Shona,' Mum said suddenly, her voice taking on a very different, bright tone. 'And we must get together some time. Perhaps lunch?'

'Shona? Mum, who the hell is Shona?'

'Next week sounds lovely. Good-bye, Shona.'

The line went dead again, and I didn't move for a few seconds. This wasn't just a bit strange; it was downright weird. Ominous weird. Mum sounded . . . scared. Yes, that was the word. She was scared. Why the hell was she calling me Shona? What was that all about? And who was the man?

'Everything okay?' Gillie asked me.

I shook my head slowly. 'I don't know,' I said. 'There's someone in my mother's house. She was really strange on the phone. Then she said it wasn't a good time and hung up.'

'Maybe she was having sex,' Gillie suggested. 'I mean, that's not a great time to be talking on the phone, is it?'

I frowned. 'She wasn't having sex. Her fiancé is in America.' Gillie raised an eyebrow. 'And she isn't having an affair,' I said stiffly. 'He left only a few days ago. They're getting married soon. Anyway, she called me Shona. Why would she call me Shona? I don't even know anyone called Shona.'

'Shona,' Gillie said thoughtfully. Then her eyes lit up. 'Maybe she's being kept hostage,' she said excitedly. 'Maybe that man's got a gun to her head and is forcing her to pretend everything's okay. That's why she called you Shona – it's what hostages do in Iraq. They write their confessions with spelling mistakes so people will know they did it under duress.'

I looked at Gillie uncertainly. 'Don't be ridiculous. And why do you know so much about hostages?'

She shrugged. 'You date a lot of men, you kind of absorb stuff. A guy I dated a while back worked for an insurance company that acted in kidnap situations. Of course, he told me that he was involved in all that stuff – you know, like Russell Crowe in *Proof of Life*. Turns out he just worked for the call center. Story of my life . . .'

'Well, she hasn't been. Kidnapped, I mean,' I said sternly. Then I frowned again. 'Although she has gone on Facebook recently. You don't think she—'

'What, attracted some weird stalker? Oh God, definitely,' Gillie said, as though it was absolutely obvious. 'The Internet's full of weirdos. He's probably got her tied up or something.'

'Or there's another, perfectly reasonable explanation,' I said, pressing redial again.

The phone rang. Then someone picked it up. 'No!' I heard Mum cry, and the line went dead again. I looked at Gillie, wide-eyed, then put the phone down, grabbed my bag, and ran to the car.

'Perfectly good explanation,' I muttered to myself as I did my best to speed down the motorway. But who was I kidding? The more I thought about it, the more my imagination ran wild. She'd tried to tell me about Facebook and I'd cut her off, and now she was probably being tortured by some homicidal maniac or something.

I put my foot on the accelerator. I hadn't had Mum for most of my life, had met her only a few months before I married Max. And I wasn't going to lose her now. No, I was going to save her from whatever that monster was doing. I was going to protect her.

By the time I finally pulled in to Grace's drive, my blood pressure was at an all-time high – even the sight of the house, which usually lifted my spirits immeasurably, didn't slow my heartbeat. It was the most beautiful house in the world: crumbling yellow brick and stone, large windows with faded curtains. It was the sort of house you could imagine full of guests at Christmas, with children outside building snowmen and adults getting slightly tipsy on sherry and mulled wine. But today it wasn't filled with guests; it was filled with danger.

I parked the car as quickly as I could, then hesitated. If there was some crazed stalker in the house, leaving my car here might not be the most sensible thing to do. He'd see it out the window. He'd be waiting for me when I got inside. With a gun. Or a knife. Or . . .

Quickly, I nipped back to the car and reversed out of the drive as quietly as I could, parking on the street instead. Then, slipping between the trees that separated the plot of my house from the house next door (or, rather, the estate next door – there was a house somewhere, but it was acres away and I'd never actually seen it), I made my way toward the back door, thanking my lucky stars for the seren-dipitous whim that had made me bring my full set of keys instead of only the front door one.

From where I was, the house looked pretty much as it had the last time I was here. No sign of a break-in. Then again, he'd probably seemed like a nice guy; I'd heard that homicidal maniacs could turn on the charm when they wanted to. I should have warned Mum about the Internet, should have stopped her from going on Facebook without proper guidance. It was all my fault. I was the worst daugh-ter in the world.

Holding my breath, I took out my key and opened the

door. It squeaked just slightly, but I managed to get in. Then I started to tiptoe down the hall. I had no idea what I was going to do, I realized, as I made my way toward the kitchen. After all, I was on my own, unarmed, and no one even knew I was here. To be honest, my planning hadn't been that great. If I were watching myself in a movie, I'd be screaming at my character not to be so completely stupid, to get the hell out of there and call the police. But what would I say? That my mother had called me Shona? That there was a strange man in the house? The police would laugh. They'd say she was probably having an affair.

I continued to creep down the hallway, wincing every time the floorboards creaked as I passed the old, dark furniture, old paintings, old drapes . . . old everything, actually. I'd brought Helen here soon after I inherited the house, and she oohed and aahed about the potential, telling me which walls I should knock down and how newer, brighter furniture would make it seem a hundred times lighter, but somehow I kind of liked the 'old'ness. Although right now I was regretting not putting down some rugs.

I heard voices and stopped dead. They were coming from the kitchen. Desperately, I looked around for something, anything, with which to arm myself. My eyes lit upon a suit of armor in the main hall; next to it was an ax. Checking that no one was watching, I picked it up. It was far lighter than I'd imagined – probably just for show, I realized. But that didn't matter. The man in the kitchen wouldn't know that. Tentatively, I approached the kitchen door. Was I going to walk in on a torture scene? Was I going to be snatched, tied up, and thrown in a cellar?

Slowly, nervously, I reached out and turned the handle, cracking the door open so that I could peek inside. And then I froze. A man was in there. He had blond-gray hair

143

and he was sitting at the table holding a knife. The hairs on the back of my neck were standing up as I inched forward. What kind of monster was he? And where was my mother? I scanned the room desperately as my stomach clenched in fear. Up until now I'd been hoping that I was wrong, that I was freaking out over nothing. But this wasn't nothing. This was very real. Too real.

I pushed the door just a tiny bit more, but as I did so I stumbled, dropping my car key to the floor with a loud clang. I started to sweat profusely, and then I heard something.

'Lawrence, was that you?'

It was my mother. I heard footsteps and ducked back. Through a crack in the door I watched my mother emerge from the pantry. 'Lawrence, did you hear what I just said? I think I heard someone moving around.'

The man looked up and grinned at her. 'Est, this is a creaky old house. There are noises everywhere – that's part of its charm. Stop being silly and eat some cheese with me.'

I stared at him. *Est?* That was a bit familiar for a kidnapper, wasn't it?

He pulled back a chair and Mum sat down. 'I really shouldn't,' she said, taking a piece from the knife in his hand. 'Very fattening. But very delicious. You're sure you didn't hear anything?'

'Not a thing,' Lawrence said.

Mum sighed. 'Must have imagined it, I suppose. I'm still not used to this house.'

'And this is her house? Jessica's? I can't wait to meet her. Can't wait to tell her everything.'

'Everything?' Mum looked at him nervously. 'The thing is, Lawrence, dear, I'm not sure your version of *everything* and mine—'

'I'm excited,' Lawrence cut in, his eyes shining. 'I want her to know. I want everyone to know.'

He grinned and leaned over to kiss Mum; she turned slightly so that he got her cheek, not her lips, but that was enough. I felt sick to my stomach suddenly. This man Lawrence wasn't a criminal. Mum hadn't met a stalker online; she'd just met a man. A normal, red-blooded, cheating man. Of course he wasn't a bloody stalker. I'd been so determined to believe that my mother wouldn't be stupid enough to have an affair that I'd let Gillie convince me of some ridiculous, paranoid story.

I shook my head in disgust. I felt so foolish, so pathetic. I'd driven all this way to see her, had worried myself into a nervous wreck – I was even holding a frigging replica ax, for goodness' sake – and for what? So that I could witness her hanging out with her new lover. In my house. Behind Chester's back.

I stepped into the kitchen, my heart beating rapidly in my chest. I wasn't afraid anymore; I was angry. I looked at them incredulously, shaking my head in disbelief, in crushing disappointment. I'd thought that Mum had grown up since she ditched me with Grandma, since she gambled her way into debt, since she faked her own suicide to get away from her problems. But she hadn't grown up at all. She was acting like a teenager and cheating on Chester. Chester, who'd offered her a proper life; Chester, who was patient and sweet; Chester, whom I liked. Really liked. Who had started to call me his prospective stepdaughter, with this little twinkle in his eye that made me want to hug him, even though he was actually a client and I was far too grown-up to need a father now, step- or otherwise.

They still hadn't seen me, had no idea I was looking at them. I took a deep breath. I was going to be calm. I was going to be calm, collected, and cool. In fact, I was going to be frosty.

'I can't believe you,' I screeched. I wasn't cool and frosty at all. Or calm, or collected, for that matter. 'I can't bloody well . . . I drove all the way here. I was worried. And you're . . . you're . . .'

'Darling!' My mother pulled away from Lawrence, shock plastered across her face. 'Darling, what are you doing here? Lawrence, let go. Jess, let me explain. I really have to—'

'No, you don't,' I said angrily, grabbing my car key from the floor. *Lawrence.* I hated him already. 'You don't have to explain anything. I understand. And now I'm going.'

'No, Jess. Don't go. You see—'

'I see what?' I said, stopping and turning on my mother. I felt furious, as if all my frustration at everything that was going wrong in my life right now (pretty much everything) finally had a focal point, a chance at release. 'You know, Mum, Chester asked me to come here. I had other things to do. Other more important things to do, like visiting my husband in the hospital. But I came, because Chester was worried about you. Because I was worried about you. Because Lawr— Because you called me Shona, and this man' – I shot a derisory glance at Lawrence – 'answered the phone and I thought he might be a gangster. Or a kidnapper. Or . . . or . . .'

I turned toward the door. I was shaking. 'I just can't believe you've been so stupid. Again.'

I started to run. I didn't want to be there anymore. I wanted to be at home, wanted to be with Max. 'Wait,' I heard Mum call after me. 'Wait, Jess, let me explain. Lawrence is . . . We . . .'

But I didn't wait for her to finish. I didn't care if he was the love of her life. She was supposed to be marrying

Chester. She was supposed to be happy and settled for once in her life, not shagging some bloke called Lawrence. I ran out the door, down the drive, and to my car; once in, I started up the engine so quickly it nearly stalled. And it was only when I put my foot down on the accelerator that I realized I hadn't even mentioned the audit. Or dropped off the trunk.

Chapter 13

❧

I'D NEVER BEEN MORE DESPERATE to see Max, never been more in need of his friendly face, his strong pair of arms to hug me. I drove straight to the hospital, parked terribly, and dashed up the stairs to Max's ward.

And then I stopped for a second. There were curtains pulled around his bed, from which Emily was emerging.

'Hi!' I said, rushing over. 'I'm not too late, am I? I really need to see Max, if it's okay.'

'I'm afraid he's asleep,' Emily said with a little shrug. 'It's probably not a good idea to disturb him.'

I met her eyes and took a deep breath. 'Actually,' I said, my voice trembling slightly, 'I don't think he'll mind.'

I moved to step past her, but she put up her arm to stop me. 'He's been in quite a lot of pain today,' she said firmly. 'He's just fallen asleep. The best thing for him is to be left alone.'

'The best thing for him is to see his wife,' I said, equally firm, forcing back the tears that were threatening to tumble down my cheeks.

She smiled tightly. 'There are only another fifteen minutes of visiting time. Do you really want to disturb him just for that? I can tell him you came and pass on anything you've brought him.' She looked down at my empty hands and her eyes glinted triumphantly. Or maybe I imagined it, I didn't know. 'Or not,' she added.

'I didn't have time to pick anything up,' I said unhappily. And it was true – I'd been in the car for more than four hours and had rushed back to the office to somehow pull together some policies for Eric in time to meet his deadline. I'd wanted to be here earlier, with delicious treats and magazines. Instead, I was here empty-handed and too late to even see him. None of my plans was working out at the moment, but the one that was failing the most was my plan to be an ideal wife. Right now I couldn't be further from one. 'But I want to see him. Even if he's asleep.'

'Jess? Jess, is that you?' A voice came from behind the curtain. Max's voice.

'Max!' I said, pushing past Emily. 'Darling, I'm here.'

I pulled back the curtain and saw Max looking up at me groggily. 'I was asleep,' he said. 'God, it's a nightmare getting to sleep in this place. Things beeping all the time, beds being moved about. What time is it?'

I looked at my watch, even though I already knew. 'Um, a quarter to nine,' I said.

Max frowned. 'Don't visiting hours end at nine?'

I nodded uncomfortably. 'Yes, they do. And I'm so sorry I couldn't be here before. It's been a bit of a day, really. But I'm here now.'

'Did you bring me any muffins?' he asked, his eyes lighting up hopefully.

My heart sank. Muffins. I'd forgotten the bloody muffins. My eyes started to well up. 'No,' I said miserably. 'No, I didn't. I . . .'

'Not to worry,' Max said, with a little shrug. 'It's no big deal.'

'But it is a big deal,' I said unhappily. 'I said I'd bring you muffins and I meant to bring you muffins, and now I'm here without them—'

'It's okay,' Max said. 'You're busy. I understand. How are things at the office, anyway?' His eyes closed briefly, then opened again.

'They're fine,' I said, reaching out to take his hand. 'You look tired.'

He nodded. 'It's the pain,' he said. 'They keep me doped up.'

'Is it still very bad?' I asked gently.

'No, it's fine,' he said, his expression suggesting that it probably wasn't. 'So you've had an awful day, have you? Are things tricky at work?'

I shook my head. 'Work? No. Nothing tricky at work. Just traffic jams,' I said, managing a smile. 'Nothing I can't handle. But I'm so sorry I wasn't here earlier.'

'Me, too,' Max said quietly, and closed his eyes again. I watched as he fell back to sleep, and then listened to his breathing become steady and soft.

Emily poked her head around the curtain. 'We really are going to have to ask you to leave now,' she said.

'I know,' I said with a lump in my throat. 'I'm going. He's asleep again.'

'Best thing for him,' Emily said. 'See you, then.'

'Tomorrow,' I said firmly. 'Tomorrow I'll be here early.'

I felt very lonely going home. I'd never minded being on my own before I fell in love with Max – I'd grown up pretty much friendless, with only Grandma for company, and had always thought of my independence as my biggest strength. But right now I didn't feel very strong. I felt vulnerable, afraid, and confused. I wanted to pull a big blanket over my head and go to sleep and not wake up until things were better again. So much for being the ideal wife. So far I'd failed on nearly every count. I wasn't honest – I still hadn't told Max about Hugh, and now I wasn't telling him about my mother, either. I wasn't good – I was having dark thoughts about Emily and was obviously a terrible 'companion.' Now it seemed I was the worst carer in the world, too. My husband was lying in a hospital bed and I couldn't even remember to bring him muffins. How long would it be before I stopped being loved, too?

Sighing miserably, I looked in my rearview mirror and indicated left. The car behind me indicated, also. It was a large black car, a Hummer – I'd noticed it parked outside the hospital. Funny, I thought, that it should be on the same road as me now, twenty minutes later. Strange how closely strangers' lives could come together sometimes. The driver was no doubt visiting someone in the hospital, too – perhaps they lived on the same road as Max and me. I indicated again; sure enough, the Hummer did, too. I smiled. Sure I felt lonely, I thought to myself, but no one's ever completely alone.

And then with a start I remembered that I'd promised to go to the resource center that evening. Yet another opportunity to show what a failure I was, how useless and pathetic, I thought, despondent. Yet another thing I was rubbish at. But then I sat up a bit and shook myself. Self-pity wasn't going to help matters any. If anyone was to be pitied, it was the poor people relying on me for companionship, or Max alone in the hospital. Not me.

Looking in my side mirror, I did a U-turn and made my way back to the main road. Ten minutes later, I parked around the corner from the resource center and went inside.

'Jessica!' Christina waved as I walked in. 'Lovely to see you!'

I found myself smiling. She looked as if she really meant it. 'Don't you ever go home?' I asked her sheepishly.

She shook her head and returned the smile. 'Rest is for the wicked. Always leads to trouble.'

My smile got slightly bigger as I made my way to the living room and sat down. It was packed and the smell was horrendous, but I barely noticed; what I did notice was the sense of camaraderie, of relief at being inside, warm, and fed. Maybe Jerome D. Rutter had a point, after all, I found myself thinking. Maybe freeing yourself from all your stuff let you focus on what was really important.

Then again, I guessed most of the people in the room wouldn't have said no to a bit of stuff. New clothes, warm bedding. No, stuff wasn't the enemy; audits were. Audits and mothers having affairs, and husbands laid up in the hospital with nurses who were overattentive . . . I took a deep breath and looked around the room. No one appeared to be looking for a companion to read to them or listen to them talk.

I turned to the woman sitting next to me. 'Hi,' I said. 'I'm Jessica.'

She looked at me, a bewildered expression on her face. 'No, thank you,' she said. 'Not today.'

'No, I don't want anything,' I said quickly. 'I just wondered if you wanted to talk. Or play a card game, or—'

'No. Thank you. Not today,' the woman repeated, then stood up. 'No, thank you. Not today, thank you. No. Thank you. Thank you, but no.' She wandered off, muttering, and I shrank back in my chair. I was obviously terrible at this companionship lark. I was scaring people away, not helping them. Maybe it had been a bad idea coming here. I was meant to be helping; instead, I was using the center to avoid going home and facing up to the stark reality that I was not only not an ideal wife but not an ideal anything, that everything was falling apart around me and I didn't know how to put it all back together again.

I would go; I'd make an excuse to Christina and promise to come back soon, I decided.

'It gets easier.' I looked up uncertainly; the person who'd spoken was Greta. 'This seat taken?' She motioned to the chair beside me, the one that had been vacated by the muttering woman.

'No,' I said. 'Actually, I was just going, so . . .'

'Takes a while, but it does get easier,' she said, easing herself into the chair.

'Thanks,' I said, slightly embarrassed, not sure if she meant being a companion got easier or if she, too, had mistaken me for another homeless person.

'Don't thank me. I'm only stating the obvious. That's all,' she said. 'But sometimes you've got to, haven't you? State the obvious. Sometimes it's staring you in the face and you still can't see it.'

I looked at her uncertainly. 'The obvious being that it gets easier?'

'Exactly,' she said. 'Everything does. Stands to reason. Things become familiar. Familiar is easier. I used to hate this place. People asking me questions. I thought they were trying to catch me out.'

'Catch you out?' I asked, curious.

She shrugged. 'Find reasons to send me back home. I didn't like home.'

Her voice was higher than I'd expected; as I looked at her more closely, I realized that she was much younger than I'd thought – mid-twenties, maybe, when I'd had her in her mid-fifties.

'You didn't?' I asked.

'I just said that.' She frowned.

'Of course you did. I'm sorry.'

' 'S all right,' she said with another shrug.

She didn't say anything for a minute or two. 'Does living on the street get easier?' I asked eventually. I didn't know if she'd bite my head off or not; to my surprise, she laughed.

'Living on the street's the easiest thing I've done. You've got to find out where you can go. But you're safe.'

'Safe?' I looked at her uncertainly. 'On the street? Really?'

She laughed again. 'Matter of degrees, I suppose. Where I left – home – wasn't safe.'

'Not safe . . . ?' I asked tentatively, not sure how to ask the question.

'Father beat me. Then my boyfriend beat me. Dunno what I did. Didn't matter, I suppose.'

'That's awful,' I said quietly.

'Maybe,' Greta said. 'But I'm here now. And it's easier. Keep to myself. I like it that way.'

I looked at her for a moment. 'But you're talking to me,' I said gently. 'You must get lonely sometimes.'

'Me?' She laughed again, this time loudly and heartily. 'I'm never lonely. Just a bit of peace and quiet. Not you, though. I see it in your eyes. You need to talk.'

'I . . . You think I need to talk?' I asked, slightly taken aback. 'No. I mean, I'm here to . . . No, that's not it at all. Please don't worry about me.'

'Worry? I don't worry about anything,' Greta said. 'But I think you need to talk. Everyone does sometimes. Even me. Not now, though. Now I'm hungry.'

She winked and stood up, shuffling out toward the kitchen. I watched her go, then stood up uncertainly. Did I need to talk? Maybe Greta was right.

I got up and made my way out; at the door, Christina stopped me. 'So, how are you getting on?'

I smiled awkwardly. 'I'm not sure I'm a very good companion,' I said. 'I think the people here feel a bit sorry for me. Greta thought I needed to talk.'

Christina laughed. 'She's very perceptive, our Greta,' she said. 'Although if you've been talking to her, you're better at this than you think. Greta doesn't talk to anyone. She's only ever said a handful of words to me in all the time I've been here.'

'Which is how long?' I asked.

'Oh, years,' Christina said. 'Eight or nine now. Greta was one of our first. Lots of them are rehabilitated – they find jobs, get housing, get their lives back on track. But some, like Greta, don't want that; this is the only home they need. It's just a shame we can't cater to all the Gretas in the world.'

'You're sure you don't want help securing funding?' I asked. 'You're absolutely sure?'

'Funding, yes. Partnerships, scrutiny, and demands for publicity, no.' Christina smiled. 'Unfortunately, it's rare to get one without the other.'

'Yeah,' I said quietly. 'I guess you're right.'

'So, you're going?'

I nodded uncomfortably. 'I'm sorry. I'm tired. I think maybe I need to get some sleep.'

'Good idea,' Christina said warmly. 'You come back when you're rested.'

I looked over her shoulder; Greta was carrying a plate of hot food back into the living area. Behind her, two men were arguing over a sleeping bag.

'Bye,' I said, turning to leave. 'And thank you.'

By the time I got outside, I already felt more positive. I might be an appalling companion, but at least I had a roof

155

over my head and a job – for now, at any rate. I had a mother who loved me, even if she was fundamentally flawed, and after all, wasn't I flawed, too? Plus I had money in the bank. A ridiculous amount of money in the bank, actually. I took a deep breath of the cool night air and let it fill my lungs. I would tackle the issue with Mum in the morning, and I would also start fresh with Eric. I would get to the hospital in the afternoon. And as for Hugh . . . I grimaced uncomfortably as I realized I hadn't responded to his text. Well, I'd do that tomorrow, too.

A car door slammed behind me and I turned, surprised to see it was the Hummer, parked on the other side of the street from me. At least, it looked like the Hummer that had been behind me earlier. I eyed it curiously, then shrugged and walked toward my own car.

I got to my car and opened the door. Just as I was about to get in, the doors to the Hummer opened and two men got out, both dressed in black. One of them was wearing sunglasses, which struck me as odd since it was dark outside. They were large men – not particularly tall but broad. Both had crew cuts, too; they looked like soldiers. Or bodyguards. They had started to cross the road and were walking toward me. Quickly, I got into my car and started the engine. They were probably only going to ask for directions, I reassured myself as I pulled away; as Greta had said, the streets were perfectly safe, and running away was a very silly thing to be doing when they might have needed my help.

But I didn't care; what I cared about was getting home, having a hot bath, and then getting into bed. What I needed, I told myself firmly as I pulled out and started to drive, was to see the end of this day and to hope that tomorrow would be considerably better.

156

Chapter 14

THE NEXT DAY, after a fitful sleep, I woke with a sinking feeling in my stomach but did my best to suppress it. I just needed some perspective, I decided, needed to see the big picture. The trouble was, even the big picture looked terrible to me. Nothing was going right; no area of my life was chugging along nicely.

I showered, did my best not to focus on the bags under my eyes as I brushed my teeth and pulled back my hair, then got out my black suit. The power suit, Max called it – it was the suit I wore to impress clients or whenever I had a difficult meeting. Today, I hoped it would act like a suit of armor, letting the world believe I was tough and strong and not falling apart inside.

And as I put it on, it began to work its magic. Just as the skirt seemed to hold my bum in place, it also seemed to streamline my thoughts, pulling them together into coherent strands instead of a huge muddle of consciousness. As I slipped the jacket on, I was already beginning to think more clearly, developing a strategy instead of sinking into a puddle of despair.

What I needed to do, I decided, as I suddenly got the urge to put on some makeup and even some earrings, was to take control. I was letting my problems get the better of me, and that was the worst thing I could do. Quickly, I grabbed an old envelope from the kitchen table, found a pen, and started to write.

Problems:

1. Max and Emily

Solution: *Visit him early today. Prioritize it above everything else. Bring muffins. Bring his laptop and some DVDs. Make him feel looked after. You are his wife; Emily is his nurse. End of story.*

2. Mum

Solution: *Go and see her. Force her to realize how stupid she's being. Tell her to ditch the Facebook guy before Chester comes back.*

3. Eric

Solution: *Breathe deeply, and it'll be over soon. Do your best in the interview. Pray.*

4. Trunk

Solution: *Take it when you go to Mum's.*

5. Hugh

I sighed. This one was the hardest.

Solution: *Tell Max.*

I bit my lip.

When he's better. When everything is back to normal.

I looked back at the list. Written down, it all looked pretty straightforward and easy. The trouble was, I knew it wasn't either of those things. I needed to be strong, clear-headed, and determined.

I picked up the phone. What I needed was Helen.

*

'So tell me about this guy with your mother again. Are you sure there wasn't some other explanation?' Helen asked me half an hour later, at a coffee shop near where she lived. 'Could he have been a plumber or something?'

I shook my head wearily. 'It's pretty hard to make that kind of mistake, Hel. He wasn't standing over something that required fixing. Or talking about something of a legal or accounting nature. He kissed her. And they were talking about telling me. His name was Lawrence.'

I didn't know why that last fact was important; it just was. Luckily, Helen seemed to understand.

'Lawrence,' she said, as though it explained everything. 'Hmmmm.'

'Yeah.' I nodded. ' "Hmmmm" pretty much sums up my life right now.'

'It's really that bad?' Helen asked, concerned.

I nodded gloomily. 'How long do you have?'

'As long as it takes.' Helen shrugged. 'I'm kind of between freelance contracts at the moment. Who knows, I might get another idea for a show.'

'Maybe Ivana can give you one,' I said, rolling my eyes. 'You know, she's got me looking after a trunk for her because she said she'd teach me to iron. Or, rather, hiding it for her.'

'Hiding a trunk?' Helen asked, her nose wrinkling.

'She brought it to my office. The trunk she used to have in her bedroom. You remember?'

'Yeah. But why?'

I shrugged helplessly. 'I don't know. It's really heavy. It's in my car. I meant to take it down to the house – I did take it. I just forgot to drop it off. You know, with Lawrence and everything.'

'Yeah, I can see how you might have had your mind on other things,' Helen said, nodding seriously.

'Then there's Max,' I said despondently. 'He's all doped up, and this nurse, Emily, is all over him. Yesterday she even tried to stop me from seeing him, because she said he was asleep and needed his rest.'

'Bitch.' Helen shook her head. 'And, what, he was wide awake waiting for you?'

'No,' I said, pulling a little face. 'Actually he was asleep. And really tired. But still.'

'Still,' Helen agreed. 'Okay, so let me recap briefly. We have a possessive nurse, an unfaithful mother, and an injured husband. Oh, and Ivana's trunk. Anything else?'

I smiled involuntarily. This was why I loved Helen; she made the terrible seem funny, made everything feel slightly less serious. 'Well, there's Eric Sandler,' I said, taking a gulp of coffee. 'He's interviewing me today, and I'm terrified.'

'You, terrified?' Helen asked, looking at me dubiously. 'Why?'

'Because he's horrible,' I said, cringing.

'That's specific,' Helen said dryly.

I relented. 'Fine. I'm terrified because this audit is very important and I think Eric's got it in for me. He's the auditor from hell. He follows me around on the pretext of talking to Caroline.'

'Ooh, furtive. You've got to hate that.'

'Yes, exactly,' I agreed, warming to my theme. 'And he's got horrible beady eyes.'

'I hate those,' Helen said supportively.

'And a nasal voice.'

'Well, that does it.' Helen grinned. 'String him up now and have the village elders throw stones at him.'

I laughed, then I sighed heavily. 'Maybe I'm the one who's been a little strung out lately.'

'A little?' Helen arched an eyebrow. 'Jess, you're a bundle of nerves. I've never seen you look so tired. When was the last time you had a good night's sleep?'

I bit my lip. The truth was I couldn't remember. Not since . . .

'Not since Hugh came back on the scene?' Helen suggested gently.

I grimaced. 'He texted again yesterday. I mean to call him, but I don't know what to say. "Hi, how much do you want? Take it! Take it all." My stomach flip-flops every time I think of calling him. I feel like I'm on a treadmill, Helen, and I can't get off. And I keep hoping it's going to slow down, but instead it's getting faster and faster, and everything's rushing by so fast I don't even know what's happening anymore.'

'So hit the button that slows it down,' Helen said, leaning forward.

'I can't,' I said despondently. 'I just can't.'

'Yes, you can,' Helen said firmly. 'Let people deal with their own problems. Your mum and Chester are grown-ups. So is Max. Hugh isn't, obviously, but even that isn't as bad as you think it is. It was just a kiss, for pity's sake.'

'I know,' I said quietly. 'It's not the kiss, though; it's the fact that I didn't tell Max. He's so honorable. He would never lie about anything or let me believe something that wasn't true. I was trying so hard to be ideal, but the fact of the matter is I'm not. Never will be. I'm just not like him. And if that changes things, then . . .' I looked away, not wanting to contemplate what that would mean.

Helen nodded, then looked up at me with a sly smile. 'You're sure you don't want to let Ivana get rid of the problem for you?' she asked, then giggled.

'Why not,' I said, managing a smile. 'I mean, she'd probably turn up at the office with a couple of dead bodies for me to hide at the house, but, hey, it's just returning a favor, right?'

Helen laughed. 'I'm sure she's not as dodgy as we make her out to be.' I caught her eye, and then we were both laughing. 'Okay, maybe she is,' Helen conceded. 'But she means well. So, okay, tell Max the truth. Pick your time well, though. And don't build it up into something it wasn't. Promise?'

'Promise,' I agreed. 'Thanks, Hel.'

'Don't mention it,' she said dismissively, then grabbed my hand. 'Ooh, I think there's a guy out there checking you out. Not really your type, but still. Nice to know you've still got it, huh?'

'No one's checking me out,' I said, rolling my eyes.

'Maybe he's checking me out, then,' Helen said thoughtfully. 'He's not my type, either, but change is good, right?'

I looked at her uncertainly. 'You want a change? What happened to John?'

Helen pulled a face. 'We kind of called it a day,' she said.

'He was married?' I asked, concerned.

'No, he wasn't,' Helen said with a little shrug. 'And once I knew that, it all got a bit . . . I don't know. Boring.'

'You're hopeless,' I said, shaking my head. 'I sometimes think you don't want to be happy, because it's too dull for you.'

'That's not true. I do want to be happy, and that means feeling excited,' Helen said, her eyes twinkling. 'Just not with John. Whereas this bloke, he's got a slightly dangerous look about him. Him and his friend. You know, maybe I could go for the short-hair-and-shades look.'

'Short hair and shades?' I asked, frowning. I turned

162

round to see who she was looking at, and immediately my heart started to thud in my chest. It was the two men I'd seen the night before, the ones who'd been in the Hummer. I was sure it was them – they had the same stocky build, the same short hair. Only in daylight they looked even scarier – they had tattoos up their arms, and one even had one on his forehead. And they were standing outside the coffee shop, talking into their mobile phones. I looked back at Helen in alarm. 'Okay, this is weird,' I said worriedly.

'What is?' Helen asked, still staring at them with goofy eyes.

'Those men,' I said, covering my face with my hands. 'They followed me back from the hospital last night.'

'They what?' Helen looked at me skeptically.

'They followed me. In their Hummer. They stopped right outside my building. And then I saw them at the resource center.'

'The what?'

'The— Oh, just this place I went. It was definitely them.'

'Okay,' Helen said hesitantly. 'So what are you saying?'

I shrugged helplessly. 'I don't know. But it's strange, don't you think? I mean, it's too much to be a coincidence. What are they doing? Are they looking at me?'

Helen took out a mirror and reapplied her lipstick. 'No. No cause for alarm,' she said, putting her lipstick down and smiling. 'They're not looking at you. One of them *has* been checking me out, though, and he's seriously hot.'

'Helen, stop it,' I said, desperate. 'Do you think they're following me? What if it's the audit? Do you think Eric Sandler has put a tail on me?'

Helen laughed heartily, throwing her head backward. 'Oh my God, Jess, you really are losing it. You think an auditor is having two guys follow you around in a Hummer?'

I had to admit it seemed unlikely. 'So why else would they be following me?' I asked defensively, taking another sneaky peek out the window. I could see only one of them clearly, but he was definitely one of the guys from the night before.

'Maybe it *is* a coincidence,' she suggested. 'They probably live near here.'

'Both of them? And they just happen to be outside this particular coffee shop now?'

'Oh, I don't know,' Helen said, exasperated. 'I can't think of any good reason why anyone would be following you at all. You don't have anything to hide, do you?'

We looked at each other for a second or two, and then we both frowned.

'Ivana?' we said in unison.

'The trunk,' I whispered. 'You don't think . . . ?'

'No,' Helen said, shaking her head vigorously. 'No. Definitely not.' She didn't look too convinced. 'Probably not, anyway. What was it she said again?'

'She asked me to hide it for her,' I said anxiously.

'That's just her poor English,' Helen said, taking out her phone. 'I'm going to call her now.' She hit a number and smiled reassuringly at me. 'Ivana? Hi, it's Helen . . . Yes, really well. You? . . . Oh, Giorgio's laughing? How cute!' She shot me a knowing look. 'So, look, I'm with Jess, and we were wondering what was in that trunk you . . . Oh. Oh, right . . . No, no, I didn't mean to . . . Okay, fine . . .'

She looked at me uncertainly.

'What?' I said worriedly. 'What did she say?'

'She told me not to call her about it again. She said you shouldn't have told me in the first place. And she said people might be . . .' She trailed off awkwardly.

'People might be what?' I demanded. 'Might be what?'

'Might be listening,' she faltered.

'You think those are the people she meant?' Panicked, I moved my head backward to indicate the men outside.

'Could be,' Helen whispered.

'So what do we do?'

'You get out of here,' she said firmly. 'I'll create a diversion, and you head to the hospital. You'll be safe there.'

'And then what?'

'Later today we'll take the trunk down to the country and hide it somewhere. Then we'll check out this Lawrence dude,' she said, her eyes glinting.

'Okay,' I agreed weakly, my heart thudding in my chest. 'Although by "check out this Lawrence dude," I take it you actually mean eject him from the house and tell Mum to ditch him?'

'That, too,' Helen said, leaning toward me. 'Right,' she whispered. 'I'm going out.'

'You're sure about this?' I asked, dubious.

'Just call me later.' Helen sounded serious. 'Okay?'

'Okay,' I said gratefully. I watched as she sashayed out of the café, then dropped her bag on the street, sending all her possessions flying. Immediately, the two men dashed over to help; Helen smiled winningly, and I grabbed my bag and legged it.

Chapter 15

❦

'HI. HI! HELLO, darling. Hi, gorgeous!' I was walking along the hospital corridor, practicing my greeting for Max. Something cheerful, not at all stressed out, something relaxed but genuine. Something that hid the fact that everything was imploding around me. Around the business he'd entrusted to me.

'Max. Hi!' I pushed open the door – and my smile froze when I saw that he wasn't alone. 'Oh, hi, Emily. How are you?' She was perched on the side of the bed. Max's bed. They were doing the crossword together.

'Jess! Hi! You made it here early!' she said easily, her face creasing into a friendly smile.

'Yes, well, I wanted to see Max,' I said briskly.

'Oh, you shouldn't worry about Max. We've been keeping each other occupied,' Emily said, grinning. 'Haven't we, Max?'

He grinned back, and I forced myself to ignore the sinking feeling in my stomach. *She's his nurse,* I reminded myself sternly. *He loves you.* 'Oh, Jess, you should've seen us,' he said ruefully. 'We were playing truth or dare.'

'Truth or dare?' I asked uncertainly. 'Really?'

'Really,' Max said, laughing. 'I haven't laughed so hard since . . . since . . . actually, I can't remember when I laughed that hard.'

'Is that right,' I said, my voice tensing slightly. 'Well, that's nice.'

I looked at Emily meaningfully. 'So, thanks, Emily, but I can probably keep Max occupied for a while. I know you must be really busy.'

Emily hopped off the bed. 'Oh, okay,' she said lightly as I squeezed gingerly past her to give Max a kiss. And not just a peck on the cheek – I went for a full-on smooch on the lips.

'How long can you stay?' Max asked. 'There's a lunch menu over there if you—'

'Not that long, I'm afraid,' I said, pulling an apologetic face. 'I've got my audit interview today, and then I've got to go and see my mother—'

'Audit interview?' Max asked, serious. 'How's it going? Anything been raised yet? Any potential problems?'

'Oh, no,' I said, rather too quickly. 'Everything's fine. More than fine. Everything's great!'

'You make it sound easy,' Max said, frowning slightly.

'Easy? Oh, it is,' I gushed. 'Don't you worry about Milton Advertising. It's easy-peasy running that place. No problem at all. So, how about you? How are you feeling?'

'Me? Oh. You know.' Max shot a little smile in Emily's direction – Emily, who, I noticed, was still in the room, hovering by the door.

'No, I don't know,' I said tightly, trying not to show my annoyance. 'Why don't you tell me?'

'Well, while you've been running everything, I've been mainlining trash television – *Countdown, Homes Under the Hammer, Flog It* . . . The list is endless,' Max said dryly. 'It's like junk food – you know it's bad for you, but you're powerless to resist.'

'Not powerless,' Emily chided him. 'Just weak.' She laughed, and I found my shoulders tensing.

'Max isn't weak,' I said, the fixed smile returning to my face. 'He's in the hospital with a broken leg. And I can't imagine there's much for him to do around here.'

'No, of course there isn't,' Emily said quickly. 'I was only joking. Of course he isn't weak. And if he is, then I'm just as bad. Honestly, those conundrums are addictive!'

'A bit like my husband, apparently,' I said, rather louder than I'd intended.

Max shot me a strange look. 'Jess, is everything okay?'

'Okay?' I answered brightly. 'Of course it's okay. I mean, you're in here with Emily having a whale of a time, which is great. Just fabulous, actually.'

'A whale of a time?' Max's expression changed. 'Is that what you call it?'

I shrugged. 'Doing conundrums, watching property programs . . . Sounds okay to me.'

'Does it? Well, perhaps you'd like to swap with me, then,' Max said, his tone harsher. 'Perhaps you'd like to be unable to walk, unable to run your business, unable to go to the bloody lavatory without help from someone.'

His eyes were boring into me, and I flinched. 'And I suppose that someone is usually Emily?' I said before I could stop myself.

'Yes, that is Emily,' Max said levelly. 'And it was Emily who went out and picked me up some toothpaste and other things that I needed.'

'But I would have done that,' I protested.

'Like the muffins?' Max shot back.

'I meant to bring muffins,' I said defensively. 'I just—'

'You've just been busy. I get it,' he said, turning away.

'Yes, I have,' I said, looking at him unhappily. 'But I'd rather have been here with you. You know that.'

'Jess, you don't have to do this,' Max said seriously. 'I get it. You don't like seeing me in the hospital. You're not a looking-after-someone kind of wife. It's like your mother said: You're an independent type. You don't need anyone. It's fine. Just go to work, do your interview.'

I felt a large lump in my throat. 'That's not true,' I said hotly. 'I'm not independent. I do need you. I want to look after you. I—'

'No, you don't,' Max said, his voice resigned. 'You don't need me. It's not your fault – it's what I fell in love with, that strength of character you've always had. I just didn't realize you don't want to be needed, either.'

'I do want to be needed,' I gulped, desperate. 'I want you to need me. I do.'

'Which is why you've been here for barely five minutes since I got here,' Max said tightly.

'Oh, that's not true,' Emily said quickly. 'She's been here more than that.'

'Yes. I have. I mean . . .' I looked from Emily to Max uncertainly. This was all wrong. She was defending me and Max wasn't even looking at me.

'I should go,' Emily said suddenly, as though she could read my mind. 'Give you two some alone time.'

'That would be great,' I said immediately. 'Thanks.'

'Oh, no problem.' She smiled winningly, then turned and left, closing the door behind her.

'She's amazing,' Max said, looking after her with a dreamy look in his eye that felt like a knife in my stomach. 'So sweet. So considerate.'

'So flirtatious,' I said before I could stop myself. Max narrowed his eyes.

'So *what*?' he asked. 'What did you say?'

I cleared my throat uncomfortably. 'So flirtatious,' I said, then looked at him awkwardly. 'Come on, Max. She is.

Doesn't mean she isn't a great nurse, but . . .' I trailed off as I saw Max's expression, saw the anger flashing in his eyes.

'I can't believe you,' he seethed. 'This lovely girl is doing everything she can to make my stay here a bit more bearable, and all you can do is criticize her? You know, Jess, I feel as if I don't even know you right now. Emily said the other day that you only learn who you can really trust, who really cares about you, when the chips are down. And now I see that she's right.'

I stared at him in disbelief. 'But the chips have been down loads with us, and we've always been okay,' I said incredulously. I could feel tears pricking at my eyes and wiped them away angrily.

Max looked away. 'Oh, so the chips have *always* been down? And that's my fault, too, is it?'

'No!' I said hotly. 'No, of course not. It's just that . . .'

'Just that what, Jess?'

I swallowed uncomfortably. This wasn't going the way it was supposed to at all. 'I miss you, that's all,' I said hesitantly.

'Miss me? Or miss the strong me? The one you don't have to worry about?'

'That's unfair and totally not true,' I said quietly. 'I like worrying about you. I—'

'You don't. I wish you'd just admit it instead of attacking Emily, who's done absolutely nothing wrong here.'

'And I have?' I asked desperately.

Max looked at me silently for a few seconds, then he shrugged. 'The difference is, she didn't have a bad word to say about you. She said there would definitely be a very good reason why you turned up so late last night and why you've been so weird when you *have* been here—'

'Weird?' I blinked back tears. 'What do you mean?'

'I mean sitting there with that fixed smile, your voice shrill, barely telling me anything about work. What, you want to run the business? You think I've been doing a bad job?'

'What?' I said incredulously. 'What are you talking about, Max? I don't want to run the company. I want you to. And since you've been in the hospital, all I've been trying to do is to keep things going so that you don't have to worry. Even though the auditor is a weasel, even though Mum's shagging some guy she met on Facebook, and Chester doesn't want to talk to me about anything apart from why she's not taking his calls. So I'm sorry if I haven't been here all day – I'd love to have been, actually, but I've been too busy trying to keep things afloat.'

'Of course you have. And let's not forget, if you were running the company we wouldn't be scrabbling around for money to pay our bills, would we? You'd solve all our cash-flow problems in a second. But we don't all have millions in the bank, Jess.'

I stared at Max indignantly. 'I've always said that's our money,' I said, the lump returning to my throat.

'But it isn't, is it? It's your money. My money is all invested in the business, which, as you've no doubt dis-covered, is at a breaking point. So right now I could do without your tight little smile and your excuses. Just go. Go and see your mother or whatever other important thing you have to do. And tell Emily to come back in when she's got a moment. Okay?'

I realized I was shaking. 'Is that what you want?' I asked. 'For me to go?'

Max sighed. 'Look, I'm tired. Let's just leave this, shall we?'

'No, I don't want to,' I said desperately, but Max had already closed his eyes. I watched him for a few minutes, then slowly, sadly, turned and left the room.

Eric was waiting for me when I got back to work, standing outside his office with folded arms. At least I hadn't noticed anyone in a Hummer following me, but then again, I hadn't noticed much on my way back from the hospital. I felt like the wind had been knocked out of me, like I'd literally been punched in the stomach. My attempts to be the perfect wife had backfired spectacularly; I had never seen Max like that before, had never known him to talk to me with such anger. And now I had my interview with Eric, after which I had to race down to Wiltshire with Helen to face my mother. All I wanted to do was curl up in a corner and cry.

I approached him heavily. 'Eric, I don't suppose you'd rearrange this, would you?' I asked. 'Today is . . . Well, it's just a bit of a hellish day, to be honest.'

Eric smiled thinly. 'I'm afraid I need twenty-four hours' notice to rearrange an interview,' he said.

'You do?' I asked. 'What, like a dentist?'

He looked at me strangely. 'I suppose.'

'But why? I mean, you're here all the time, aren't you? Couldn't we please rearrange for tomorrow?'

'It's a rule,' he said firmly. 'Being ethical also involves being punctual, after all. Being polite. Giving people notice if you are unable to make an appointment.'

I didn't feel very ethical, or polite, I realized. 'Is that right?' I asked stiffly.

'Yes, it is,' he said, equally stiff.

'Then I guess we'll do the interview now, then,' I said.

'I suppose we will,' he agreed.

He walked into the office, sat down at Anthony's desk, and I sat down opposite him.

'So, Mrs. Wild Wainwright,' Eric said, looking at me closely. 'I've heard so much about you.'

'You have?' I looked at him warily. 'From whom?'

His eyes flickered slightly. 'From a . . . source.'

'A source?' I narrowed my eyes. 'You mean a colleague?'

'Perhaps,' Eric said vaguely.

I stared at him uncertainly. If it wasn't a colleague, who was it? To whom else had he been talking?

'They certainly had lots to say,' he continued.

'They did?' I asked flatly. 'Who was it? Surely you have to tell me.'

'I'm afraid my sources are strictly confidential,' Eric said.

'Well, what did they say?' I asked impatiently.

Eric studied his notebook. 'I am not at liberty to divulge that information,' he said.

'Great,' I said sarcastically. 'So you'll talk to people about me, but you can't tell me what they said or who they are?'

Eric drew his mouth in; he looked as if he'd just eaten what he thought was a slice of orange but turned out to be lemon. Then something occurred to me: Anthony had been interviewed yesterday. Which meant he probably told Eric all about our history. I sighed inwardly. I was going to have to explain that Anthony's version of what happened was very different from the truth of the matter. My life might be in a state of collapse, but I still had to at least try to pass this stupid audit.

'Was it Anthony?' I asked. Eric didn't say anything; I took that as a yes. After all, no one else that I could think of would talk about me behind my back. 'Because if it was, you shouldn't believe everything that you hear,' I continued.

Eric nodded slowly. 'If you say so,' he said, writing in his notebook.

He wrote for quite a long time. Too long. 'What are you writing?' I asked suspiciously.

'I'm just noting your comments on Mr. Milton,' he said, not looking up.

'My comments?'

'About his being a liar,' Eric said. 'He's the former director of the company, isn't he? Didn't he set it up?'

I swallowed uncomfortably. 'Yes. But Max runs the company now. And he's not like Anthony at all.'

'They're good friends, are they not?'

I frowned. 'Yes, they're friends, I suppose,' I said hesitantly. 'But let's not talk about Anthony, shall we? I mean, you've interviewed him already, so—'

'Such good friends that, after Mr. Wainwright bought the business from Mr. Milton, he still welcomed him with open arms and gave him his old office back?'

'Well, yes, but that's because Max is such a good person,' I said quickly. 'You know, honorable and—'

'And yet he has brought a man whom you describe as untrustworthy and no judge of character back into the firm to tout for new business?'

I looked at Eric worriedly. This was all going wrong. 'Actually,' I amended, 'Anthony really isn't all that bad. I was just . . . you know, joking.'

'You didn't mean what you said about him?'

'No,' I said with relief. 'No, not at all.'

'So he is a good judge of character?' Eric's eyes were triumphant, as if we were playing a game of chess and he'd put me in check without me realizing.

'Sure, why not,' I said tensely, trying not to get annoyed. I took a deep breath. 'Look, do you think we could start this again? I feel like maybe we got off on the wrong foot.'

'Start again?' Eric asked curiously.

'Yes, you know, just scratch what we've said so far and go back to the beginning?'

'You mean pretend that the past five minutes hasn't happened?'

I nodded in relief. 'Exactly. That would be great.'

Eric nodded back, and I felt my shoulders relax slightly.

'So,' I said. 'Where do we start?'

'Start?' he asked. He had pale, watery eyes, I noticed, and he could do with a few days in the sun; his skin was pale and washed out, and his pale-gray ill-fitting suit did nothing to warm his complexion.

'Yes. Aren't you going to ask me some questions?'

He smiled. 'Right now, Mrs. Wild Wainwright, I'm trying to decide how to phrase your request to pretend that the first few minutes of this interview didn't happen.'

'Phrase it?' I looked at him in confusion. 'For what?'

'For my report,' he said, his lips curling upward in a most unattractive way.

'Your report? I thought we were going to start over.'

'My job is to report what is said during the interview, then to analyze the interview, requesting supporting evidence should I deem it necessary,' Eric said. 'So I'm writing down everything. This isn't the first time you've attempted to start over, after all, is it?'

I looked at him for a moment. And then, without warning, I started to cry – stupidly, embarrassingly. Big fat tears were wending their way down my cheeks, and there was nothing I could do to stop them. He was right. It wasn't the first time I'd attempted to start over. I kept doing it, over and over, and it never made things better – it only made

175

things worse. 'You're right,' I sobbed. 'I thought I was making myself a better person. I thought cooking and being supportive and . . . and listening . . . and trying new things in the bedroom . . . I thought they'd make things better. I thought I'd deserve Max more. But I don't. And everything's just got worse.'

'Right,' Eric said, clearing his throat uncomfortably. 'What I meant was—'

'I thought if I reinvented myself, it wouldn't matter about Hugh Barter,' I said miserably. 'But it turns out Hugh isn't important. I mean, he isn't the reason Max has totally fallen out of love with me. I managed that all on my own. I didn't bring him muffins. That's all he asked for, and I didn't bring him any. And Mum kept trying to talk to me and I wouldn't listen and now she's shacked up with some . . . some . . . person called Lawrence, and when Chester finds out, he'll . . .' I sniffed loudly, and Eric handed me a tissue, his eyes as wide as saucers. 'He'll pull his account, is what he'll do,' I sobbed. 'And Max will be ruined and it'll be all my fault. And as for this . . . this . . . audit, well, I've screwed that up, too, haven't I? I mean, how am I ethical? I'm being blackmailed by Hugh Barter and I'm being followed by the Russian Mafia. Really ethical.'

'Okay,' Eric said nervously. 'Now, back to the interview. So, Mrs. Wild Wainwright, you have been working at Milton Advertising for . . . five years, is that right?'

'Five years.' I nodded wretchedly. Then I looked up. 'I wouldn't have had a shrill voice or tight smile if she hadn't been there all the time. I mean, nurses are meant to nurse, right? Not watch *Countdown*. Not play truth or dare. Right?'

'Right,' Eric said awkwardly. 'Now, about your recycling habits . . .'

'And he thinks because I've got money . . . he thinks that

I've found running this place easy. Is he crazy? It's been a nightmare. I haven't stopped for a second since he went into the hospital. I just didn't want him to worry, that's all.'

'No, I'm sure you didn't,' Eric said, looking over at the door as though hoping for an interruption. 'So what about charitable giving?'

A hollow laugh erupted out of my mouth. 'Charitable giving? Let me tell you about my charitable giving. I wanted to help. Wanted to be a good person, right? So I went to a soup kitchen. A resource center, they call it. And Christina, the woman who runs the place, asked me to be a companion. But you know what? Turns out I'm crap at that, too. I'm the one who goes there for companionship. That's how sad I am. The people there take pity on *me*!'

Eric cleared his throat. 'Now, moving on to your habits. Do you gamble, Mrs. Wild Wainwright?'

I shook my head and Eric smiled, evidently pleased to be able to cross something off his checklist. 'And how would you view your attitude toward risk? When it comes to investments and the like?'

'Investments?' I looked at him blankly.

'What do you do with your money? Your savings?' he prompted.

'I . . .' I frowned. 'Nothing,' I said.

'Nothing,' Eric said, nodding. 'Is that because you have no savings or because you prefer not to invest?'

'You know what?' I said, standing up. 'I think we should stop this.'

'You do?' Eric asked nervously.

'Yes,' I said. 'Let's stop dancing around, shall we? I am not ideal, not at all. This company probably isn't ideal – I mean, can you think of one that is?'

'Well, I . . . Let m-me think n-now . . .' Eric stuttered.

'I'm not ideal,' I repeated, with a little shrug. 'I'm imperfect. I'm flawed fundamentally. What I need isn't to try to be ideal but to accept what I am. Don't you think?'

'Ah, acceptance,' Eric said, his eyes lighting up. 'Jerome D. Rutter has a chapter on acceptance in his book. I was talking to Caroline about it just this morning. Now, there's someone who's ideal.'

'Rutter?' I asked.

Eric looked down. 'No. I . . . So, anyway, you were talking about acceptance?'

'Exactly,' I said. 'I accept that I'm not ideal. I'm rubbish. Isn't that great?'

Eric pulled a face. 'It is?'

'I love Rutter. The man's a genius,' I said happily.

'Oh, he is,' Eric said sagely. 'What he says about possessions weighing down the soul, it's inspired. They hold us back, they entangle us in the selves of our past, the selves we wish to break away from and the lives that others have set for us—'

'Yes, that,' I said excitedly. 'He's right!'

'Well, of course he's right,' Eric said. 'And when we're free from material bondage, we can speak the truth.'

'The truth! Exactly,' I said triumphantly. Then I took a deep breath. 'I have to go,' I said.

'Go?' Eric asked. 'But I haven't told you about what happens when you speak the truth. You can rescue others. Rescue yourself with the wisdom of the—'

'I really do have to go,' I interrupted.

'But you can't go,' Eric protested.

'Yes, I can,' I said, smiling through my tears. 'I really can.' I opened the door to leave, then froze. There, in reception, were the two men. The men who had been following me. They were talking to Gillie, who was pointing toward my desk. Maybe I couldn't go after all. Quickly, I shut the door again.

Eric looked at me strangely. 'You're not going now?' he asked.

I scanned the office desperately. There was one window; I could probably climb out it if I tried. But what would I say to Eric?

I opened the door again, just slightly; the men were talking to Caroline now. And suddenly something occurred to me. That look on his face when he'd mentioned Caroline's name. Something Helen had said. I swung round. 'Eric?'

He had a slightly terrified look in his eye. 'Yes?'

'You like Caroline, don't you?'

He went bright red. 'Caroline? I . . . I don't know what you mean. I . . .'

'Do you? Like her? You can tell me if you do.'

He looked at me hesitantly, then managed a half-nod. 'I . . . She's very nice. A nice girl. Way too good for me. And totally against the rules. She's a client. But if you're asking if I . . . like her, then yes, all things considered, when you put it all into—'

'There are two men hitting on her,' I cut in.

'Hitting on her?' Eric stood up, a look of outrage on his face.

'I don't like the look of them,' I said, holding the door open so that he could see. 'It seems to me that she could use some help. Some rescuing.'

'You think?' Eric asked, wide-eyed.

'I think,' I answered, nodding.

'Right, then,' he said, taking a deep breath. 'Right, then, here goes.' He half skipped to the door, then turned back. 'You won't . . . tell . . . ?'

'I won't say a word,' I promised. I watched as Eric ran toward Caroline and pulled the men away from her. Immediately, I grabbed my bag and ran – out of Eric's office, through reception, out the door, and down to the car park, as fast as my legs could carry me. I jumped into my car and sped off. I was going to the resource center to finally do something useful. But before I did, I had a few calls to make; the first one was to Ivana. As I'd expected, no one picked up. 'Ivana,' I said, when asked to leave a message. 'It's Jessica. It's about the trunk . . .'

Chapter 16

༒

THE ROAD DOWN TO WILTSHIRE seemed longer than usual. Helen was in the front of the car with me, and Giles was in the back; he'd called me to ask how things were going and had immediately offered to come when I told him. He was the last person I'd spoken to – after Ivana, Hugh, and Chester, and after my visit to the resource center. I'd been jubilant by the time Giles called – I felt amazing for having spoken my mind. I still did – confident and finally in charge of things. Even the men in the Hummer didn't seem quite so ominous. Anyway, they were in London. And London was getting farther away by the second.

'I've never been chased by the Russian Mafia before,' Giles breathed as we drove down the motorway.

'Try acting as a decoy for them,' Helen said dramatically. 'I had to keep them occupied so that Jess could escape this morning. Honestly, it was terrifying.'

'Was it?' I asked worriedly. 'God, what happened? I saw you drop your bag.'

'What happened?' Helen asked, turning round so Giles could hear. 'I'll tell you what happened. I dropped my bag, and one of the guys came up and started to help me. But the other one saw you and wanted to get the first one back in the car to go after you.'

'You're joking!' I breathed. 'So what did you do?'

'Well, I had to stop them,' Helen said, her hands going up

181

in the air for dramatic effect. 'So I burst into tears. And that made the first guy feel sorry for me. He was asking me what the matter was, and I had to make up this whole story while the other one was chomping at the bit. And I knew that at any moment they could have taken out a gun or something. It was pretty intense, I tell you.'

'Wow,' Giles said. 'You're amazing.'

'Oh, it was nothing,' Helen said airily.

'Were they Russian?' I asked.

'I don't know,' Helen said. 'I think so.'

'What was the accent of the one you spoke to? Was it Russian?'

'Oh, um, yes. Yes, definitely Russian,' Helen said author-itatively.

'Shit,' I said. 'So they must be the Russian Mafia. I was hoping they might be something else. You know, like the police chasing me for a speeding fine or something.'

'In a Hummer?' Giles asked, raising an eyebrow.

'I said "hoping," not "expecting." Actually, it was more like praying, to be honest.'

'A Russian accent doesn't mean they're necessarily the Russian Mafia,' Helen said. 'They could have been any Russian organized-crime gang. Or maybe they were former KGB agents.'

I was about to tell her that didn't exactly reassure me, but I felt my phone vibrate and saw Hugh's number flash up. Quickly, I rejected the call. Then, for good measure, I turned my phone off. I'd said all I wanted to say to him in my message; frankly, I never wanted to hear his voice again as long as I lived.

'And they came to your office, Jess?' Giles was saying.

'Yes,' I said, feeling a little less confident, a little less in charge. 'Yes, they did.'

Helen turned round to look out the window. 'Are they behind us now?'

I checked the side mirror nervously. 'No. No one there.'

'Okay, then. We've shaken them,' Helen said, turning to Giles. 'See? I promised you it would be exciting.'

I looked in the rearview mirror and saw Giles pull a face.

'Tell me again about this Lawrence person,' he said, apparently keen to change the subject. 'Your mother met him on Facebook?'

'I guess,' I sighed. 'I mean, one minute she's asking me how to upload photos, and the next minute some guy called Lawrence is in the kitchen kissing her and she's hanging up on me.'

'Sounds steamy,' Helen said.

I cringed. 'Please, Helen. We're talking about my mother.'

'So you're going to chuck him out?' Giles asked, leaning forward. 'Tell your mother to stop messing around and get married to Chester?'

I shook my head. 'No,' I said.

'But I thought that's why we're going down there.' Helen looked confused. 'To make sure Chester doesn't flip his lid when he gets back.'

'It was,' I said with a little shrug, 'but I've kind of changed my mind.'

'You have?' Helen asked interestedly. 'Why?'

'Because . . .' I took a deep breath, then let it out again, slowly. 'Because it's not up to me how she lives her life. I mean, I'm hardly a shining example of how to go about things, am I?'

'You're not having an affair,' Helen said.

'No,' I conceded, 'but I am being blackmailed, and I do have the Russian Mafia on my tail, and I did just walk out of

183

an interview that I needed to pass in order to salvage my husband's advertising firm and retain our key client.'

Helen digested this for a moment. 'You walked out?'

'There wasn't any point in staying,' I said lightly.

'What happened to being ideal, then?' Giles asked, leaning forward into the front seat. 'Correct me if I'm wrong, but walking out of the interview probably doesn't constitute ideal-wife behavior.'

'Yeah, well, I'm not ideal,' I said. 'I realize that now. I don't think I ever will be.'

'Thank the Lord!' Helen said. 'And Max loves you all the same, right?'

I shook my head. 'Actually, I don't think he does,' I said quietly. 'But that'll just make it easier when I tell him about Hugh, won't it?'

'But—' Helen looked thoroughly confused.

'It's okay,' I cut in. 'Max said I'm not a looking-after sort of a person, and he's right. He'll find someone else, and I'll . . . Well, I'll be fine.'

'You're not a what?'

'A looking-after sort of person,' I said, choking up slightly as I remembered the way Max had looked at me – disappointed and resigned.

'Max said that?' Giles asked incredulously.

I nodded. 'It's no big deal. Actually, it's a good thing. I'd never have measured up to Max. This way I don't have to.'

'But—' Helen protested.

'But nothing,' I said firmly. 'That's the end of the matter.'

'So we're going down to Wiltshire to . . . what, meet Lawrence?'

'To talk to Mum. And to hide the trunk,' I said.

'Doesn't sound very exciting after all,' Giles said disappointedly.

'We're still being chased by two men in a Hummer. Two Russian Mafia men,' Helen reminded him.

'That's true,' Giles said, brightening slightly. 'And, on that point, is there any reason that we're driving below the legal speed limit? Shouldn't we be racing against the clock or something?'

'I'm tired of racing,' I said. 'Anyway, Ivana's trunk is really heavy. I think that's slowing us down. Besides, we're here now. Look.'

Giles's eyes were out on stalks as we pulled into the drive. 'Oh my God, is this it? It's amazing. It's huge. It's like a stately home!'

'Yeah,' I said, then frowned when I saw a car I didn't recognize in the drive. Helen caught my look.

'That's his car?' she whispered.

'I guess,' I said.

'So are you ready to face your mother's lover?'

I nodded. 'I'm ready,' I said.

I got out of the car, and Helen and Giles followed. I didn't know whether to ring the doorbell or use my key, or what on earth I was going to say when I saw my mother – or Lawrence, for that matter.

But my mind was made up for me; the door opened and my mother appeared, her expression apprehensive. 'Jess. You're here.' She smiled at Helen and Giles. 'Hello,' she said warmly. 'So nice to see you both.' Then she looked back at me, her face anxious again. 'I'm so glad you came. I need to talk to you. I need to tell you something.'

'I know,' I said quietly. 'But first let me say something. I'm sorry I didn't let you explain yesterday. If you're in love with this Lawrence guy, then that's fine. I'll be supportive. If you want me to tell Chester that the wedding is off, I will. You're my mother and I love you, and so whatever you want to do is fine by me. Okay?'

'Okay,' Mum said uncertainly. 'If you say so. But—'

'But nothing. You heard her,' a voice said; Lawrence was walking toward us. 'She wants you to cancel the wedding, Esther. I say do it. I say let's tell Jess here the truth and start our lives together.'

'The truth?' I looked up in alarm. 'So the wedding really is off?' I'd kind of hoped Mum would tell me that Lawrence had been a big mistake – or, better, a misunderstanding.

'No,' my mother said quickly.

'Yes,' Lawrence said, equally quick, then he smiled at me. 'The thing is, Jess . . . The thing that your mother wants to tell you is . . .'

'Is?' I asked, turning to my mother when he trailed off.

She met my gaze awkwardly. 'It's about your father, Jess.'

It took me a few seconds to digest what she'd said. 'My father?' I eyed her suspiciously. As far as I knew, I had no father. Well, obviously I had a father, but not one I could track down. He was an impoverished student who had moved to the States when I was a baby. My mother was afraid that he wouldn't be able to provide for us, so she'd dumped him and told one of her rich suitors that *he* was the father. It had worked, too – for all of a few months. Then she'd got tired of the drudgery of motherhood and started to gamble, using his money. When that dried up, she turned to dodgy moneylenders, who became so keen to get their money back that she faked her own death and dumped me with Grandma.

'The thing is, darling, Lawrence . . . Well, he's your father.'

'Father?' Okay, I wasn't expecting that. I looked at Mum

uncertainly. 'You're joking, right? Because it's not funny. It really isn't.'

'I'm not joking,' Mum said fretfully. 'He found me on Facebook.'

'On Facebook,' I said, turning to stare at this man – Lawrence – who was apparently my own flesh and blood.

'He . . . he just turned up,' Mum said. 'I tried to tell you, but—'

'She's right. I'm your long-lost dad, Jess,' Lawrence said, grinning at me. 'The moment I saw Esther's picture on that website I knew I had to see her, knew I had to find you. The fact is, Jess, I've come home.'

I looked at them in disbelief. I could feel Helen and Giles standing stock-still behind me, waiting for my reaction. I watched my mother scrutinizing my face for a clue to what I was thinking. I didn't know myself. I felt suspended in time, as if nothing was real, as if I was dreaming. I was finding it hard to breathe. It was the excitement. The fear. The surprise. I felt hot. I felt clammy. 'Jessica? Jess? Jess, are you all right?' a voice said, and then there were dots in front of my eyes, dancing, getting bigger and closer. I tried to nod, I tried to speak, but I couldn't; I was slipping downward. I couldn't stop it, couldn't stop the walls from closing in on me, blocking out the light as I fell to the ground.

And then everything went black.

'Jess! Jess, are you okay?'

I opened my eyes groggily. I was on the doormat outside the front door. Oh God. I pulled myself up to sit. I felt terrible. I'd fainted. I mean, what was I, the heroine of some swoon-fest or something?

'Darling, you look awful. I'm sorry. I didn't mean to shock you like that.'

'I'm fine,' I said, as Helen and Giles helped me to my feet and through the door. Mum led the way to the kitchen. 'I don't know what happened. I just . . .' I stopped suddenly; the dots were there again, closing in on me, threatening to topple me once more. I took a deep breath and leaned on Helen, letting my head drop, trying to work out what was going on. I was at the house. Mum had been telling me about . . .

'He's really . . .' I looked back to see Lawrence walking behind me. 'You're really—'

'Your dad. Yes, I am,' he said. He spoke easily, as if it was no big deal.

We'd gotten as far as the kitchen; Helen guided me toward a chair. 'I think you need to sit down,' she suggested.

'He's my father,' I said, my eyes wide as I sank into the chair. 'I've got a father.'

'I know,' she said. 'I know.'

Father. It felt strange even hearing the word. I'd never had a father. Not even a surrogate father. Grandpa hadn't been around when I was growing up, and I'd kind of gotten used to the idea that I didn't have a dad, had convinced myself that I didn't need one. But saying the word brought back a whole bunch of memories – of being at school and listening jealously to the other girls talking about their overprotective fathers, about their dads' new cars, new jobs . . . It had seemed like an exotic world that I would never enter, where the sun shined just a little bit more, where things were all a little bit easier. Fathers, as far as I could deduce with my limited experience, made decisions quickly, were strong, loyal, and protective. When they turned up at school, there was a different energy about the place. I felt awkward around the other girls' fathers, self-conscious, as though they could tell I didn't have one. And yet at night I dreamed that mine would come back for me and rescue me. He would turn up with a fast car, an easy smile, and strong arms to wrap around me.

And now here he was. My real-life father. Part of me wanted him to scoop me up in his arms right that minute. I wanted that moment in *The Railway Children* when their father returns from prison and everything's okay again. I wanted to see Pa Walton striding in, a look of grit, determination, and love on his face. I wanted Harrison Ford, Father Christmas, and my old headmaster, the man who'd told me I could do anything I wanted, who'd told Grandma that it would be a travesty if I didn't go to university even if she thought it was time for me to stand on my own two feet. I wanted them all, wrapped up in one person.

Except . . . except . . .

My mother was looking at me tentatively. Lawrence came in and leaned down to look at me. 'You okay, kiddo?'

'You're . . .' I cleared my throat and stood to stare at him properly. 'You're my father?'

He was older than I'd thought he was when I'd seen only his back. Fifty-something maybe. He had blond-gray hair, a tan, blue eyes. He was slim, fine-boned. Handsome, even.

'Jess,' he said, reaching out his hands, 'I can't tell you how great it is to finally meet you.'

'Really?' I didn't know what to say, how to react.

'Really,' he said, letting his arms fall back to his sides. Easily. Unfazed. Was I really related to this man? He was nothing like me. He was a stranger. There ought to be something, a feeling or an understanding; we should be looking into each other's eyes with a deep recognition. Something. Instead, I was staring at him blankly, my nails digging into my palms, aware that everyone was staring at me and expecting something that I couldn't deliver. 'You okay?' he asked, a look of concern on his face. 'I guess this is a lot to take in, me turning up like this. I'd have come before, only . . .'

'Only what?' I asked quietly. 'Why didn't you come before? Why didn't you get me from Grandma's?'

He looked slightly uncomfortable. 'I guess it was difficult. I didn't know where you were, for one thing. Esther here . . . Well, after she left with you, we lost touch. Then I heard she died, and—'

'And you didn't think that was a good moment to try to track down your daughter? Your flesh and blood?' My voice sounded more irritable than I'd intended it to. I noticed Lawrence shrink back slightly.

'You're right, of course,' he said, attempting a smile. 'I should have. All I can tell you is that I was young. Young and pretty stupid, if I'm honest. I'd moved to the States, and I guess it didn't feel real.'

'It was real for me,' I said.

'I know. I know that now.'

I took a deep breath. 'And now you're back?' I looked at Mum. 'He's back? With you? After all this time?'

She opened her mouth to say something, but Lawrence got there first. 'After all this time,' he said, smiling again. 'The three of us, Jess. How about it?'

How about it? My long-lost father had dropped back into my life and wanted to know what I thought about it? I looked at him uneasily.

'If you're here for a kidney, you can forget it,' I said quietly.

He looked at me strangely. 'A kidney?'

I nodded. 'I've seen *Lost*. I know all about long-lost fathers who turn up out of the blue. And I'm not falling for it. So if you want a kidney, you're going to have to find some other sucker, okay? Because you're not getting one of mine.'

His eyes widened in surprise, then he grinned. 'Okay, well, that's good to know. No kidney. I'll . . . bear it in mind. In the future, if I ever wind up needing one.'

I realized he was laughing at me. His eyes were twinkling the way Max's did when he was teasing me.

'It's not funny,' I said stiffly.

'No, it's not,' my father agreed, his mouth still creasing upward. 'Well, only a little bit.'

'Not at all.'

'What about something smaller?' he asked.

I frowned. 'Smaller? What do you mean?'

'I can see how you wouldn't want to give me a kidney,' he said thoughtfully. 'Big operation, nasty scar. But could you maybe give me a wisdom tooth? Or, I don't know, your appendix maybe? Something you don't need so much?'

I looked at him uncertainly. 'No.'

'Nothing?' He shook his head and whistled. 'Man, you're tough. Esther, are you hearing this? Not even a wisdom tooth for her old man.'

My mother, who seemed rather flummoxed, looked at him anxiously. 'I don't understand,' she said. 'You don't want her teeth, do you? Why would you want her teeth?'

I caught my father's eye. And immediately I had a flash of something, of a life that could have been: of in-jokes, of teasing Mum, of being part of something that couldn't be broken.

Except it hadn't existed, I reminded myself. And it *had* broken. It had never really been in the first place.

But I knew one thing: He was my father. It wasn't his eyes, or his lips, or his hair color, or anything else. It was his sense of humor. Grandma never got my humor, nor did Mum. They thought I was being stupid or ridiculous. They rolled their eyes and changed the subject or looked the other way.

'You can have a bit of toenail, if you really want,' I said dryly, looking up at him warily. In the pit of my stomach was something approaching excitement, and it scared me.

'Toenail.' He nodded thoughtfully. 'And would there be strings attached, do you think?'

'I'd be wanting a cup of tea for that.' I shrugged. 'And probably a biscuit.'

'Esther? We got biscuits here?'

My mother nodded. 'Of course we have biscuits. But I still don't understand,' she said. 'Why do you want a toenail? Jess, is there something going on here that you're not telling me?'

I allowed myself a little smile. 'No, Mum,' I said. 'Nothing at all. But you,' I said, turning back to my father, 'you have got some explaining to do.'

He met my eyes and looked at me seriously. 'And that's exactly what I'm going to do,' he said, sitting down at the table and motioning for me to do likewise.

I looked at my watch. 'Now?'

'Why not now?' Lawrence said, returning my smile.

Why not? I thought for a moment. Any moment now, Chester could arrive, discovering my mother and Lawrence. Any second now, Russian Mafia agents could bang on the door, demanding Ivana's trunk. Any minute, Eric might fail Milton Advertising's ethical audit on the basis that its acting chief executive abandoned ship in the middle of an interview. And Max was no doubt lying in bed waiting for me to arrive full of apologies, bearing muffins. I knew what I should do. I didn't have time to sit here and find out about the father I'd never known about.

Then I looked back at him. 'Okay, tell me,' I said. 'Tell me everything.'

Chapter 17

'RIGHT, THEN.' MY FATHER – it felt weird using the word in relation to me – smiled broadly. 'Well, my name is Lawrence, as you know. Lawrence Green. Born just outside London, lived there most of my preadult life. Went to school in Oxfordshire, then on to university in London – the London School of Economics. Got myself a degree in politics and economics, got interested in technology, and stayed on to do a master's in business studies. And that's when I met your mother.'

I looked at her. 'You said he was a doctor,' I said accusingly.

'Did I?' she said rather coyly. 'Yes, you're right.' She turned to my father. 'You *were* a doctor, weren't you? Training to be one?'

He raised his eyebrows. 'I was planning to do a doctorate.'

'There, you see?' Mum said.

She placed some hot mugs of tea down on the table. Giles and Helen took theirs silently; they'd even scraped their chairs back a bit, evidently aware that this was a family thing, that they were here to play supporting roles only. My father winked at Mum; she offered him a faltering smile and joined us at the table.

'So you were at LSE. Did you two go out for long?' I asked. 'Were you serious?'

He met Mum's eyes again goofily. 'I was serious,' he said. Mum opened her mouth, then closed it.

'Then?' I prompted.

'Well, then you came along. Or, rather, the prospect of you.' He cleared his throat and took a slug of tea.

'And?' I persisted.

'And.' He sighed. Then he looked me in the eye. 'I'm not going to lie to you, Jess. It wasn't what I was expecting. It . . . it threw me, I don't mind saying. I wanted to do the right thing, of course I did. But we were having fun, your mother and me. It was never going to be—'

'You weren't serious,' I said flatly.

'Nothing was serious in those days,' he said, shaking his head. 'Nothing.'

I digested this. 'So?'

'So,' my father continued, putting down his mug, 'we did the best we could, I guess. But it wasn't exactly working. I had no money, your mother wasn't happy living in my tiny room, I couldn't get any work done . . . I mean, you were amazing. Truly, utterly amazing. You had the cutest smile, and you used to lie on this cushion looking up at me like . . . like a little angel. But it was hard. The sleeping. The—'

'The expectation that I would do everything single-handedly,' Mum chipped in. '*That* must have been hard for you.'

My father looked rather uncomfortable. 'Look, I'm the first to say I didn't do a great job. I wanted to. I just . . . I didn't know how to. Not back then.'

I looked at him carefully. 'You mean you did it again? You were better the second time?'

'Yeah,' he said quietly. 'I got married. Later. Much later. Had three children. And a dog.'

'A dog.' I nodded slowly. 'You got a dog.'

He grinned ruefully. 'I tell you what, if you think a baby's a pain in the arse, you try having a puppy. You can't put a nappy on a puppy. Can't put a puppy in a playpen. Well, you can try, but they just crap all over it. And the clothes aren't half as good. Jeez, I tell you, never again. N-E-V-E-R.'

I nodded, keen to cut him off. I didn't want to hear about his little domestic idyll, thank you very much. 'So. You had me; it wasn't working out. What happened next?'

'Sorry,' he said. 'You're right. I always jump around too much when I'm telling a story. Bad habit.'

He looked at me as though expecting me to say something, but I didn't. I waited.

'Right,' he said. 'Okay. Well, you know, we tried. We really did. But then one night your mother decided to take off.'

'I decided to look after the best interests of my child, you mean,' Mum said tersely.

'She left. Moved in with another guy,' my dad said, a sad expression on his face.

'And that's it? You didn't come looking for us?' I demanded.

'I tried, I guess. Kind of. But your mother made it clear that she was better off without me, that both of you were. She moved into some swanky apartment and got some other guy to pay for everything. I figured you were better off. To be honest, I was kind of relieved.'

I digested this for a few seconds. 'Relieved,' I said eventually. 'Well, thanks for the honesty.' I turned to Mum. 'The swanky apartment – that was the rich guy? The one you suckered in? Told him he was the father?'

Mum looked down at her tea. 'Darling, in times of need,

we do what we can. Sometimes we have to bend the truth slightly.'

'Bend it?' I asked incredulously. 'You did a 360-degree turn.'

'I thought we were talking about your father,' Mum said. 'Weren't we?'

'Hey, that's pretty much all there is to tell,' he said. 'A few months later I got offered a place to do my doctorate in the States and off I went. End of story.'

'End of story?' I looked at him carefully. 'I don't see how.'

'You don't?' He seemed a bit embarrassed. 'No, I guess you don't. Look, I'm not proud of skipping off like that, but I thought it was the right thing to do, you know?'

I shook my head. 'I didn't mean that. I meant why are you back now? Why aren't you still in America with your wife and children and dog? What, you were just surfing Facebook, saw Mum's photograph, and decided to ditch them all?'

'I, uh . . . Well, let's not get bogged down in detail, huh?' he said dismissively. 'The point is, I'm here now, and we're all going to have a great time getting to know one another again. What do you say, Jess?'

I looked at him for a moment. In my mind's eye I could already see us all as one big happy family; I could move back in with them and we could go to Disney World together and sit around playing board games and I could forget all about work, Max, and everything else.

'You're really my father?' I asked.

'I really am.'

'Wow,' I said. 'It's a lot to take in.'

'So you take it in. I'm going upstairs to make a call. You drink tea, talk with your friends, with your mother, and then we'll regroup. Huh? How does that sound?'

'Sounds good,' I said weakly, as he got up and left the kitchen. Giles patted my shoulder in a concerned but ineffective way, and I rounded on my mother as soon as Lawrence was out of earshot.

'My father?' I asked incredulously. 'He's my father? When were you planning to tell me that?'

'I was planning to tell you as soon as he got here,' Mum said crossly. 'Every time I tried, you said you were too busy to talk.'

'But . . . but . . .' I sputtered, 'I would have made time if you'd told me who he was.'

Mum sighed heavily. 'What am I going to do?'

'What do you mean?' I asked. 'Looks like you've got it all sorted.'

'But he thinks we're getting back together,' Mum said worriedly. 'He won't listen. I keep telling him that Chester's coming back.'

'You mean you don't want to get back together with him?' I asked uncertainly.

'Of course not!' Mum said. 'He turned up out of the blue, and I couldn't send him away. I'd given him my address only so he could send me some photographs. And when he turned up, I was flattered, of course. I was still cross with Chester, so I thought frankly it would serve him right. But now Lawrence won't leave. He keeps talking about being a happy family.'

I frowned. 'You don't want that?' I asked.

Mum shook her head, exasperated. 'I hardly know the man, darling. I haven't seen him for a very long time. And we went out for only about a year. Long enough for me to get pregnant, have you, and realize that he wasn't the right man for either of us.'

'But I saw you kissing him.'

'Kissing him? Darling, I haven't kissed him. Not at all. He's tried to kiss me, believe me, but I'm getting married to Chester soon. At least, I would be if I had a bit of time to plan the wedding. Having a houseguest is very time-consuming. Particularly one who thinks he isn't going anywhere.'

'So what are you going to do?' I asked.

'I hoped you might tell him to go home,' she said.

'Me?' I looked at her in horror. 'I can't do that!'

'Oh, but you can. You're so much better at that sort of thing than I am,' Mum implored me.

I looked at her levelly. 'I'm not telling anyone anything,' I said. 'This is your problem and you need to deal with it. I, on the other hand, have problems of my own.'

'You do?' Mum sounded unconvinced. 'Really?'

'Really,' I confirmed. 'I've got a trunk in the car and I need to hide it here.'

'Hide it?' Mum frowned. 'Hide it from whom?'

'From the Russian Mafia,' Helen said.

'The Russian Mafia? You're joking, of course,' Mum said, her eyes widening.

'Not really.' I shrugged. 'They're definitely Russian; we're not sure about the Mafia connection as of yet. But we need to put the trunk in the cellar just in case.'

'Oh, for goodness' sake,' Mum grumbled. 'Very well. You can put it in the cellar, but only if you promise to talk to your father afterward.'

'It's my cellar!' I protested.

'But I'm living here,' Mum pointed out.

'Oh, fine,' I sighed. 'I'll talk to him.'

'Good!' Mum smiled. 'Now, where is this trunk? In the car?'

I nodded and walked to the front door; as I opened it, the doorbell rang. And then my mouth fell open.

'Chester,' I gasped. 'What the hell are you doing here?'

Chapter 18

CHESTER LOOKED AT ME UNCERTAINLY. 'Not much of a welcome. Are you going to let me in? Is Esther at home?'

'I . . .' I stared at him, at a loss for words. 'I thought you were in the States.'

'I was.' He shrugged. 'Decided to come back early. Figured loose ends could stay loose for a bit longer. Esther was right – I didn't need to stay away that long. So, is she home?'

I gulped. 'You should have called.'

'I did.' Chester frowned. 'Your mother didn't pick up. Oh, but I got your message when I touched down at Heathrow. Something about the ethical audit not going so well?'

'Oh, yes,' I said, stepping out onto the doorstep with Chester. 'Yes, I need to talk to you about the audit. Maybe we could go for a walk?'

'Or maybe I could come in and see your mother,' Chester said firmly, pushing the door open. Mum appeared behind it.

'Chester! Darling!' she said, throwing herself at him and wrapping her arms around his neck. 'Oh, it's so lovely to see you.'

Chester grinned. 'Likewise. Now, this is more like the reception I was hoping for! Instead, I get Jess wanting to talk to me about the audit.' He rolled his eyes, and I shot a meaningful look at Mum.

'Ah, the audit,' she said immediately. 'Well, you must talk about it. You must.'

'No, we mustn't.' Chester wrinkled his brow. 'You always say I talk about work too much, and you're right. It hit me in New York. I was in this meeting – this really boring meeting – and I suddenly realized that I was never going to get that time back again. You can't replace it. Once it's gone . . . well, it's gone. And, frankly, I don't want any more of it wasted on business meetings. I'm going to get a new personal assistant, like you suggested. I'm going to get one who knows how to say no.'

Mum glowed with pleasure. 'Oh, darling, I'm so pleased. And you're so right.' There was a noise upstairs – footsteps. Lawrence's footsteps. Mum heard them, too – her face whitened visibly. 'But,' she said quickly, 'I still think you should talk to Jess. She's very worried. And she's my daughter.'

'So? I'm tired. I've just spent two hours in traffic after a long plane ride. What I want is to sit down and get a foot rub. With a glass of whiskey in my hand.'

'Or,' Mum said, urging him out of the house, 'a walk. With Jess.'

'With Helen,' I said quickly, mouthing 'trunk' to Mum, who nodded.

'With Helen,' she corrected herself. 'Fresh air – it'll do you a world of good, Chester.'

'Who the hell's Helen?' Chester asked, confused, as she appeared in the hall at the sound of her name. 'And I don't need fresh air.'

'After being on a plane? Of course you do,' Mum said firmly, manhandling Helen out onto the doorstep with Chester and me. 'They starve you of oxygen. All sorts of bugs circulating. And think of your heart. Sitting down all that time – you could have thrombosis. A clot could be wending its way around your body as we speak. No, Chester, it is of paramount importance that you go for a walk now. With Helen. Jessica's best friend. Her brides-maid, if you remember? You need to learn to notice things, Chester. If you're going to be a good stepfather, you need to bond with Jessica's friends, so off you go. Out of the house. Away from here. For an hour or so. If you don't, I shall be very cross.'

Helen forced a smile. 'Hi, Chester. I'm Helen. And I'd really love to go for a walk.'

Chester looked at her vaguely, then turned back to Mum. 'You'll be very cross?' he asked disbelievingly. 'I come back early from the States and you'll be very cross if I don't go out right away?'

'Extremely.' Mum nodded. 'I'll see you later. Good-bye, darling.'

'I'll . . . see you inside in a second, Mum,' I said, pulling the door shut. 'So, you guys, the village is that way, if you fancy that, or if you go the other way, you'll come to the river, which is really pretty.'

'The river or the village,' Chester muttered darkly. 'Either your mother's going mad or I am. Or both of us are. Or maybe it's you?' He peered at me, and I shrank back.

'No one's mad,' I said hesitantly. 'Mum's right – a walk will do you good. Clear the cobwebs away. And Helen's really nice. She works in television.'

'She works in television,' Chester repeated. 'Well, that makes sense. I feel as if I've arrived on the set of *The Twilight Zone*.'

'Then you'll have lots to talk about,' I said weakly. 'See you later!'

I watched as they disappeared down the drive, Chester

shaking his head in disbelief and Helen chattering away about . . . well, I didn't know what. Didn't care. The important thing was that they were gone.

I pushed the door open to find Mum and Giles waiting expectantly for me.

'Okay,' I said. 'We need to get rid of Lawrence. And we need to do something with the trunk.'

'That blasted trunk,' Mum sighed impatiently. 'You do complicate matters, darling. You really shouldn't have brought it down here.'

I raised an eyebrow. '*I* complicate matters? You're the one with the little love triangle going on, remember?'

'It is not a love triangle,' Mum said stiffly. 'He just turned up—'

'What's that about a love triangle?' Lawrence said, coming down the stairs. 'It's lies, all of it.' He winked at me. 'So, Jess, have you had some time to think? Are you ready to get to know your old man?'

'I . . .' I looked at him uncertainly. 'I am,' I said. 'But I just have to . . . talk to my friend first.'

I grabbed Giles, who looked poised to go somewhere but with no idea where. 'Get the trunk out of the car and into the house,' I whispered. 'Put it in the cellar – Mum will show you where that is.'

'Where are you going?' Giles asked, a look of alarm on his face.

'I'm going to take Dad out of the house,' I said, then realized I wasn't ready to use that word yet. 'Lawrence, I mean.' I turned back to Lawrence and smiled. 'You know, maybe you and I should take a walk. Get to know each other.'

'What a wonderful idea,' Mum said immediately, clapping her hands together. 'Yes, you go now.'

204

'Right now?' Lawrence asked uncertainly. 'It looks like it's going to rain.'

We all looked out the hallway window; sure enough, ominous dark-gray clouds were gathering overhead.

'No, it's not,' I said briskly. 'The clouds are always like that round here. Then they clear up again. It's nothing to worry about.'

'You're sure of that?' Lawrence asked, unconvinced.

'Absolutely,' I lied. 'Shall we?'

'Okay, then,' Lawrence said, grabbing a coat. I turned back to Mum and pulled her out of earshot.

'You pack up his stuff,' I told her. 'Erase all traces of him. Put his bag in my car – I'll drop him at the airport on my way back to London.'

'Oh, darling, thank you. Chester wouldn't understand, you see.'

'No, he wouldn't,' I agreed tersely. 'And show Giles where the cellar is – he's going to get the trunk out of the car.'

'Are we going, Jess?' my father called from the front door.

'Coming,' I said brightly, rushing over to him. 'Right,' I said, taking his arm and doing a quick mental calculation. Chester and Helen would almost certainly have headed toward the village, I decided; neither particularly liked the countryside, so a river was unlikely to hold much appeal. The village, on the other hand, had shops Helen loved and pubs that might entice Chester with the promise of whiskey. 'Let's head toward the river,' I said firmly. 'It's this way.'

'So,' I said, a few minutes later. We were walking down a country lane. On either side of us were perfect little cottages with lovely thatched roofs and people outside who wouldn't have looked at all out of place in an episode of *Marple*.

'So,' Lawrence parroted, looking around. 'It's nice here, huh? Nice little arrangement you've got.'

'Arrangement?' I frowned.

'House. Area. You know,' he said.

'Oh, I see. Well, yes,' I said, 'although I'm not sure I'm using it as Grace intended.'

'Grace?' he asked.

'A friend of mine. The one who left me the house.'

'Ah. Her.' Lawrence nodded. 'Why? What did she want you to do with it?'

'Live in it,' I said with a half-smile.

'And you don't because . . . ?'

I hesitated for a moment. 'Because of work,' I said. 'It's too far a commute into London.'

'It's not such a long way,' Lawrence said. 'What, an hour by car?'

'In good traffic.'

'So leave early.'

'It's not that easy,' I sighed.

There was a bench by the side of the road, and Lawrence walked toward it. 'You mind sitting?' he asked. 'Not that I don't love walking, but it's quite a view here, don't you think?'

I looked around – he was right. The bench was on a rise, and the road led downhill from there. In the distance was the river, which met the thunderous clouds seamlessly – it looked like a Turner painting. 'Sure,' I said, sitting down next to him.

'Why isn't it that easy?' he asked. 'Why on earth would you choose to live in London when you can live here?'

'Oh, lots of reasons,' I answered quickly. 'I mean, it's

too big for only Max and me. And the commute, like I said. And . . .' I frowned. There were other reasons; I just couldn't remember them. I tried to hear Max's voice, remember what he always said. 'Being in London is important if you're in advertising. And Max works long hours, so . . .'

'So he doesn't want to move?' Lawrence asked gently.

'He does want to,' I said. 'But . . . not now.'

'He's given you a time scale?'

I shook my head.

'Maybe when you have children?'

'Maybe,' I said quietly.

'And that'll be when, do you think? You've been married, what, a year, your mother said?'

'Yeah, about a year. And we'll have children, you know, when things settle down a bit. I mean, the recession doesn't help.'

Lawrence laughed. 'I'm sure it doesn't. But if everyone thought like that, no one would have had children in the whole of the 1970s. Or during the Great Depression. Most of the world wouldn't have them at all.'

'Yes, well, we'll get round to it. Eventually. Maybe,' I said, feeling less and less confident the more I spoke.

'Maybe?' he asked.

I sighed heavily. 'We had a fight. Max and I,' I said. 'So right now everything's kind of in the balance, you know?'

He laughed again. 'Oh, I know. If there's one thing I know about, it's fights.'

I frowned. 'You fought with your wife? A lot?'

'Of course,' he said. 'Everyone does. She'd pick fights with me, I'd pick fights with her, we'd bicker and complain and then forget all about it for a while. It's called marriage.'

'Really?' I asked uncertainly. 'That's normal?'

'That's good,' Lawrence said wryly, putting his arm around me. 'It's when you can't forget that you know things are bad.'

'Huh,' I said thoughtfully.

'Huh,' he agreed.

'So you're really my father,' I said, turning to look at him.

'I really am,' he said with a little shrug. 'You know, you turned out well. Considering that your grandmother brought you up. She was some witch.'

I grinned. 'She wasn't so bad. She meant well.'

'If you say so.'

We sat in silence for a while, watching the purple and gray clouds gather. And then I heard something, something that sounded remarkably like Chester's and Helen's voices coming down the road toward us. They mustn't see us, I thought frantically. We had to move. With my heartbeat thudding in my head, I grabbed my father's hand. 'You know what? I think we should walk again.'

'You do?' he asked uncertainly. 'But it's nice here, just sitting.'

'It'll be nicer walking,' I insisted, pulling him up. 'This way.' I started to drag him away from the bench, down toward the river.

'It's starting to rain,' he complained. 'Let's go back to the house, have a nice cup of tea.'

'But you haven't seen the river close-up,' I said, urging him to walk more quickly.

I could still hear Chester and Helen behind us; they were headed the same way we were. If we headed the other way, we'd pass them. That was unthinkable – Chester would want to know who I was with. The only thing keeping us hidden was the steep incline of the road; once it flattened out, we'd be clearly visible in front of them. I looked around frantically for a path, anything that would take us off the lane. And then I stopped still, because the loud sound I now heard reminded me a great deal of something I very much hoped it wasn't. I turned round to look up the hill; sure enough, in the background I could see a large black car headed our way.

It was a Hummer.

Gulping, I grabbed Lawrence's hand. 'You know what?' I asked frantically. 'Maybe you're right. Maybe we should go back to the house.'

'Okay, but isn't it that way?' he asked, frowning as I pulled him toward a hedgerow. 'Jess, I don't think there's any way through that . . . Oh . . . oh, okay, I see you're going to make a way. You know this coat I'm wearing was quite expensive, Jess . . .'

I barely listened as I forced my way through the brambles into what turned out to be a field. All I knew was that we had to get back to the house. The Russians had found me, and I needed somewhere to hide.

'Jess! Lawrence!' Mum had a smile fixed on her face when she opened the door twenty minutes later. 'You're back!'

'Yes,' I said, pushing past her. 'We need to get inside.'

'Rain,' Lawrence explained.

'Rain. Right,' I said, hurriedly closing the door behind him. Mum still had the frozen smile on her face; behind her, Giles was motioning frantically toward the sitting room.

'Chester,' he mouthed. 'In there.'

I gulped, then turned to my father. 'Okay,' I said brightly, 'let's have that tea. In the kitchen. Right now.'

'Sure,' he said easily. 'Let me just take off my coat and shoes. They're wet through from all the—'

'No need!' Mum trilled. 'And you'll need your coat in the

kitchen. No central heating. In fact, I might put my coat on now. You should, too, Jess.'

'Absolutely,' I said weakly. 'Come on, Dad. I'll race you there.'

He stopped and smiled. 'You just said "Dad."'

I stopped, too. 'You're right,' I said, biting my lip. 'I did.'

'I liked it.' He smiled, putting his hand on my shoulder and giving it a squeeze.

'I did, too,' I agreed.

'You'll like it even more in the kitchen,' Mum said forcefully; immediately, I snapped to and nodded, pulling Dad down the corridor and sitting down at the table with a sigh.

'Phew,' I said.

'Phew?' Dad asked, uncertain.

Our eyes met. 'Brew. I said brew. As in let's brew a cup of tea,' I managed to say. 'I'll put the kettle on.'

I got up and rushed to the counter, nearly falling over in the process. 'What the—' I looked down to see Ivana's trunk on the floor.

At that moment, Giles's head appeared around the door. 'You're probably wondering about the trunk,' he said.

I nodded frantically and he ran toward me. 'Your mother couldn't find the key to the cellar,' he whispered worriedly. 'So we thought it would be safe in here.'

'Safe?' I hissed. 'I just saw the Hummer on the road. That's why we're back so early. The Russian Mafia Hummer, Giles. The trunk isn't safe here, and we're not safe with it here, either.'

'The Hummer?' Giles's eyes widened with fear. 'They followed you here?'

I nodded uncomfortably. 'We have to move it,' I said decisively.

'But how? Chester's in the sitting room.'

We stared at each other for a few seconds. And then the doorbell rang.

'Oh God,' I whispered.

'Oh dear,' Giles whispered back. He was trembling. We both were.

'Go and see who it is,' I said anxiously. 'Don't let anyone open the door.'

'Right you are.' Giles nodded, took a deep breath, said what looked like a prayer, and dashed out of the room.

'He all right?' Dad asked curiously. 'What were you two whispering about?'

'Um . . . girl trouble. I mean . . . boy trouble,' I said, my voice faltering slightly. 'Nothing important.'

'If you say so.' Dad shrugged.

Giles reappeared, a strange look on his face. I beckoned him into the room. 'So?' I whispered. 'Was it them?'

He shook his head.

'Then who was it? What's the matter?'

He looked like he really needed to pee. Or had just been stung by some nettles in a very personal place.

'It's . . . it's . . .' he stammered.

'Oh, for goodness' sake,' I said impatiently, marching out of the room. 'I'll look for myself.' I strode up to the door and looked through the peephole. And then it was my turn to pull a face. Incredulously, I opened the door and the visitor stepped inside.

'Hugh Barter,' I said in utter disbelief. 'What the hell are you doing here?'

Chapter 19

'I GOT YOUR MESSAGE,' Hugh said, gazing around the hall-way in wonder. 'This is really your house?'

I nodded curtly. 'What, going to try to get that, too?' I asked, my eyes narrowing.

'What? No. No, I just . . . It's amazing. It's huge! And was that . . . I mean, did I see your friend Giles? Is he here?'

'Yes, he is, not that it's any of your business. Now tell me what you want and then go. I'm very busy,' I said.

'Who's that?' I heard Chester's voice from the sitting room. 'Was that someone at the door?'

Mum poked her head round the door, saw Hugh, and turned her gaze on me worriedly. 'What is . . . he doing here?'

'I don't know,' I said. 'I'm trying to find out.'

'What's who doing here?' Chester asked. I shook my head at Mum, mouthed at her to keep Chester occupied, then dragged Hugh toward the kitchen.

'No one,' I called back to him. 'Just a . . . delivery.'

'A what?' Hugh asked uncertainly. 'Was that Chester Rydall?'

'None of your business. Now . . . come in here.' I took him into the pantry, for no other reason than it seemed to be the only free room.

Hugh spun round. 'This is bigger than my kitchen,' he breathed. 'It's enormous. And it's just for storage.'

I looked around the shelves and shrugged. 'Yes, it is. Now tell me what you're doing here. I thought I made it perfectly clear in my message that I'm not being black-mailed anymore. You can do what you want and say what you want to whomever you want. You're not getting any more money out of me.'

'But that's the thing. I haven't blackmailed you,' Hugh said, a pained expression on his face.

I laughed dryly. 'Do you prefer the term "extortion"?'

'No!' Hugh said, shaking his head. 'Look, I needed some money. I ran out. And I don't know anyone else with any spare cash.'

'So you threatened to tell Max about us in return for a handout. Yes, I can totally see how that isn't blackmail,' I said sarcastically.

Hugh looked uncomfortable. 'Okay, I can see how that looked.'

'You can? How nice,' I said with a sigh. 'So you'll under-stand how much I want you out of my house, then?'

'Yes. Of course. But the thing is, what I mean to say is . . .' He trailed off, his eyes looking at something behind me. 'Who's that?'

I turned to see my father standing in the open doorway. 'Is this him?' he asked.

'Him?'

'The one Giles has just told me all about. Hugh Barter, was it?'

Hugh nodded and held out his hand. 'Very nice to meet you,' he said. 'And you are . . . ?'

'Jessica's father,' Dad said, drawing back his arm and, before I could do anything to stop him, punching Hugh right in the nose.

Hugh fell back onto the floor, clutching his face. 'Bastard!' he yelped. 'What the hell was that for?'

'For treating my daughter like your personal ATM,' Dad said, standing over him, a strange smile on his face. He looked at me with wide eyes. 'I haven't punched anyone since I was at school,' he said excitedly. 'I forgot how good it feels. Hurts, though. Look at my hand.'

He showed me his hand, which was shaking slightly.

'Sod your bloody hand,' Hugh said angrily from the floor. 'My nose is bleeding.'

It was, too – all over Hugh's shirt and the floor beneath him. He sat up, looking very sorry for himself.

'Jess?' I heard Chester's voice approaching and felt my heart stop briefly. 'Jess, where are you? I need to talk to you.'

'Who's that?' Dad asked. 'Who's here?'

'No one. You two stay here,' I ordered. 'Don't move. Don't you dare make a sound.'

'No one? That wasn't no one. That was Chester, wasn't it?'

'You know Chester?' Hugh asked.

'Not exactly,' Dad said. 'But I do want to meet him.'

'Not now,' I whispered urgently. 'If you want a relationship with me in the future, you will stay here and be quiet. Do you understand? You, too, Hugh.'

Hugh shrugged, Dad nodded, and I quietly stepped outside, closing the door of the pantry behind me.

'Chester!' I exclaimed, as he walked toward me. 'How was your walk?'

'Wet,' Chester said grimly. 'And bizarre. That friend of yours takes some getting used to, kept talking to me about reality television. She's on the phone to someone now telling them I've agreed to appear on *Private Banks Go Head to Head*. And I've done nothing of the sort.'

'That's Helen,' I said affectionately, leading him away from the pantry and wondering where my mother had got to. 'She's great, isn't she?'

'I'd prefer to reserve judgment, if it's all the same to you.'

'Of course. No problem at all. So, what can I do for you?'

'You can tell me what the hell's going on,' he said, taking my arm. 'And don't try any of your shenanigans. I'm not a fool, Jess. I know when something untoward is happening. And being sent for a walk with that crazy girl, then being shut in the sitting room with Esther and the crazy girl, suggests exactly that. I want you to tell me what is going on.'

'Going on?' I asked, my voice quivering slightly. 'I don't know what you—'

'Yes, you do,' Chester cut in firmly. 'What is it? Because if your mom is having second thoughts, I need to know. I won't be taken for an idiot, Jess.'

'No one thinks you're an idiot, Chester,' I said weakly. 'It's just that . . .' I thought frantically, trying to think of something, anything, to say that wouldn't devastate him and Mum.

'That what, Jess?' Chester asked, bearing down on me. 'Tell me now or, damn it, I'm leaving.'

'Okay,' I sighed. 'Look, Chester, what you have to understand is—'

The doorbell rang, and I looked up in alarm.

'Yes?' Chester pressed. 'What I have to understand is what?'

'Is . . .' I stared at the door worriedly. 'Is . . .' I looked at Chester imploringly. 'Chester, would you mind seeing who that is? Don't open the door – just look through the peephole.'

'Look through the peephole?' Chester asked uncertainly, and I nodded.

215

He sighed wearily and walked over to the door. 'It's a man,' he said.

'A man in black with sunglasses on?' I asked worriedly. 'What's he wearing?'

'A pretty cheap suit, far as I can see.' Chester shrugged. 'And there's a girl with him. Hey, I recognize her. Karen. No, Caroline. Your assistant.'

'Caroline?' I looked at him dubiously. 'Are you sure?'

'Hey, she's your assistant. You take a look,' Chester said impatiently. I ran to the door.

'It is Caroline,' I gasped. 'And Eric.'

'Eric? Who the hell's Eric?'

Giles, Helen, and my mother had all appeared in the hallway with worried expressions on their faces. 'Eric?' they asked in unison.

'Eric.' I nodded helplessly. This was the last thing I needed. I'd planned my whole conversation with Chester, the one where I'd tell him that I'd screwed up, that it wasn't Max's fault, that if there were any problems with the audit I took full responsibility. Having Eric show up out of the blue was so not part of the plan. 'Look, maybe you should all go back to the sitting room,' I said.

'Why?' Chester's eyes narrowed suspiciously. 'Who is this Eric?'

Biting my lip, I said, 'Chester, Eric is the auditor, and if he knows you're here it'll . . . well, it'll confuse client–auditor relations.'

'It will?' Chester asked. 'How?'

'Oh, Chester, just do as Jess says and let her get rid of him,' Mum said impatiently, and ushered everyone into the sitting room, leaving me to open the door.

*

216

'Jess,' Caroline breathed as she rushed through the door and gave me a hug. 'Eric told me about the interview. He's come to say sorry, haven't you, Eric?'

She looked at Eric pointedly; hanging his head, he walked in behind her.

'I am sorry,' he said. 'I didn't mean to make you cry.'

I stared at him. 'You came all this way to say that? How did you even know where I was?'

'I guessed,' Caroline said with a shrug. 'Eventually, I mean. We tried your apartment first and then the hospital. Actually, it was Max who said to come here. He gave us the address.'

'Max?' I felt my heart thud. 'You saw Max?'

'Yes,' Caroline said. 'Didn't we, Eric?'

Eric nodded sheepishly.

'How was he?' I asked nervously. 'Was he really angry with me?'

'Angry with you?' Caroline looked at me. 'No, not at all. He said to tell you something.'

'He did?' I asked apprehensively. 'What?'

Caroline frowned. 'Oh God, what was it? Eric, can you remember?'

Eric shook his head.

'Oh, come on. You must remember!'

Caroline closed her eyes. 'He said . . . he said . . .' Then she opened them again. 'I remember!' she said triumphantly.

'So what was it?' I asked, holding my breath.

'He said he'd tell you himself,' she said happily.

I sighed. 'Great. Thanks.'

'You're welcome!' Caroline beamed.

Eric was looking around the hallway, wide-eyed. 'This is your house?' he asked. 'It's got a coat of armor.'

'Yes, it does,' I said. 'So that's it? Is that what you came all the way down here for? To say you're sorry?'

Eric smiled. 'Actually,' he said nervously, 'I was hoping you'd do me a favor.'

'A favor? Seriously?' My eyebrows shot up into my forehead. 'What is it with people wanting favors today?'

Eric cleared his throat. 'The thing is, I . . .' He looked over at Caroline, who nodded in encouragement and mouthed something at him. 'The thing is, I didn't mean to be so harsh. I really need this job. And if you tell Chester Rydall I made you cry, and he tells Josh, then I'll be out of a job, and I need the money.'

I frowned. 'Josh will fire you if he finds out you made me cry? But surely he'll think you were just being thorough.'

Eric grimaced uncomfortably. 'Josh says the audit should be a pleasurable experience for all concerned. Making people cry doesn't quite fit with that.'

I thought for a moment. 'Okay, but I didn't cry because of you. It was more about my own issues,' I said. 'However, I wouldn't say you made the audit pleasurable for me. I mean, you've been quite horrible.'

It felt great being so honest. Eric looked slightly green.

'I know,' he said miserably. 'I didn't mean to. I just . . . got a bit carried away with the character.'

'With the character?' I looked at him closely. 'What character?'

'The auditor character.' Eric's voice changed suddenly, becoming deeper, more resonant, with a slight Midlands accent. 'Look,' he said heavily, 'the truth is, I was a car salesman until a few weeks ago.'

'A car salesman?' I stared at him suspiciously. 'What are you talking about?'

'It's true.' He shrugged helplessly. 'I was making good

money, too. I had this great character, Eric the salesman. I had a cheap shiny suit and referred to women as "ladies." But no one's buying cars at the moment, so I got laid off; the next day I saw this ad for ethical auditors, and I thought, you know, what the hell?'

I held up my hand. 'Wait,' I ordered. 'Let me get this straight. You were a car salesman? You had no auditing experience whatsoever?'

'None,' Eric said with a sigh. 'I met this guy Josh who said he had this great way of making money. He put me on a two-day training course, and you were my first assignment. I thought it would be good to be tough, you know? I thought it would be more authentic. I'm an actor, you see? That's my real vocation. The other jobs only pay for acting classes and for food and rent. My ethical auditor was one of my best characters, I thought. I believed in him. It just felt right, him being an arsehole, you know?'

I didn't say anything for a while. Then my eyes narrowed. 'You have got to be kidding me. Caroline, he's kidding me, right?'

'No,' she said, looking at me awkwardly. 'He only told me today. He's really nice actually, Jess.'

'And I'm going to tweak the character. You know, make him more of a mellow guy,' Eric said seriously. 'Still on top of things but less aggressive. I thought maybe a bit like Columbo. The detective?'

'Columbo.' I nodded, my brain spinning. 'Columbo sounds like a good way to go.'

'The voice should stay, though, right?' he asked. 'The whole nasal thing. You believed I was an auditor with that voice, didn't you?'

'I guess,' I said.

Eric sighed in relief. 'Great. Okay, look, I've got lots to

219

work with here. I know I can make this work. So you won't tell Chester Rydall? Or Josh? You'll keep it between us?'

'Won't tell Chester Rydall what?' Chester asked, appearing suddenly. Eric's eyes widened in alarm.

'Chester,' I said weakly. 'You're not meant to be here. You're meant to be—'

'Um, Jess?' Giles said, suddenly appearing at my side and lightly touching my arm.

'Not now, Giles,' I said quickly.

'No, you have to listen,' he whispered, tugging at my arm insistently. 'It's your father . . . Lawrence . . . Well, he doesn't want to be in the pantry anymore. He wants to talk to your mum. He's getting a bit antsy so I had to lock the door.'

'Oh God,' I said.

Giles nodded. 'Just thought you should know. And Hugh's not very happy, either. He says he needs to go to the hospital or else he'll need plastic surgery on his nose. I told him that he'd be fine – he's got amazing bone structure. In a way, a broken nose could make him even more handsome – you know, in a . . .' He caught my expression and trailed off. 'Not handsome,' he corrected himself. 'Not handsome at all. Only in the sense that he's not ugly, that's all . . .'

'What is going on around here?' Chester asked. 'Why does everyone keep whispering and sending me off places?'

'Nothing! We're whispering because . . .' I said, racking my brain for a plausible reason. And then it came to me. 'Because we're planning a surprise party!'

'A party? Who for?' Chester frowned.

'You, of course,' I said immediately. 'It's a welcome-home party!'

Chester's frown deepened. 'But you didn't know when I

was coming back. How could you have been planning a party for today?'

'Because . . .' I said, looking at Mum desperately.

'We didn't plan it for today, of course,' Mum said, rolling her eyes. 'Then you turned up and everything changed.'

Chester's eyes lit up. 'So that's why you sent me out on a long stupid walk?'

'That sounds like a good reason, yes,' I said happily. 'And it's why I need you to go back to the sitting room now. We don't want you seeing any more party guests, do we?'

'Eric and Caroline are party guests?' Chester asked, confused again. 'I thought you were surprised when you saw them.'

'Yes,' I said, thinking on my feet. 'But it's a surprise party, remember? Full of surprises. Lots and lots of surprises.'

'I guess,' Chester said uncertainly.

'So we're invited to the party?' Caroline asked excitedly. 'Really? Oh, that's so nice of you. Eric, didn't I tell you how lovely Jess is?'

'Okay, then.' I clapped my hands together. 'That's all set, then. Chester, you go to the sitting room and . . . Mum, I need to talk to you. And Helen. And Giles.'

'Guess I'll go on my own,' Chester said. 'Unless you two would care to join me?'

Eric immediately resumed his nasal twang. 'Yes, sir. I'd be delighted, sir. And I'm very sorry about the mix-up. I really am.'

'A party?' Mum said when she'd finally closed the door on them all. 'We're having a party now?'

'Don't use that tone of voice with me,' I said indignantly, my mind whirring. 'Dad is in the pantry getting agitated, and Hugh Barter has a bloody nose—'

221

Mum's eyes widened. 'Did you find out why he's here?'

'Long story,' I sighed. 'The important thing is that we get rid of Dad and hide the trunk, because the Russians are here.'

'Where?' Mum asked worriedly, looking around as though they might pop out from behind the curtains.

'I saw their Hummer on the road,' I said ominously.

'Well, we shouldn't hide the trunk in the house, then,' Mum said briskly. 'If they know you're here, they'll search the house. The best thing is if you take the trunk with Lawrence in your car and dispose of it.'

'How?' I asked, wrinkling my nose.

'Chuck it in the river for all I care,' Mum said firmly. 'Just get rid of it. And Lawrence.'

'Fine,' I sighed. 'Hel, Giles, would you help me get the trunk into the car? Then we need to figure out how we're going to convince Dad to leave.'

'Tell him *you* need a kidney?' Helen suggested archly.

'Take him sightseeing?' Giles recommended. 'He's been in America for years, hasn't he? He's effectively a tourist. We could take him to the Tower of London.'

'And lock him up in there,' Mum said.

I shook my head crossly. 'That's my father you're talking about,' I said. 'Okay, well, we'll think of something. So, trunk?'

'Trunk,' Giles and Helen agreed.

I ran to the door and opened it slightly – there were two men standing there. Immediately I shut it again and turned round, my eyes wide with fear.

'What?' Mum whispered anxiously. 'What is it now?'

'It's them,' I gasped. 'They've found me.'

'Who?' Helen asked, drawing back the curtains on the window next to the front door to take a little peek.

'Oh shit,' she said.

'Who is it?' Mum asked, her voice agitated. 'I can't see.'

'It's them,' I said desperately. 'It's the Russians.'

Chapter 20

❀

'WHAT DO WE DO? They saw me. They know someone's here.'
I looked from Giles to Mum to Helen. I couldn't breathe –
panic was rising up my throat.

'I think the important thing is to stay calm,' Helen said,
seeming anything but. 'You think they followed us?'

I shook my head. 'If they'd followed us, they'd have been
here at the same time as us. Which means . . .' My forehead
creased with worry. 'They got this address from somewhere.
They're going to find me wherever I go.'

'Like the Terminator,' Helen said seriously as the doorbell
rang.

I shot her an agitated look. 'Hide,' I mouthed, and we
all drew back from the window. 'What the hell is in the
trunk, anyway?' I wailed. 'Why did Ivana have to give it to
me?'

'Because she didn't relish having these men following
her around, I should think,' Mum whispered crossly as the
doorbell rang again. 'I'm going to call the police. It's the
only sensible thing to do.'

I sighed. Ivana hadn't returned any of my calls – what
else were we supposed to do? 'Okay, call them,' I said.

Mum nodded brusquely, and we all ran down the hallway to the telephone outside the kitchen. She picked up the
phone book and started to flick through it.

'Call "999,"' Giles said.

224

'That's for an emergency,' Mum said. 'We should call the local police station.'

'But this is an emergency,' I said. 'They're right outside. They've probably got guns.'

'Yes,' Mum said, 'but the local police are closer and will be able to respond more quickly.'

'No,' Helen added, shaking her head. 'They've all got radios. If you call 999, they'll get in touch with the nearest patrol car.'

Mum considered this for a moment, then sighed. 'Very well, I'll dial 999.' She dialed, then waited a couple of seconds. 'Hello?' She looked at us meaningfully. 'Police. I would like the police, please.'

'Esther?' A voice came from the pantry. 'Esther? Will you open this door? That crazy friend of Jess's has locked us in here. Esther? Can you hear me? Open this door. Otherwise I'm going to break it down.'

Mum grimaced, then shook her head. 'He'll never do it,' she said. 'The door's far too strong. He's not the athletic type at all.'

'I heard that,' Dad muttered from inside the pantry.

Mum chose to ignore him. 'Oh, hello? I'm terribly sorry about that. Yes, I want to report a—'

'Esther? Jess?' It was Chester's voice. We turned round desperately. 'There are two people at the door who say they need to talk with you urgently.'

'You . . . you opened the door?' I gasped.

'That's usually what you do when someone knocks, isn't it?'

This was it. I was going to die. We all were. Horribly. We'd be in the newspapers. Max would read about it . . . 'So they're . . . in the house?' I managed to say. I felt like collapsing on the floor.

'Yes,' Chester said slowly, 'they are in the house. Am I not making sense? And what the hell is that banging?'

'Banging?' I faltered. 'Oh, it's . . . it's—'

'It's part of the surprise,' Helen said. 'It's for the party.'

'Yes,' Mum added. 'Chester, please go back to the sitting room. You're really going to ruin everything. If you haven't already . . .' I felt her hand grip mine, and I squeezed it. She put the telephone receiver down, then looked at me. 'Come on, Jess,' she said stoically. 'Let's go and see what they want.'

'They want the trunk,' Helen said. 'Just give it to them.'

'What trunk?' Chester asked.

'That trunk,' Giles said, helpfully pointing to Ivana's trunk, which was still on the kitchen floor.

I took a deep breath. 'Okay,' I whispered. 'I'm ready.'

Reluctantly, I started to walk toward the front door. I felt like John Wayne, or like Harry Potter facing Voldemort. I would be brave, I told myself. I would look them in the eye and tell them that no one else here had anything to do with the trunk, that I alone was responsible, that . . .

I stopped uncertainly. There were two people in the hallway, but they weren't the Mafia men. One had gold teeth and was holding a baby, for a start.

'Ivana?' I asked incredulously. 'Sean?'

Sean looked at me grimly. 'Is it here?' he asked. 'Did she give it to you?'

'Did she give what to me?' I asked weakly. 'Did you see the men who were here a second ago?'

Sean shook his head. 'I didn't see anyone. Just tell me yes or no, Jess. Is the trunk here?'

Ivana was glaring at me, her eyes flashing. She was shaking her head only enough for me to see. My face crumpled in confusion. 'I . . . I . . .' I said uncertainly. 'I . . .'

226

'Yes, the trunk is here,' Mum said, stepping forward. 'As are the two Russian Mafia men who have been chasing my daughter around ever since you gave it to her. I think you owe us an explanation, Ivana, and an apology.'

'Russian Mafia?' Sean looked at Ivana, bewildered. 'You've got your clients following her, too?'

Ivana shook her head. 'Of course not,' she said irritably. 'I no know vat she saying. I give trunk. I think she hide for me. I no realize she no can kip secret.' She folded her arms and shot a severe look in my direction.

'I *can* keep a secret,' I said, outraged, as a huge crash made everyone jump. I carried on regardless. I was beyond fear now, beyond normal reactions to anything. 'I kept your trunk hidden for you. But two men in a Hummer have been following me around. They're everywhere I go. And they're here now. So whatever's in that trunk, I'd get it a long way away from here if I were you. Because they'll be back any minute.'

I realized that no one – not even Ivana – was listening to me; they were all staring at something behind me. I turned slowly to see my father and Hugh, their clothes covered in dust.

'Not athletic,' Dad said with a snort. 'I'll show you who's not athletic.'

'You're *not* athletic,' Hugh said irritably. 'I broke the door down; you just barked orders. Fat lot of use you were.'

'Someone had to devise the strategy and implement it,' Dad said indignantly. 'Who are you?'

He was looking at Ivana and Sean, who were looking right back at him.

'More to the point,' Chester said, staring at Dad, 'who are *you*?' Then Chester turned to me. 'And what the hell is

Hugh Barter doing here? Is he invited to my surprise party, too?'

'Um, yes,' I said falteringly. 'Yes, he is.'

'You invited the guy who screwed my company over to my surprise welcome-home party?' Chester asked incredulously. 'The guy who tried to ruin Milton Advertising and leaked my corporate secrets to *Advertising Weekly*?'

Hugh cleared his throat. 'About that,' he said. 'I wanted to apologize. You know, set the record straight. I accept that there were misunderstandings, and I regret—'

'You,' Ivana cut in, looking at Hugh, her eyes hostile. 'I heff seen you before.'

'No,' Hugh said, shaking his head thoughtfully. 'No, I don't think so.'

'Yes,' she said. 'I see you in bar. I see you in photograph. You are man kiss Jessica. You are man bleckmail my friend.'

'Oh, for the love of God, I didn't blackmail her,' Hugh said, rolling his eyes. 'You lot are so melodramatic. I just begged a few favors, that's all, and . . .' He trailed off as Ivana stalked toward him, slowly, deliberately. 'I'm sorry,' he stammered as she approached him. 'I didn't mean to . . . I really didn't . . . Ow. Fuck. Damn it.' With one fell swoop, Ivana had floored him.

'Who is this girl?' Chester asked, looking at her in surprise. 'She's amazing.'

'My bloody nose,' Hugh moaned. 'My poor bloody nose.'

'Next time will be more than nose that hurts,' Ivana said darkly.

'Ivana,' I said seriously, 'I think you'd better hide. Those men will be back soon.'

'Which men?' she asked.

'The men in the Hummer,' I said. 'The Russian men. The . . . you know, the Mafia.'

'Mefia?' Ivana's face creased in confusion. 'I no know why you talk Mefia. Why Mefia here? You liv message, message about men in Hummer. I no know vat you are minning.'

I sighed. 'Ivana, what's in the trunk?'

'You don't know?' Sean asked, stepping forward.

'No, I don't know,' I said tentatively.

'But I think it's time we all found out,' Mum added.

'They're right,' Sean said firmly. 'So, Ivana, are you going to show us?'

Ivana looked away angrily. 'I no see trunk, anyway.'

'It's in the kitchen,' Giles said, with an awkward smile. 'I can get it, if you want.'

Sean nodded and went to help; Ivana was looking in the opposite direction with her nose in the air, as though trying to pretend that the rest of us didn't exist.

We all waited in silence as Giles and Sean heaved the trunk down the corridor and deposited it in front of Ivana. Sean looked down at it angrily. 'You just had to keep it, didn't you,' he said, shaking his head. 'You couldn't give it up.'

'Why should I?' spat Ivana. 'You no give up your work because you are father.'

'I don't work as an escort,' Sean said levelly, as Ivana leaned down to open the trunk. We all watched in silence as she took out a key, opened the padlock, and lifted the lid.

I shrank back, not sure what to expect. And then I frowned. It wasn't drugs. Or dead bodies. Or even cash. It was . . .

'Fluffy handcuffs?' Helen said incredulously. She squatted down next to Ivana and started to pull things out. 'Metal chains? Leather corsets? Are you kidding us?'

'Is my work,' Ivana said with a shrug, then stared at Sean

icily. 'He say I nid get rid of it. I no vant to. So I give to Jessica to hide for me.'

'You lied to me,' Sean said angrily. 'You said you'd thrown it away.'

'I said,' Ivana corrected him, 'that it no here anymore. I no lie.'

'Let me get this straight,' I cut in. 'This trunk is just your work stuff? I was only hiding it from Sean? And that's why you hung up on me and refused to talk to Helen or me about it on the phone?'

Ivana nodded. 'I tell you no spik on phone, no call me. But you liv message. Sean hear message. And now he know trunk not thrown away.'

Helen and I looked at each other. 'So . . . who are the men in the Hummer?' she asked nervously.

'Men in a Hummer? What men in a Hummer?' Dad said suddenly.

'Oh, keep up,' Helen groaned. 'Two men have been following Jessica around in a Hummer. Men with a funny accent, wearing shades and black suits.'

'A Russian accent,' I added.

'Maybe Russian.' Helen shrugged.

'You said it was definitely Russian.'

'I know,' Helen said defensively, 'and it probably is. Or it could have been South American. One or the other.'

'What?' My face creased in confusion. 'But they're not alike at all. Which one was it?'

'I don't know.' Helen pouted. 'Does it really matter?'

'Of course it matters,' I said incredulously. 'If they're not Russian, then they're not going to be the Russian Mafia, are they?'

'Well, then, they're the South American Mafia,' Helen argued.

'Is there even such a thing?' I sighed.

'I don't know and I don't care,' Sean said firmly. 'All I know is that this trunk is going in the skip.'

'Or the river,' Mum suggested. 'That's where we were going to put it.' She caught my expression and corrected, 'If the Mafia came. Only if they threatened our lives.'

'Trunk is not going in river or in skip,' Ivana said flatly. 'Is my trunk. Is my things.'

'Things that belong to a previous life,' Sean corrected her. 'You're a mother now. You can't go out working all hours with dodgy men.'

Ivana turned on him. 'Escort is vat I do. Strip is vat I do. I do well. I mek lots money. You know this about me. I vant work. I no like asking for money. I no like.'

'So get a job,' Sean said with a sigh. 'Just not . . . this.' He picked up a leather thong and let it fall sadly back into the trunk.

Ivana bit her lip. 'Vat else I do?' she asked, her voice rather smaller. 'Vat else I *can* do?'

'You can work for me,' Chester said, stepping forward.

Ivana looked at him dubiously. 'You merry Jess mother. I no tek client if friends or femily.'

'Not as a client,' said Chester patiently. 'I run a bank. I could use someone like you as my personal assistant.'

'Personal assistant?' Sean asked suspiciously. 'Just how personal are we talking?'

'Not that personal,' Chester assured him. 'I need an assistant who's a bit of a rottweiler. Guard my door. Stop my diary from getting filled with unnecessary meetings.'

'Rrrilly?' Ivana looked at him uncertainly. 'Me? Personal assistant?'

Chester nodded. 'If you're interested.'

Ivana considered for a moment, then shrugged. 'I think

231

yes,' she said. 'I think I em very good personal assistant.' She folded her arms. 'I nid flexible hours for look after bebe, and I no wear suit – I no like.'

'Okay,' Chester said. 'No suits and flexible hours. Anything else?'

'No,' Ivana said, her mouth breaking into a huge smile that revealed her two gold teeth. 'No, I think this is good. I think mebe is good thing Jess call about trunk.'

'Well, that's great.' Chester smiled back, then turned to Mum. 'There's just one more thing.'

'Yes?' she asked happily. 'What is it, darling?'

'That man,' Chester said, looking around. 'The one who was here a minute ago.'

Mum looked around, as did I, and then we looked at each other uncertainly. Dad had vanished.

'Which man, Chester?' Mum said quickly. 'I don't know who you're talking about.'

'The man,' Chester said deliberately, 'who was in the pantry with Hugh. The one who developed the strategy for breaking the door down.'

'He didn't develop any strategy,' said Hugh, still clutching his bloody nose. 'He just stood there shouting orders.'

'Ah, so I have someone who agrees that he exists. Or existed,' Chester said, raising his eyebrows. 'Now, Esther, perhaps you'd care to tell me who he is and what he was doing locked in there in the first place? And don't tell me he was another guest at my surprise party. Frankly, I'm not convinced that this party isn't just an elaborate cover-up for something else.'

'A cover-up?' Mum looked at him with a hurt expression on her face. 'Darling, how can you even suggest such a thing?'

Chester sighed. 'Okay, fine, the party's genuine. But you still haven't answered my question.'

'No,' Mum said with a sigh. 'No, Chester, I haven't. And I must. I really must. The fact of the matter is, that man, Lawrence, well, he's—'

'In a great deal of trouble,' a voice said from behind her. We all turned to look and my nails dug into my palms. It was them. It was the Russians. Or South Americans. And they were holding Dad by the arms.

'I'm sorry,' Dad said.

'You're sorry?' Mum said uncertainly. 'About what? Where have you been? Who are these men? Why are they holding you like that?'

'And let's not forget,' Chester added, 'what were you doing in this house in the first place?'

Chapter 21

⚬‿⚬

'YOUR HUSBAND IS A VERY naughty boy,' one of the men said.

'Husband?' Chester turned to Mum. 'Husband?'

'He's not my husband,' Mum said impatiently.

'Husband-to-be,' Lawrence said with a hopeful smile.

'Absolutely not,' Mum said firmly, leaving Dad with a slightly wounded expression.

I eyed one of the men with the sunglasses and then the other. Something wasn't adding up. And then suddenly I realized what it was.

I looked at Helen. 'Funny, these guys don't seem to have Russian accents. Or South American accents,' I said.

'Russian accents? What are you going on about?' one of the men said.

'They're Londoners.' I folded my arms and looked at Helen expectantly.

She smiled weakly. 'So they are,' she said, clamping her teeth together. 'I . . . must have been mistaken.'

'You mistook a London accent for a Russian one? Or South American?' I deadpanned.

Helen cleared her throat. 'Fine, so maybe I didn't talk to them.'

I stared at her, and she went red. 'They didn't actually help with my stuff at all. But someone else did, and when I looked up, they'd gone. I'm sorry – but you asked and I kind of got carried away.'

234

'I can't believe you,' I said, rolling my eyes. 'I thought the Russian Mafia were on my tail. You said they sounded really dangerous.'

'I know,' Helen faltered. 'But I think we're missing the big picture here, aren't we? They're holding your father. Not you.'

She had a point.

'Your father?' Chester asked. 'I'm sorry, did you just call this man Jessica's father?'

'Keep up, Chester,' Helen said, with a little smile that he didn't return.

'So *this* is the big secret? This is the big surprise?' he asked Mum.

She hesitated, then answered. 'Yes, Chester, but before you jump to any conclusions, before you get angry—'

'Yes?' Chester demanded. 'Before that what?'

'Well, I want you to know that I didn't invite him here. He just turned up. Out of the blue. And I couldn't turn him away. He'd come all the way from America.'

'America?' one of the not-Russian-Mafia men asked, grinning broadly. 'Is that what he told you?'

'Yes,' Mum said, frowning. 'New England, wasn't it, Lawrence?'

Dad looked at her uncomfortably. 'Actually, Esther, I might have exaggerated a little.'

'How can you exaggerate where you live?' Chester said evenly. 'You either live somewhere or you don't. It's not a matter of degree.'

Dad cleared his throat and shot Chester a look that wasn't exactly friendly. 'Fine,' he said tightly. 'So I didn't come from America.'

'Then where did you come from?' Mum asked, her eyes wide.

'Epping Forest,' the other not-Russian-Mafia man inter-jected. 'He disappeared, didn't you, Lawrence? Thought maybe we wouldn't find you. But we don't like our debtors vanishing into thin air.'

'But you've been following me,' I said, frowning. 'I saw you.'

He shrugged. 'We thought you might lead us to him, and we were right. Didn't know he had a daughter, to be honest, but we found your name written down when we searched his house. Wasn't too hard tracking you down.'

'Damn,' Dad said irritably.

The man smiled. 'Yes, but good for us. So, Lawrence, got our money, have you?'

Dad looked down. 'No. I . . .' He looked at me hopefully. 'Unless you . . . I don't suppose—'

'*That's* why you came,' I said, the truth suddenly so blindingly obvious it hurt. 'You didn't come to make us a happy family. You came to get money out of me.'

'No,' Dad said. 'I didn't know about your money. Not until Esther told me.'

'You bastard!' Mum launched herself at him, battering him with her fists. 'You utter bastard. You told me you were madly in love with me.'

'I thought I was,' Dad said sheepishly. 'Thought I could be, anyway. You know. I just needed a new start. Needed to get away. And then I saw you on Facebook, and it felt kind of serendipitous. Like it was meant to be.'

'And to think I felt sorry for you,' Mum said, outraged. 'All this time I've been trying to get rid of you without hurting your feelings, when you just saw me as an escape route. Me and Jess.'

'You've been trying to get rid of him?' Chester asked hopefully.

236

'Of course,' Mum said angrily, rounding on Lawrence. 'Oh, I could kill you.'

'Don't worry, we're going to do that for you if he doesn't have the money,' one of the men said, smiling blankly. 'So, come on, Lawrence, are you going to cough it up? Or is anyone here?'

My dad looked at me beseechingly. 'Jess, I'm sorry. I'm a terrible father, always have been. But help me out? It's only twenty thousand. I'll never ask you again. But you heard them – they'll kill me if I don't pay them. You've got the money. Help out your old man? Please?'

I bit my lip. 'I can't,' I said quietly.

'Yes, you can,' he said desperately. 'I'm not a good person, Jess. Never have been. I went to the States, got thrown off course, came back here, and never even tried to find you. I know I'm no good. You're better off without me. But don't let me die. Not like this. I'll pay you back. Somehow. Please? Please?' He was trembling, and it made my stomach lurch.

'No, you don't understand,' I said unhappily. 'I want to. I mean, you are a terrible person, but you're still my father. And you punched Hugh. I'd give you twenty grand for that alone.'

'I only did what he's doing!' Hugh exclaimed. 'I hope the irony isn't lost on you.'

'He's just asking for money, not blackmailing me,' I said tightly, then turned back to Dad. 'The thing is, Dad, I really can't. I don't have the money anymore.'

'What do you mean, you don't have the money anymore?'

'I gave it all away.'

There was a shocked silence. 'You gave it away?' Helen asked slowly. 'To whom, may I ask?'

I cleared my throat. 'To a soup kitchen. Resource center, actually. They're going to buy new premises.'

'You gave it all away to a soup kitchen?' Mum asked.

'Like, *all* of it?' Helen gasped. 'To a bloody soup kitchen?'

'All of it.' I nodded. 'And it's a resource center.'

Helen shook her head. 'You're obviously deranged. Look, don't worry. When we're back in London, we'll go and explain that you're having a meltdown and you didn't know what you were doing. They'll have to give it back. Trust me.'

'But I don't want it back,' I said quietly. 'I never really wanted it in the first place.'

'Didn't want it?' Helen snorted. 'You went through that whole thing with Anthony Milton because you didn't want to inherit four million pounds?'

'I wanted to save the house from developers,' I said. 'The money's been a burden ever since I got it. It's the reason Hugh blackmailed me; it's the reason Max feels he can't talk to me about the business. And it's just been sitting there making me feel guilty because I'm not doing anything with it. So now I am. I've given it to people who actually need it. And now I'm free.'

Helen looked at me indignantly. 'I don't believe this,' she said. 'You ask my advice on everything but then go and give away four million pounds. When did you get that crazy idea in your head? Why didn't you tell me? Why didn't you at least give a bit of it to me?'

'I only decided when I was in my interview with Eric today,' I said wearily. It had only been that morning but it felt ages ago. 'I stopped off there before coming down here. It felt like the right thing to do. It still does.'

'It felt like the right thing to do,' Helen said lightly. 'Oh, well, that's okay, then.'

'It . . . really?' Mum asked, looking dumbfounded. 'It really felt like the right thing to do, to give away all that money?'

I found myself smiling. 'It did. It felt like a huge weight was lifted from my shoulders. I'm me again now – I'm not me with four million pounds in the bank, I'm just me. I can do what I want, be who I want.'

'No,' Mum said, frowning. 'With four million pounds you can do what you want; now you can't do anything. You had all that opportunity and you've . . . wasted it. I can't believe it, darling. I'm sorry, but I just can't believe it.'

'I haven't wasted it,' I said stiffly. 'Having it sitting in the bank was wasting it. And I still have opportunities. But I have to make them for myself instead of buying them. You know, ever since I got the money I've been a bit lost. Now I know who I am again. I've got my drive back.'

Helen let out a long breath. 'Well, if it's really what you want to do . . . You're sure you didn't keep a bit back? A few hundred thousand?'

'Maybe twenty grand?' Dad asked hopefully.

'Nothing.' I shook my head. 'Not a penny.'

'Well, that's not great news for you, is it, Lawrence?' one of the not-Russian-Mafia men said. 'Seems as if you're coming with us.'

Dad looked at them with terror in his eyes. 'Give me a bit longer,' he begged. 'A few weeks. A month, tops. I'll come up with the money.'

'No, Lawrence,' the man said, shaking his head slowly. 'You'll only run away again. You've demonstrated that you are an unreliable debtor. And you know what happens to them. We've got to send a message that this kind of behavior can't be tolerated.'

'Wait,' Chester said. 'Twenty grand, you say?'

'To be precise, £20,201.'

Chester sighed. 'I'll give you your money.'

Dad's eyes lit up. 'You will? Really?'

'If you promise to leave my future wife alone.'

Dad nodded immediately. 'No problem. None at all. She's not really my type, anyway. Never was. Too high-strung, to be honest.' He caught Chester's eye and blanched. 'Not that she's not cracking,' he said quickly. 'A real catch. Lovely woman. Mother of my child, you know—'

'Get out of here,' Chester said in a low voice. 'I'll settle up with these gentlemen. And Esther will send your things on to you.'

'Right you are,' Dad said gratefully, then looked at me. 'I'll be in touch. If I may?' he asked. 'It's been a pleasure. An honor.'

'Yeah,' I said quietly. 'Do get in touch. I'd like that.'

He walked to the front door, opened it, then turned back to me. 'One other thing,' he said. 'Don't leave this place empty when your mum moves out. This house needs a family, like that woman Grace said. You should move here, Jess. It suits you. Sort things out with that husband of yours. You can't let fights get in the way of your future, however serious they are.'

'I couldn't agree more,' a voice said, and I looked up, frozen on the spot.

'Max?' I said tentatively. 'Was that Max?'

'It was,' Max said, hobbling in on crutches through the front door. He glanced around with a confused expression on his face, then looked back at me. 'I came to say I'm sorry,' he said seriously.

'Sorry?' I asked.

'For being an arse.' He hung his head.

'You weren't an arse,' I said, incredulously. I wouldn't believe he was here – wouldn't believe this was all actually happening. 'I was. I'm so sorry, Max. I was trying so hard to be the perfect wife, and the more I tried, the more I realized that I wasn't, that I couldn't be, that I was never going to be perfect.'

'But you are perfect,' Max said, looking bewildered.

'No, I'm not,' I said, sniffing. 'I'm not good, I'm not caring, I'm not honest, and I'm not . . . At least I didn't think I was . . . I mean, I'm not sure really, but . . .'

'But what, Jess?' Max frowned. 'What aren't you?'

'Loved,' I said in a small voice.

'Well, that just shows how little you know,' he said, his voice quivering with emotion. 'Because you are totally loved. Totally and utterly. And you are caring. Caroline told me about what's been going on at work and that you kept it from me because you cared. And I got annoyed because you didn't bring muffins? I'm an idiot, Jess. I was in pain, I was cranky, I was feeling insecure, and what I said was unforgivable.'

'No.' I shook my head. 'I was the one who was unforgivable. I was jealous of Emily, when all she was doing was looking after you. Which is what I should have been doing.'

'No,' Max said. 'I asked you to run the business, and you did that. And Emily . . .' He looked at me awkwardly. 'Well, as it turns out . . .'

He pulled a strange face, and I frowned. 'What? As it turns out what?'

He grimaced. 'She tried to kiss me,' he said sheepishly. 'She said she'd felt some . . . I don't know . . . connection or something.'

'She what?' I felt my entire body bristle.

'I realized you'd been right all along,' Max said helplessly. 'Please forgive me.'

'Of course I forgive you,' I said, blinking back the tears that had suddenly appeared in my eyes. He opened his arms and I rushed toward him, then stopped. 'But there's something you need to know,' I said anxiously.

241

'What?' Max asked. 'Tell me anything.'

'She gave away her money,' Mum blurted out. 'I'm sorry, darling, but he needs to know. She gave it away, Max. To a soup kitchen!'

'Is that true?' Max looked at me, incredulous, then his face fell. 'Because of what I said? Oh, Jess, tell me you haven't done anything stupid. You shouldn't have listened to me. I told you, I'm an idiot.'

'Not because of what you said,' I said calmly. 'Because I wanted to. I've been helping out at this place. They prefer "resource center" to "soup kitchen." Anyway, they need new premises and . . . Look, I never wanted the money anyway. So I gave it to them. You don't mind?'

'Of course I don't mind,' Max said quietly. 'I didn't even know you'd been into a soup kitchen. I mean . . . resource center.'

'I hadn't,' I said awkwardly. 'Not until . . . Well, I was trying to be good, you see. It was part of Project Ideal Wife.'

Max looked at me uncertainly. 'There was a project?'

'Yes,' I said. 'Sort of. You know, the whole cooking thing?'

Max shook his head. 'God, I really am an idiot,' he muttered. 'You did all that for me?'

'For us,' I whispered.

'I'm so proud of you.'

Max looked at me for a moment, and I felt something intense, something I hadn't felt for a very long time. I felt happy. Not cheerful, or upbeat, or pleased, but *happy*. Truly. Perfectly. But then my happy glow gave way to something else, a sense of foreboding. 'Well, anyway,' I said. 'That's not the thing I need to tell you. There's something else.'

'Something else?' Max asked lightly. 'Whatever it is, you can tell me. I couldn't love you more at this moment, and I certainly won't ever love you less.'

'You might, actually,' I said, biting my lip. 'It's about Hugh.'

'Hugh?' Hugh put his hand up, and Max suddenly noticed him standing behind Giles. 'Hugh. What the hell are you doing here?' he asked, his voice rising.

'He came to see me,' I said, looking at Max tentatively. 'He . . .' I took a deep breath. 'Last year, when Mum said that she'd slept with Hugh, that she'd told him about Chester's business plans, she was lying. For me.'

Max looked as if he'd been punched in the stomach. 'You slept with Hugh?'

'No,' I said. 'I didn't. But I did kiss him. I was drunk. I thought you were having an affair. And I kissed him. And—'

'And it was my fault,' Hugh said suddenly. 'I took advantage of her, Max, and I've been doing it ever since.'

'What do you mean?' Max asked levelly.

'He's been asking her for money,' Mum said. 'Little weasel.'

'He's been what?' Max's face darkened, and he walked toward Hugh. 'You have been extorting money from my wife?'

'No. I mean yes, but . . . it's not like that,' Hugh said, stepping backward. 'Jess, tell him. Please.'

'But you have,' I said, as Max hobbled toward Hugh angrily.

'Not my nose,' Hugh wailed, stepping back in alarm. 'Not my bloody nose again.'

'It'll be more than your nose if I have anything to do with it,' Max said angrily, grabbing Hugh by the shoulders. 'How dare you? How bloody dare you?'

Chester pulled Max off, and Giles grabbed Hugh. 'Easy there,' Chester said. 'Come on, Max, he isn't worth it.

243

Although I have to say, I'd like to punch him myself after all the damage he's done.'

Max was staring at Hugh like a bullfighter staring down his bull. 'Don't you ever come near either of us again,' he said. 'Ever. Do you understand?'

'Fine,' Hugh whimpered. 'I didn't want to, anyway. I only came to ask Jess for a favor.'

'And I've told you,' I said. 'I've given all my money away, so there's no point in asking anymore.'

'Not that kind of favor,' Hugh said unhappily. 'No one ever listens. I came here because I wanted a real favor, not money.'

I looked at him suspiciously. 'What kind of favor?'

Hugh sighed. 'I was hoping you'd introduce me to your friend Giles.'

'Me?' Giles asked, his eyes widening.

'Yes, you,' Hugh said, looking down in embarrassment. 'I . . . well, I'd seen you around, and someone said you were friends with Jess here, and . . . Look, it's no big deal.'

'No big deal?' I asked. 'Hugh, you came all the way here. To Wiltshire.'

'Only because you left a message telling me not to blackmail you anymore. I didn't want you telling Giles. That was the other favor I was going to ask you. I've turned over a new leaf, you see. I read this book by Jerome D. Rutter, and it really spoke to me. I've decided to set myself up as a self-employed life coach. That's why I wanted to borrow some money. To get things started. I've already got three clients – I'll be able to pay you back in a couple of months.'

I frowned. 'You mean you honestly were just borrowing the money?'

'Yes, I was,' Hugh said miserably. 'And now my nose is broken and Giles here obviously thinks I'm the lowest of the low, which I was, I admit, but . . . but . . .' He sniffed loudly, and Giles, who was still holding him back from Max, gave a shrug.

'But you've changed, right?'

'Right,' Hugh said quietly.

Giles looked at me awkwardly, then shook his head. 'I couldn't,' he said. 'Jessica is my friend.'

'You can if you want,' I said, with a little smile.

'Really?' Giles's eyes lit up. 'I mean, really?' he said, trying to sound less excited this time. 'Well, maybe one date, then. You know, see how it goes.'

'Did I hear someone say Jerome D. Rutter?' We all turned to see Eric and Caroline emerging from the sitting room. Max grinned at them.

'So you found the place, then?' he asked.

Caroline grinned back. 'You're out of bed!' she said. 'Oh, you look so much better.'

'That's Jess's doing,' Max said, hobbling toward me and putting an arm around me. 'I was missing my perfect wife.'

'Not perfect,' I corrected. 'Quite flawed, actually.'

'That makes two of us,' Max insisted.

'Oh, include me in that,' Chester said wholeheartedly. 'Jeez, I'm as flawed as they come. I'm a workaholic. Although you're going to keep that in check, Ivana, right?'

Ivana nodded firmly. 'I heff way of meking you do vat you're told,' she said, raising an eyebrow. Then she turned to Sean with a shrug. 'End me, mebe I em not so perfect mother. I nid more. I nid more than just bebe.'

'Hey, that's not a flaw,' Sean said with a sigh. 'It's who you are. It's a good thing. And I should have known it, too. I knew you were independent, and I tried to turn you into something you're not. I'm the one who's flawed.'

'Hey, if we're talking flaws, I win hands down,' said Dad,

245

who was still standing in the doorway. 'I've never held on to a job in my life. Or held on to anything, for that matter.'

'Oh, bully for you,' Helen said. 'I've never held on to a relationship. I chase a man until he commits, and when he does, I get bored. I couldn't be more flawed.'

'I'm a terrible auditor,' Eric put in, shaking his head sadly. 'And I've broken the code of auditors, too. Fraternizing with clients. Unforgivable.'

I looked at him curiously. 'Is that you talking or Eric the auditor talking?'

He grinned. 'Oh, I was back in character,' he said. 'But I'm flawed, too. I mean, I'm out of work and in love with someone who's way out of my league.'

'You are?' Caroline said, looking devastated. 'Who?'

'You, dummy,' he said sheepishly.

'Oh, Eric,' she gushed, throwing her arms around him. 'I'm not out of your league at all. I'm very flawed, too.'

'You are so not flawed,' I said, rolling my eyes.

'I am, too,' she said, swinging round. 'Sometimes I don't separate my recycling properly. And I haven't cleaned under my sofa in about a year.'

The two not-Russian-Mafia men looked at each other guiltily. 'We're not the best debt collectors, either, if we're honest,' one of them said.

The other one nodded. 'We wouldn't really have killed you, Lawrence. We're good with the threats—'

'But not the follow-through,' the first one cut in sadly.

'So none of us is ideal?' I asked.

We all looked at Mum, who held her head up defiantly. Then she sighed. 'Oh, okay, if I must. I suppose I'm not entirely perfect.'

'You're not?' Chester grinned. 'Tell me, my angel, what faults could you possibly have?'

246

'I'm sometimes too much of a perfectionist,' Mum said airily, then looked down. 'And maybe I can be a little on the demanding side.'

'I wouldn't have it any other way,' Chester said warmly. 'You demand away.'

'So we're okay?' I asked Max hopefully. 'You forgive me?'

'There's nothing to forgive,' he said quietly. 'You are the sweetest, most wonderfully not-quite-perfect girl in the whole wide world.'

'Even though we're going to fail the audit?' I asked tentatively.

Max chuckled. 'Chester, I'm afraid we might have failed your audit. Fact is, we're a good company – in my view, a great one. But we're not perfect, so you're going to have to settle for imperfect if you want to work with us.'

'*If* he wants to work with us?' I whispered incredulously. 'This is Chester we're talking about. Our number-one client.'

Max shrugged. 'And I have enough confidence in us to stand up and speak my mind,' he said into my ear. 'So, what do you say, Chester?' he continued, more loudly.

'I say,' Chester said thoughtfully, 'that we're lucky to have such a committed and talented partner in Milton Advertising. And that I'm beginning to realize that sometimes our flaws are what make us great.'

'And the audits are pretty much a load of old hooey,' Eric said with a shrug.

'That, too.' Chester grinned. 'Although I will be wanting my money back. Obviously.'

'Whatever,' Eric said. 'I'm resigning tomorrow, anyway. Take it up with Josh.'

'So we're all good?' Chester asked. 'Everything's okay?'

'Everything's perfect,' I said happily. 'Imperfectly perfect.'

Postscript

∽

DAD WAS RIGHT ABOUT THE HOUSE. It does suit me. Actually, it suits us – we moved in just a couple of months ago. That's Max and me. And mini Wild Wainwright. She isn't born yet, but she will be in three months, and we couldn't be more excited. As is Ivana. She's pregnant with her second, but it hasn't stopped her being the most formidable personal assistant ever. Chester says he doesn't know how he coped without her and is spending far more time at home with Mum these days – he's even gotten his golf handicap down. He's taking early retirement next year; he says now that he's married, he doesn't want to waste a single minute in meetings.

Caroline and Eric are engaged, too, and moving to Hollywood – turns out that although he was a rubbish ethical auditor, he's actually a very good actor and he's got a part on a long-running sitcom out there. Caroline's sad to be leaving Milton Advertising, but as Jerome D. Rutter apparently says, change is to be embraced, because without it things would stay the same. And I thought his book was full of platitudes!

Helen's doing all right, too. Her new show, *Reality Wives,* is already a huge hit, and her love life's looking up. She bumped into Anthony at Mum's wedding (Mum booked the Hilton's ballroom for the wedding and didn't realize how big it was. She needed to boost numbers and invited everyone

248

from Milton Advertising, even Anthony), and the two of them hit it off like wildfire. She asked me if it would be all right, of course, and I told her that she was absolutely welcome to him if she really wanted. And for two commitmentphobes, they're doing pretty well – even talking about buying a place together.

Hugh and Giles are still an item, although prone to the odd explosive argument. They've merged their life-coaching and flower/wedding-planning businesses into one big lifestyle concierge company, and Hugh has paid me back every penny, plus interest.

As for the resource center, it is now the proud owner of a huge building in Clerkenwell, complete with eat-in kitchen, three living areas, and enough beds to cater to a hundred people a night. And I've continued to be a companion, although I'm still not sure I'm a very good one. Greta's looking forward to meeting the baby. She says I can use the place as a nursery when I want to go back to work; she would love nothing more than to take the baby for walks around London.

So while I'm still not an ideal wife – not really – I'm loving my imperfect life.

'Darling? Is supper nearly ready? I'm famished.'

I look at my watch, then smile up at Max. 'Should be ready right about now,' I say, standing up.

'You're sure you don't want a hand? I can't help you with anything?' Max asks.

I shake my head. 'No. You wait here.'

'I'll tell you what.' Max grins. 'That cookery course you went on was a master stroke. Your lasagna is the best I've ever tasted. Maybe you should go back? Learn a few more dishes?'

I shoot him a look. 'I thought we agreed – you're the cook.'

'I know,' Max says, his eyes glinting. 'But nothing I make compares to your lasagna, even if you do only make it three times a year.'

'Three times a year is quite enough,' I say firmly. 'Makes you appreciate it more, anyway.'

'Fair point,' Max agrees. 'Shall I set the table?'

'Thanks, darling,' I say, walking off toward the kitchen.

'Jess? Is that you?' a voice whispers.

'Yes. Are we set?'

'All ready to go,' Mary Armstrong says, appearing from behind the pantry door. 'The lasagna is in the oven and the salad's in a bowl. Are you sure Max doesn't suspect anything?'

I grin. 'Not a thing. See you in four months?'

'Four months,' Mary says, with a little nod. 'And you're absolutely sure you don't want me to teach you how to make it yourself? It would be so much easier.'

'But then I really would be the perfect wife,' I say, winking. 'And everyone knows that perfection isn't good for anyone.'